Praise for Jen

"Jenny Hale writes touching, beautifu
Bestselling Author RaeAnne Thayne

One of "19 Dreamy Summer Romances to Whisk you Away" in ***Oprah Magazine*** on *The Summer House*

One of "24 Dreamy Books about Romance" in ***Oprah Daily*** on *The Summer House*

Included in "Beach Reads Perfect for Summer 2020" in ***Southern Living Magazine*** on *Summer at Firefly Beach*

"Touching, fun-filled, and redolent with salt air and the fragrance of summer, this seaside tale is a perfect volume for most romance collections."—***Library Journal*** on *The Summer House*

"Hale's impeccably executed contemporary romance is the perfect gift for readers who love sweetly romantic love stories imbued with all the warmth and joy of the holiday season."—***Booklist*** on *Christmas Wishes and Mistletoe Kisses*

"A great summer beach read." —***PopSugar*** on *Summer at Firefly Beach*

"This sweet small-town romance will leave readers feeling warm all the way through."—***Publisher's Weekly*** on *It Started with Christmas*

BOOKS BY JENNY HALE

Butterfly Sisters

The Memory Keeper

An Island Summer

The Beach House

The House on Firefly Beach

Summer at Firefly Beach

The Summer Hideaway

The Summer House

Summer at Oyster Bay

Summer by the Sea

A Barefoot Summer

A Lighthouse Christmas

Christmas at Fireside Cabins

Christmas at Silver Falls

It Started with Christmas

We'll Always Have Christmas

All I Want for Christmas

Christmas Wishes and Mistletoe Kisses

A Christmas to Remember

Coming Home for Christmas

The Christmas Letters

JENNY HALE
USA TODAY BESTSELLING AUTHOR

HARPETH ROAD PRESS
Nashville

HARPETH ROAD

Published by Harpeth Road Press (USA)
P.O. Box 158184
Nashville, TN 37215

Paperback: 978-1-7358458-9-0
eBook: 978-1-7358458-8-3

THE CHRISTMAS LETTERS: A heartwarming, feel-good holiday romance

First printing: October, 2022

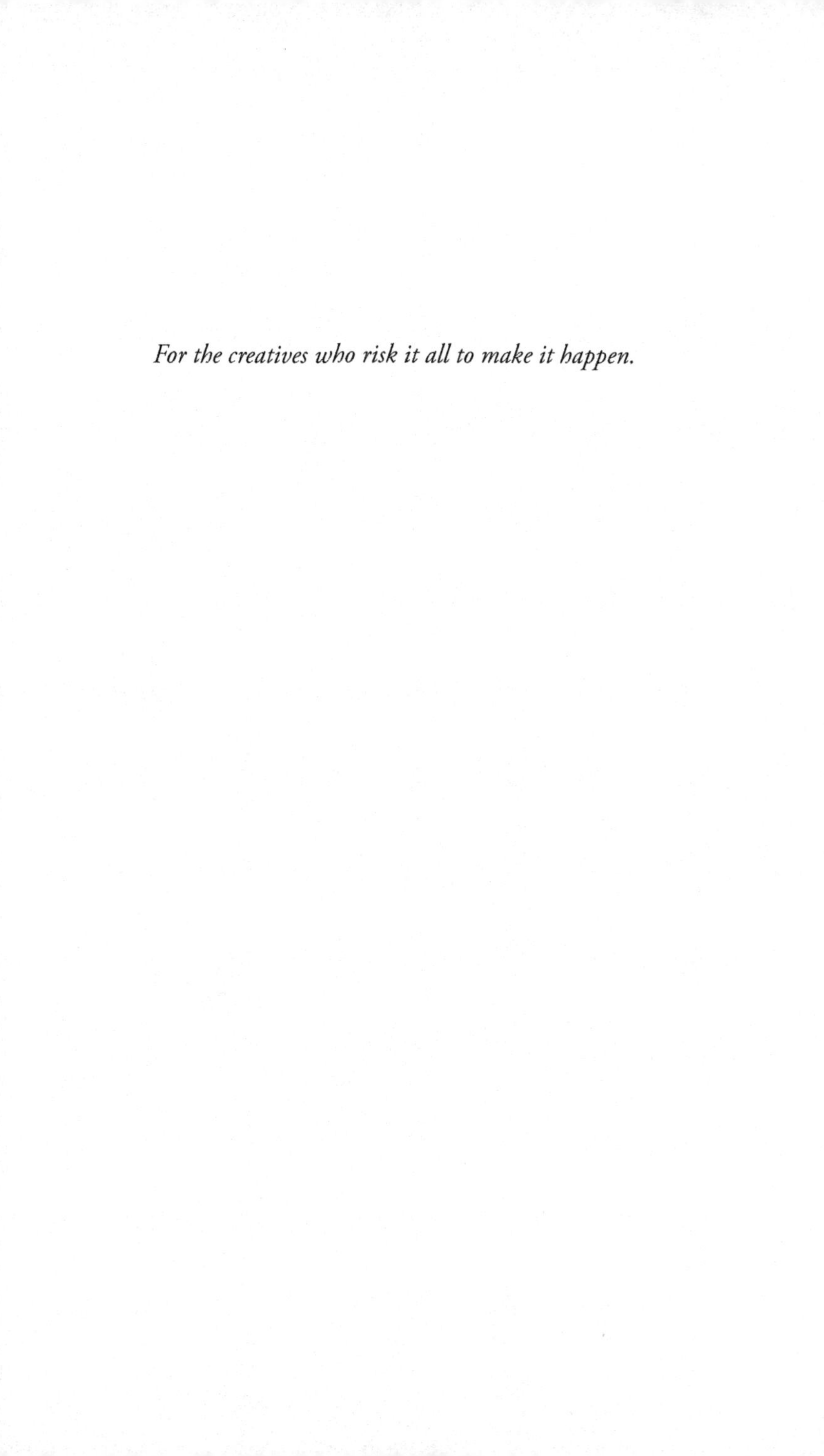

For the creatives who risk it all to make it happen.

Prologue

"I'm so sorry, Mama, I can't talk right now," Elizabeth Holloway said gently, the phone pressed to her diamond-studded ear, as snow fell like feathers against the glittering buildings of the New York City skyline. "I'll call you back first thing tomorrow, I promise."

"Liz," her mother, Loretta, breathed anxiously down the line in that southern accent that used to sing Elizabeth to sleep at night.

If Elizabeth closed her eyes, she could almost hear her mother's melody over the chirping of the crickets out back of Nan's old farmhouse in Mason's Ridge, Tennessee, the rustling of the trees in the apple orchard, and the squeak of the screened door as Mama stepped through it onto the front porch. While they'd lived just down the road, Nan's little farmhouse tucked away in the hills had been where both of them had spent most of their time.

Having been so intent on getting out of her hometown, it had taken Elizabeth years to realize how much she missed those sounds.

Growing up, Elizabeth had wanted to get a degree in social work and then go into the Peace Corps, leaving everything behind to learn and work in faraway places. She'd been constrained by her small town and had never really felt as if she'd belonged with the people in it. They were all invested in their land and their place within the community, yet she'd wanted to spread her wings. However, she'd only managed to accomplish one of her goals: she'd left that little town, and everyone in it, over a decade ago.

Now her mother was tending to the aftermath of handling Nan's will and her belongings all by herself, and she had tons of questions about taxes and the legalities of how to assume ownership of Nan's property. Elizabeth had been trying to support her with it all as much as she could from New York, but it was proving difficult to do.

"I need your help with this," Mama said, bringing Elizabeth back to the present. "I'm worried it ain't gonna wait too long."

A pinch of guilt took hold of Elizabeth's chest. She wanted to speak to her mother, but the charity benefit that had kept her in New York instead of back in Mason's Ridge was starting. Nothing could be done with whatever the issue was at this hour, and she needed to take her seat.

"I wish I could discuss this right now," Elizabeth said, "but I'm on my way in to the event I told you about." Holding the phone, she put one stiletto heel out of the limo and took the bellman's gloved hand, the man guiding her out of the car outside The Plaza where she planned to have drinks, chat with important people, and, if she was lucky, get to do the waltz on the dance floor—her favorite thing at these events. She raised her bright-red ball gown to keep the satin from grazing the snow that had piled up in the gutter, a chill slithering down her limbs. Her mother continued to speak, but Elizabeth struggled to concentrate on her words with all the commotion.

The mammoth building in front of her gleamed like a golden torch, surrounded by dazzling Christmas trees, but Elizabeth barely gave it a thought. Her long-time boyfriend, Richard Oppenheim, was already out of the limo and on the sidewalk, standing opposite her in his tuxedo with a collar that showed off his strong jawline. He ran his hand through his salt-and-pepper hair that had come early for his age, making him look distinguished. Then, spinning a finger in the air impatiently, he indicated that she should wrap up the call before they went inside.

Elizabeth knew that if they didn't get in to speak to Richard's potential client before the event started, they might not have another chance until after Christmas, and an enormous diamond sale for his company depended on it. When Elizabeth had procured the invitation to the event, it had lit up Richard like a Christmas tree. She'd begun attending charity events like these as a way to be of service, but slowly, like everything in her life, they'd become more about Richard and propelling his business forward. Everything he'd done in the last two weeks had been in preparation for this.

Elizabeth looked away from him, focusing on the snowy curb next to her heel. "I need to go," she said to her mother, shame and sadness over not being back home to help Mama bubbling up as she cradled the phone, wishing she had time to say more to ease her mother's mind. Everything in her body wanted to reach through the line, wrap her arms around her mom, and comfort the woman who'd given her so much over the years.

Richard tugged at Elizabeth's arm, practically pulling the phone from her ear.

"I'll call you later." Elizabeth ended the call, glaring up at him, letting him know what she thought of his behavior.

He offered his arm in a huff, as if she'd already ignored some prior clue to take it.

The call had been bad timing—she wasn't denying that—but rushing her off, when Elizabeth was already aware that she needed to hang up, had been uncalled for. The only attention she'd gotten from him in weeks and it was out of frustration.

Biting her tongue to keep the peace, she took Richard's arm, and he whisked her up the stairs and past the dazzling holiday wreaths on either side.

The large doors swished shut behind them, the marble floor stretching out like a runway toward the most festive event of the year, but she didn't feel the least bit celebratory. How different her life had become from the days when she'd left everything she'd planned for herself behind because she'd thought her prince charming had swept her off her feet.

"Why did you even answer the phone?" Richard asked, shaking his head as he guided her past a group of people.

"She called twice. I didn't want her to worry," Elizabeth replied, trying to keep her tone in check so they didn't have an argument right there in The Plaza. Yet, as her frustration with his behavior mounted, she blurted, "But this *is* my mother we're talking about. I can answer any time I want. And you *can* wait."

Richard produced the frown that formed whenever he was annoyed with Elizabeth, which seemed to be a lot lately. No one made Richard Oppenheim wait. "What was all the drama about anyway?"

"I'm not sure." Elizabeth dropped her cell phone into her clutch and snapped it shut. "You didn't give me a chance to find out. I'll call her tomorrow when I have time to give her my full attention and apologize."

Crossing under the enormous chandelier in the lobby, they continued on, past a towering Christmas tree that stretched up to the ornately painted ceiling, and Elizabeth tried to ignore the feeling that something was incredibly wrong back home. She decided that once they'd gotten their seats, she'd dip into the ladies' room and call her mother back.

Richard leaned in, his breath at her neck, the gesture so foreign now that, given her train of thought, it startled her. She jumped, stumbling a bit in her heels, but he caught her. "I try to lighten the mood and you flinch. I can't even *attempt* to make you romantic," he said with an aggravated exhale.

His low blow stopped her in her tracks. "I'm sorry?" she asked, knowing she was still stuck on the phone call, her mind not yet on the fabulous charity event and Christmas party they were attending, but he could cut her some slack. Her grandmother had passed away a year ago, but both she and Mama were still swarmed by grief over it—Mama so much so that she'd only just now been able to get around to doing the paperwork to inventory all of Nan's assets, settle her last few debts to some of the merchants in town who'd allowed extra time, and transfer the farm into Mama's name. Richard could, at the very least, give her a second to soak in her surroundings before accusing her of not being romantic.

"If you're holding out on me to pressure me into having kids, it's not going to work," he said into her ear, completely missing the point of her irritation.

She gawked at him, her jaw falling open. They'd had discussions about whether they'd wanted kids or not, and they'd disagreed on the subject, but she hadn't said a thing about that tonight. His remark had come out of nowhere. And, suddenly, as she looked at him, she realized that he'd been stacking up all their disagreements, forming a wall of anger that she hadn't truly acknowledged until this very second.

"What's all this about?" she asked, but the sinking feeling in her gut and the past ten months of arguing gave her the answer already.

"Look around you, Elizabeth. *This* is what excites me."

They'd had a rough time romantically over the last year. She often questioned Richard's brutal fierceness in the workplace and his neglect of their relationship because of it. But the gentle smile she'd seen from him when they'd first met had stayed with her. After seven years together, however, she'd expected to have more from him than she had, and he'd yet to pop the question. Not to mention that when she'd remarked how wonderful it would be to hear the patter of tiny feet coming down the hardwoods on Christmas morning, he'd told her that kids were definitely not an option. Ever.

"I'd never pressure you into anything," she said through her teeth, tucking a runaway tendril of her chocolate-brown hair behind her ear. "I want you to *want* it." The words stuck in her throat, because she knew deep down that, given his workaholic nature, he never would come around and she hadn't fully explored what that meant for her or for them as a couple.

Richard threw his hands up in the air as if he'd been wrestling with the issue the whole limo ride over. "You're not even present anymore. We're at The Plaza, for God's sake. And you're on the phone to Podunk, Tennessee."

Elizabeth sucked in a breath of indignation. "How dare you," she said, tears welling up as if they'd been waiting for the cue. She blinked them away, her red lips wobbling.

Richard didn't have the kind of relationship with his family that Elizabeth had. When they'd first met, she'd thought she could show him what he'd been missing. As the years went on, she pushed away the reality that perhaps she never could.

A couple walked by, eyeing them, and Elizabeth flashed an uncomfortable smile.

Richard's gaze rolled upward to the ceiling before landing back on her, surrender in his eyes. "Elizabeth, I don't think we can keep going like this anymore."

"I know," she said. "The last thing I want to do is fight."

"No," he said. "We can't do *this*—" He waggled a finger between them. "You and me."

The first thing she noticed was the jingle of the metal chain of the jeweled clutch in her trembling hands, her body reacting to the fact that her life was changing in front of her eyes before her brain had caught up. She stared at him, words escaping her.

Right there, in the cheerful, bustling, Christmas-tree-covered lobby, she knew exactly what was happening: they were breaking up. And the worst part about it was that, even after seven years of being together, she didn't really feel like she was losing much. While her limbs were responding to the fear, in a strange way she realized that what she really felt was relieved—relieved from the pressure of a relationship that she knew hadn't been working for quite a while.

"I'll get a room here at the hotel and let you… get your things together back at home," Richard said, his gaze distant, that glimmer of attraction that had been in them when they'd met long gone.

Elizabeth nodded, tears now brimming in her eyes, the end still hitting her hard, despite her rational side telling her it had been necessary. She struggled with whether her sadness was because she'd wasted so much time on someone who wasn't the right person for her, or the fact that she'd given up everything for him and now, at the age of twenty-nine, she had no idea what to do.

"This is it?" she asked, her words breaking on her emotion.

"This is it," he replied, his words so final and resolute that she wondered why he'd bothered to go through the formality of getting dressed up tonight. But then she remembered that it had all been about him and his business. She'd just been tagging along, like she had in everything they'd done since they'd met.

He turned around and walked away, leaving her alone, in her red satin gown, just twelve days before Christmas.

Chapter One

A week later

The one thing Elizabeth hadn't been banking on as they pulled into Mason's Ridge, Tennessee was to encounter an establishment that looked as if it had been built after the 1960s. She decided that, given what she'd been through, it was a gift, sent specifically for her from above.

"Coffee..." Elizabeth said to herself, perking up just a little at the idea of a warm, frothy latte, when the brand-new sign slid past. Her voice was raspy from exhaustion and the low emotional state that had settled upon her like a murky haze.

She pressed her nose against the glass of the window in the darkness of the December evening, fogging it, while sitting in the only occupied seat of the shuttle van she'd hired to transport her through the snow from the airport south of Knoxville, as it idled at the stop sign. Her head pounded from the changes in altitude, her swinging emotions, and a lack of caffeine.

"Pull off here for a second?" she asked the driver as they rolled forward. She picked up her handbag and stood in the aisle. It had been a long flight, and the warm liquid would center her before she had to face Nan's farm, whatever her mother had to tell her, and, eventually, everyone else she'd left behind. She wasn't quite ready to go home just yet, and coffee would be the perfect diversion. Scooting her carry-on bag out of the aisle, her handbag slung over her shoulder, Elizabeth made her way toward the front.

"Ma'am, we really can't make stops," the shuttle driver told her impatiently when his gaze met hers in the oversized rearview mirror above his head.

"But it's just us. Pretty please?" Her heart hammered at the idea of facing Nan's and also having to figure out what to do with her life after leaving New York.

With a loud exhale, the driver looked at his watch and then pulled off to the side of the road outside the small coffee shop. It's sign read: High Peak Coffee. The new building and its full parking lot were sitting where there used to be only woods, the large area Elizabeth's playground as a child. She and her best friend, Naomi White, had played hide-and-seek there on their day-long hikes across town that had always ended in a thirty-five-cent popsicle at Ford's.

It was an unusual sight in the insignificant town of Mason's Ridge, only a few minutes from Crestwood Farm, her late grandmother's home. She'd not traveled this route when her mother had picked her up at the airport for Nan's funeral last year, but it would've been just like Mama to avoid the "traffic," the word she used for any road with more than two cars.

Elizabeth paused, suddenly wondering if she'd bump into anyone she knew in there. She ran her fingers through her unbrushed hair and tried to get it into some kind of order, peering at herself in the shuttle's window. She could see the circles under her eyes and the paleness of her skin even in the poor reflection. She hadn't bothered with makeup since the night at The Plaza, not really seeing the point. But as she considered whether she might come across any acquaintances, she doubted very seriously that anyone who'd grown up in the fields with her would be excited about an overpriced latte with little hearts in the foam—and by the look of the place, that was what she was expecting.

"I repeat, I'm not supposed to make unscheduled stops," the shuttle driver said to her, his lips pursed in disapproval. He raised a finger at the sign bolted to the front of the van with the same message in blue block print.

"I'll only be a minute," she assured him, her eyes pleading. "And I'll buy you a coffee. My treat."

The driver perked up at the offer, putting the vehicle in park. "Strong, black, two sugars."

"Done." It was the least she could do, given the fact that he'd actually stopped for her. "Thank you," she said to the shuttle driver with true gratitude in her tone, knowing the man might have a family of his own to get home to. "If I take too long, you can honk and I promise I'll run right back out." Although she hoped he would at least give her a little time to sit and get her head together.

She'd managed to avoid Richard all week while she'd packed up her entire life, putting most of it in storage and shipping the rest to the farm. As partner in the company and director of merchandise, personally overseeing all purchases over a quarter of a million dollars, he'd easily kept his schedule full with so many celebrities in town for the charity event and the holidays, and had stayed at The Plaza until she'd gotten everything out of their penthouse, only returning on the day she was leaving. With her hand on the doorknob, her bags packed, Richard had told her he'd placed ten thousand dollars in her account for "living expenses," like some sort of final peace offering.

"I don't want it," she'd told him, even though she needed it. She hadn't held a job in almost a decade, and all the money they'd lived on had been Richard's.

"It's yours. Your work on getting us into the No Lost Children benefit brought in more than enough revenue for me. This could be your cut."

Elizabeth had ignored the fact that her "cut" of a franchise deal that had brought him well over a million in revenue would be a mere ten thousand dollars. But it didn't matter. As volunteer coordinator of a network of charities in the city, she'd never agreed with his tactic of pretending to be invested in the organizations just so he could schmooze with the high-rollers at galas and then promote his family's latest diamond line. While living on Richard's money had never bothered her before, now the handout felt like a weighted chain around her ankles, the final tether holding her to her old life. She'd buy a thousand coffees just to rid herself of it if she could.

The driver opened the shuttle's folding door, jostling the little sprig of greenery affixed to it. Elizabeth buttoned up her coat, stepping into the winter air, her boots sinking to her ankles in fluffy white snow. The stillness was quite a change from the busy streets of New York.

When she'd made it to the covered porch of the coffee shop, she pulled open the heavy door adorned with a festive wreath of balsam and red berries and stepped inside, the heat from the stone fireplace at the end of the room a welcome reprieve. Surprisingly, both given the location and the late hour, the place was full to the brim with people gathered around tables, sipping from their mugs and nibbling on pastries. She nervously scanned the crowd for any familiar faces, but, to her relief, she didn't find any. Some people were on laptops, while others quietly read books by the fire, the mantle dripping with more fresh holiday foliage. She certainly hadn't expected something as sophisticated as this.

She meandered through the crowded tables to the coffee bar, fatigue from everything she'd been through setting in, burning her eyes. Forcing her overworked brain to push past the thoughts of leaving New York and getting on a plane with no real destination other than the farm where she would stay with Mama until she could devise a plan for her life, she peered up at the menu.

Focus.

The buzz of the crowd in her ears, Elizabeth scanned the milk options and the syrup flavors, still blown over by the number of people inside. Until now, Mason's Ridge had been a farming town, and the closest thing to a coffee shop had been the stale pot sitting on the help-yourself electric burner of Ford's Corner Market that wasn't on a corner at all but a long stretch of road, both ends leading to nowhere. Mama had never mentioned this place. Although, Elizabeth hadn't really given her much opportunity to…

Pushing away her remorse, she stepped up to the counter. "Is this place new?" she asked the barista as she rubbed her tired eyes and unwound her scarf, leaving it hanging down from either shoulder.

The unfamiliar woman with short, spiked hair and red lipstick—also uncharacteristic for this area—offered her a confused stare. "We've been open for almost a year."

Elizabeth winced at the swell of shame for having been gone so long. With Richard's schedule and her busy life in New York, she hadn't been to the farm for any length of time, returning only for Gramps's funeral and then a mere two days when Nan had died. At the time, her reasons for staying away had felt legitimate, but now they seemed flimsy at best.

She broke eye contact with the barista, who'd left her to tend to another customer, only for Elizabeth's attention to land on a man sitting at one of the communal tables, a frown etched on his face while he typed on his laptop. He looked up at her as if she'd pulled him away from his work by some cosmic force.

Elizabeth's cheeks burned with the fear that he might be someone from high school. She was in no shape to go through the whole what-have-you-been-up-to chat. She was liable to stare at him blankly if he did, having absolutely nothing to say. She searched the man's face for any familiar characteristics, but couldn't find a single one. His crystal-blue eyes held her there for a tick until she tore herself away at the sound of the shuttle van's horn outside.

"What'll it be?" the barista asked, after stepping back in front of her.

"I'll have an almond-milk latte and a black coffee, strong, with two sugars."

"What sizes?"

Elizabeth forced herself to hear the question, her mind on the van. "Whatever your regular is."

The woman grabbed two mugs.

The horn honked again.

Elizabeth sucked in a flustered breath. "Could you hang on for a sec?" Rubbing the pinch in her shoulder, she avoided the glances of the man at the table and wound her way back through the crowd to the door, sticking her head out and indicating for the driver to come inside.

The driver grumbled something and the van began to move through the piled snow, its tires spinning furiously until it pulled to a stop in a nearby parking space, where he got out and met her at the door.

"This is the last leg of my workday," he said, narrowing his eyes at her. "And that storm out there isn't getting any weaker." He jutted a finger at the dark, starless sky.

She pulled him inside, and he brushed the snow from his gray curly hair. "I didn't catch your name," she said kindly.

"Terrence," he replied, his jaw tightening as if she hadn't caught the fact that he was not thrilled to be there.

"Well, Terrence, you are a wonderful man for stopping for me. I needed it. I'll hurry." She pulled out a chair at the table across from Mr. Blue Eyes, who was clicking madly again on the keys of his laptop. "Rest and I'll bring your coffee to you."

The woman next to them scooted her notebook closer to her to make room as Terrence dropped down into the seat and Elizabeth made her way back to the counter.

"That'll be seven eighty-three," the barista said, sliding the two mugs of coffee toward Elizabeth.

She dug around in her handbag for cash, located a wad, and passed it over. "Keep the change," Elizabeth told her, taking the coffees back to where Terrence was sitting.

"No to-go cups?" he asked, his disapproval clear.

"I forgot to ask," she said honestly, feeling more awful by the minute for disrupting Terrence's plans, and rethinking the whole idea. She surveyed the now-full table awkwardly, with no place to sit, and made sure not to connect with the mystery man across from them, who she seemed to keep distracting. The man's phone went off, and he answered it, turning away, thank goodness.

"You can have my seat," Terrence said, getting up. "If I can't be by my own fireplace—where I should be in about an hour and thirty minutes—then I'll at least settle in by the one over there."

"I'm sorry, I won't be long," Elizabeth said, wanting to crawl into a bed somewhere and sleep until the next season.

Terrence's face softened as he studied her, and she knew that in the light of the coffee shop, he could see how worn-out she was. "Take your time."

"Thank you," she told him as he moved away, emotion welling up without warning. Swallowing it back down, Elizabeth set the coffee in Terrence's spot and shrugged off her coat, draping it on the back of the chair, along with her scarf. With a release of stress in the form of a loud exhale, she sat down, wrapping her fingers around her mug. There was no question that this place was cozy and inviting on a cold winter's evening, but as she looked around at the other patrons on laptops and tablets, she was willing to bet that the reason the place was so busy was because it probably had the only Wi-Fi in the entire area.

The man across from her was quietly talking into his phone. "Yes," he said. "I spoke with the contractors and I think we can get it done for under 2.3 million. This was literally a Christmas miracle..."

Elizabeth sipped her coffee, still stunned at how much this area had changed. In the past, she'd have never encountered a businessman making million-dollar transactions in the middle of Mason's Ridge.

"Tough day?" Mr. Blue Eyes asked cautiously from across the table after he'd ended his call. His voice was like a silk blanket falling over her, with a sympathetic tone that she didn't need to hear at that moment or she might break down right there at the coffee shop. He shut his laptop and set his phone face down beside it.

She looked up, his comment giving her reason to notice the gold stubble around his jaw and the way his lips looked as if he were smiling even though he wasn't. Given the events of the week prior, the last thing she wanted in her state was some tourist hitting on her, even if he was easy on the eyes.

"You have no idea." She lifted the coffee to her lips, savoring the hearty, smoky taste of it to keep the tears from coming, despite the upbeat holiday music that was tinkling above them.

She hadn't meant her answer to be a conversation starter, but he produced an adorable pout with a subtle nod, his expression attentive, as if he were pulling the events of last week through the air between them and into his own mind. Yet he couldn't possibly guess all that had happened to her. He had no inkling of what she was dealing with.

"I just arrived in Mason's Ridge. I'm here for the week." He flashed a little smile and, when it faded, she realized that it was because she hadn't responded to it like she normally would have. Instead, her mind was elsewhere. "How about you?" he asked.

"Sorry," she said, forcing herself to offer him a consolatory smile. "I'm from… Here."

He nodded again, but it was clear that he was trying to figure out why she didn't look like she belonged there. "Do you come here a lot?" he asked.

Elizabeth suppressed the urge to tell him flat out that she just wanted to be left alone. But that would be rude. He was only enjoying his trip; he didn't need some jaded woman ruining it. It wasn't his fault she was a train wreck.

"No," she replied, mustering another half-hearted smile. "I left here for good when I went away to college. I've been in New York for the last eleven years." Just saying it out loud made her head begin to pound. She turned slightly away from him, hoping he got the message without her seeming completely impolite.

But, instead, he reached across the table and offered his hand in greeting. "Paul Dawson."

Frustration crawled up her spine. With the storm and Terrence needing to get on the road, clearly, she wasn't going to get even a moment to collect her thoughts, *and* she had to be nice to this perfectly innocent stranger when she wanted to run the other way. Instead of telling him all this, of course, she extended her hand and shook his, his gentle but firm grip causing her shoulders to hike up near her ears. She pulled back and picked up her mug again awkwardly.

"And you are?" he asked.

"Elizabeth Holloway."

He squinted at her, as if something were occurring to him, spiking her fear that he was an old classmate, and she hadn't placed him. Finally, he asked, "Have you always gone by Elizabeth?"

She forced a pleasant expression before hiding behind her mug, her pulse racing, the anxiety swelling with a vengeance. "I… went by Liz when I was a kid," she said. Elizabeth set her coffee down, the white heart in the foam having dissipated and spread out, forming an unshapely figure. She studied it like she had the puffy clouds while on her back in the meadow when she was a girl, but no images came to her tonight, the shape unrecognizable, like her life. With a sigh, she looked back up at him.

He smiled, the reaction oddly calming her.

"Why do you ask?" She swallowed, repeating the name Paul Dawson in her mind to see if it had any connection to her youth, but nothing came to her.

"You just look more like a Liz or Beth than Elizabeth to me." Paul's eyes penetrated hers as if he could read her. "Are you always this quiet?" he asked.

His general interest in her was unsettling, given her fragile state. Didn't he have work to do?

No, but if I don't get a moment to myself, I might stand on this table and scream. "Only sometimes," she replied instead, her words snapping more than she'd wanted them to.

He seemed to finally get the message, fiddling with his empty coffee cup. She inwardly scolded herself when the playfulness left his eyes. She didn't need to let anyone else down. To avoid the guilt, she lifted her latte, drinking almost half of it in a few gulps.

Paul's phone went off with the ping of a text and he studied the screen, firing off a quick response. "Well, *Elizabeth* Holloway, it was very nice meeting you," he said before he stood and took his coat off the chair, sliding his phone into the back pocket of his jeans, ready to exit her life as quickly as he'd arrived.

"Wait," she said, putting her drink down. Why was she stopping him when everything in her body told her to let him leave her in peace so she could unwind?

He paused, those intense blue eyes on her.

"I don't mean to be a jerk," she said, surrendering to the moment. "I've had a pretty insane week, and I'm on my way to visit my mother who's barely seen me in eleven years, so I'm not really myself."

The compassion in his gaze slammed into her like a ton of bricks. She'd only just met this guy, and he was showing her a kind of empathy that Richard never had.

"That's a long time not to see your mother," he said, something flashing in his eyes that she couldn't decipher.

"I know." She picked up her latte again but didn't take a drink this time, the acidity of it turning her unsettled stomach. She couldn't even do having coffee right anymore—one of her favorite things. "I've been in New York and I just didn't make the time," she admitted, aware that his gentle demeanor had encouraged her to divulge more than she normally would have. She blinked away more tears, mortified that he might see them. “I feel awful about it.”

Paul nodded, pursing his lips as thoughts raced through his eyes. “I get it,” he said. “I haven’t seen my grandfather much in the last year…” He didn’t finish his thought, and she wasn’t present enough to hear it anyway. “But you’re making time now.” Paul clearly shifted the focus back to her. “Is she meeting you here?”

“No, but I’m on my way to see her.”

“I hope you don’t live far. That storm coming in is no joke.” He pulled on his coat and tucked his laptop under his arm.

Her eyes found Terrence over the now-thinning crowd, knowing he needed to be home and not in some coffee shop on the side of the mountain. “I’d better go too.” She stood up, grabbed her coat, scarf, and handbag, and set her mug in the dishes bin before she went around to Paul’s side of the table to get to Terrence.

“Maybe we’ll run into each other again,” he said, looking down at her, his woodsy scent making every nerve in her body tingle despite the emotional shape she was in.

“I doubt it, with this snow,” she replied, allowing a polite smile. “But it was nice to meet you.”

“Same,” he said, that empathy written on his face.

With a little wave, Elizabeth moved past him, headed for Terrence. When she finally allowed herself to look over her shoulder, the door was swinging shut and Paul Dawson had walked out into the snowstorm.

“Thank you again for stopping,” she said, coming up behind Terrence and pulling her woolen beanie and mittens out of her handbag. “I’m ready now.” Even as she said it, she still wasn’t entirely sure she was ready for any of it.

Chapter Two

Elizabeth yanked her beanie over her snow-covered hair, protecting her ears, the frigid wind snaking through the valley of the Great Smoky Mountains, as she stood at the edge of Nan's farm. Her warm memories of it were clouded by the blanket of white stretching from where Elizabeth stood to the green clapboard house with its stone chimney and matching barn, all nestled into the hillside among the apple orchards. The winding lane leading up to it was lost in the blizzard that was upon them. Before Terrence drove away, the van's tires sliding precariously in the snow, he gave a tap on his horn and Elizabeth waved.

Turning back to the farm that she'd wanted so badly to leave when she was in her youth, emotion rose in her throat. She sucked in a mouthful of freezing air to combat it, but tears swelled under the rims of her eyes anyway. She felt as though she were seeing the snow-covered fields that used to be so familiar through someone else's eyes. That little girl she'd been, spending dreamy days there with Nan and her family, so long gone and clouded now in both grief and her own discontent that it all seemed a figment of her imagination.

The last time she'd been to Crestwood Farm had been a blur. She'd flown in for two days to bury Nan at the cemetery across town, and then she'd rushed off under pressure from Richard to return to New York, her charity schedule filled to the brim with events that she'd coordinated and he had wanted to attend. This time, while she walked through the meadow, there was no more rushing, no more lists of things to get done, no sobbing relatives and friends to comfort, no demands from Richard pulling her away.

To avoid a lashing of wind, Elizabeth turned her head east, past the skeletal apple orchard, the trees' limbs barren and draped in ice, and focused on the small stone cottages across the farm that belonged to the hired farmhands, their chimneys belching smoke in an attempt to combat the frigid temperatures.

Elizabeth continued to trudge through the field toward the house that glowed like a beacon of warmth for her already frozen body. With every icy step in her designer boots—the closest thing she had to appropriate attire, the thin leather doing nothing to shield her feet from the elements—she forced more tears away, trying to focus on the snowy railings and the sparkling tree on the front porch, along with the Christmas lights through the window, to keep her mind off the fact that her life was in shambles. She needed to channel the strength her nan had shown.

Nan and Gramps had run this farm together, until Gramps had passed away a few years ago. Even in her older age, Nan had gotten up with the rooster every morning, tilling areas of the fields and driving the plow.

"Why don't you get more farmhands?" Elizabeth had asked her once, when the woman had come in dog-tired and covered in dirt.

"Because I love it," she'd said, unexpected emotion showing in her eyes. "You can't always control what life gives you, but you can control your destiny within it. This farm is my destiny…"

As Elizabeth plodded through the snow, the large, wet flakes coming toward her at a slant made her squint, blocking her view and freezing to her numb cheeks. The old tree swing—a plank of wood hanging low by two ropes under the oak tree—rocked in the gusts as if it were shivering in the cold, a mound of snow collecting on its wooden seat. So much had changed since her bare feet had dangled above the ground from it, her little hands gripping the ropes while she sailed through the air, feeling as if she were flying. In the howling wind, she could still hear the whisper of her laughter lifting into the sky with the cinnamon-colored barn swallows that had built a nest above her. She tried to keep the image in the front of her mind so she didn't pay attention to the chugging of her breath, her muscles aching under the weight of her luggage, and the strain of moving through the thick snow.

What do I do now, Nan? she asked, praying her grandmother's spirit had stayed there to watch over them and not yet made the journey to her final resting place, but all Elizabeth received in response was the rustle of the dead leaves in the oak trees as they fought the cold.

"Oh, my stars, Liz!" her mother called from the now open front door of the farmhouse. She wrapped the belt around her coat and tugged on the worn saddleback boots that she'd always kept by the door for fetching firewood. "Let me help you!" She worked her way down the three icy steps, the snow settling in her gray hair.

"Hey, Mama," Elizabeth said, while her mother reached out and took one of Elizabeth's bags, tossing it onto the porch, the designer leather skidding across the wood floor. Mama struggled in the deluge of snow to get the other suitcase, all the months after losing Nan showing under her eyes and in her jawline, giving Elizabeth a punch of sadness.

Her mother grabbed her arm and drew her up the slippery steps, past the gleaming Fraser fir tree and the battered wooden rocking chairs on the porch. As they entered the front door that opened into the small living area, the heat from inside spread over Elizabeth's skin like a burning wildfire. Mama knocked the snow off her boots. She closed the door, set them by the front mat to dry, and then wrapped Elizabeth up in a big hug.

Elizabeth's muscles immediately reacted to it, releasing the tension with every breath of Mama's rose-scented lotion. She buried her face into the crook of her mother's neck and sobs rose in her throat as if the floodgates for everything she'd been through had opened, leaving her scrambling to figure out how to shut them again.

Mama took her by the shoulders and pulled away, getting a look at her. Elizabeth choked back the ache, tried to wipe her gushing tears on her sleeve. Mama tilted her head sympathetically. "What happened to that bright, shinin' girl who flew out of here on her golden wings?"

Elizabeth crumpled, falling onto the sofa. "I don't know."

Mama handed her a box of tissues from the side table. "I'll make us some tea," she said, but the way her gaze lingered on Elizabeth spoke to her concern.

"Who helped you cut that down?" Elizabeth asked, her voice breaking as she tried to change the subject. She threw her thumb over her shoulder toward the tree on the front porch, covered in white lights just like Nan had always done, before balling up a tissue and dabbing under her stinging, puffy eyes.

"Percy," her mother replied, while tapping the thermostat, fiddling with it.

"Percy? He's got to be pushing ninety by now." Elizabeth recalled Percy White, the grandfather of her childhood best friend Naomi. He and Naomi's father, Travis, owned the farm next door.

"And still strong as an ox." Mama came over from the kitchen area and scooted the larger of the suitcases to the side of the room while the kettle warmed. "He and Naomi's dad, Travis, are runnin' the Christmas tree lot in town."

The fact that Mama had felt the need to remind Elizabeth of the name of her childhood best friend's father hadn't been lost on her. Mama must have really felt the years that Elizabeth had been away, and being back here, Elizabeth felt it too. She breathed in through her mouth to calm more tears, her nose so sniffly she couldn't get a breath.

"I saved that one from disposal." Mama nodded toward the window with a view of the festive tree on the porch, clearly keeping the conversation light for Elizabeth's benefit. "It's missin' branches on the backside."

Elizabeth pulled off her hat and set it on the table with her scarf, while her mother meandered through the rest of the luggage and went to warm her hands in front of the roaring fire in the stone fireplace. Elizabeth's vision finally clearing as the tears dissipated, she peered down at her footwear against the old woven rug, the high-end leather of her boots stained by the snow.

The smell of cedar and burning wood instantly reminded Elizabeth of Nan, and she sat still to take in the house where she'd spent so much of her childhood. It looked different without the many visitors who'd filled it a year ago for Nan's funeral. Those two days, Elizabeth had been on autopilot, and with such a colossal bereavement, she'd failed to even notice the other loss she'd suffered: somewhere along the line, she'd lost track of who she'd wanted to be.

Nan's writing desk still faced the view out the front window, the crocheted blanket that Elizabeth used to wrap up in while Nan made her pancakes in the mornings hung on the arm of the sofa, and the old black rotary phone sat on the little table next to the corner chair.

Nan's words from their last phone call floated into her mind: *I won't be around forever and I want you to hear this. Foundations aren't all we need. They're nothing if we don't give them shape and form, Liz. Build your foundation, but plan more than just the ground level, see it through, and nurture it.* Elizabeth knew now exactly what she'd meant. Nothing had been nurtured in Elizabeth's adult life or in her relationship with Richard, and look at how both had turned out. She should have listened, should have spoken to Nan more regularly instead of putting it off because of plans she had with Richard. She'd never get the chance now.

Since it was the first moment that Elizabeth had really been back there for any length of time, it was surreal to be in that modest, quiet house, without the endless tasks of a funeral, the memories hitting Elizabeth one after another. She took in an unsteady breath and fixed her gaze on the greenery-draped mantle. Mama had arranged Nan's Santa collection along the top.

Elizabeth blinked away the tears that had sprung to her eyes once more, trying to feel *normal* as she got up and walked around Nan's living room, but she felt like an outsider.

"How long are you staying at the farm?" Elizabeth asked, following her mother over to the small kitchen table that sat at the edge of the open space between the kitchen and living room, next to the bay window. The view showed off the back of the mountain, the trees draped in fluffy snow. Nan's absence was painfully obvious in the silence that hung between them.

Mama pulled the kettle off the gas burner and poured water into two mugs, handing a steaming cup of lemon tea to Elizabeth. "I sold our house and I've moved in here full time. I kept running from our house to Mama's to tend to the farm and it didn't make sense after she passed to keep both."

"You sold it?"

Her mother's eyes became glassy and she cleared her throat, busying herself with stirring her tea. Elizabeth considered what Mama had gone through in the days, weeks, and months after losing her mother. How many nights had she spent alone in Elizabeth's childhood home without a single person to talk to? It only made sense that Mama would want to feel closer to her childhood by being back in this house. A shiver of regret ran through Elizabeth's limbs.

"I'm sorry it's been so long since I've been back just to visit," she said, following her mother with her gaze as Mama fluttered around, wiping the counter in the small kitchen.

"Baby girl, you were busy makin' a life for yourself," she said. "How can anyone blame you for that?"

Elizabeth bit her lip, Mama's grace only serving to make her feel worse.

A knock at the door silenced them both.

"I'll get it," Mama said. "You just sit back down on the sofa and try to enjoy your tea."

While Mama stepped over Elizabeth's designer makeup bag, Elizabeth breathed in the lemon scent from her mug, closing her eyes and trying to center herself. But the click of the latch and the swirl of frigid air distracted her.

"Well, I'll be…"

Elizabeth opened her eyes and turned toward the familiar heavy voice.

Travis stepped inside, handing Mama a heavy grocery bag. "I was at the market and with the snow comin', I thought you might need some milk. You can never have too much, right?" He grinned at Mama.

He had the same Wrangler jeans Elizabeth remembered from her youth, appearing soiled even when they were clean and frayed at the back hems where his work boots rubbed against them. He crossed his arms over his thick coat as he studied her.

Yes, go ahead, she thought, *judge me for leaving.*

"You don't look too good," he said instead, his gruff voice as soft as he could make it.

Elizabeth shook her head, not responding further for fear that she'd fall apart all over again.

"Thank you for this," Mama said with a look of warning to him that Elizabeth could clearly read, letting him know to be easy. Her mother went over to the kitchen and unbagged the milk, putting two jugs into the fridge.

Travis took off his coat, hanging it on the hook by the door. "Naomi know you're back?" He sat down next to Elizabeth on the sofa.

Elizabeth shook her head again, her lips beginning to wobble at Travis's mention of his daughter. Things had been strained when she'd seen Naomi last year at Nan's funeral. She'd been focused on all the tasks that had to be completed and, before she knew it, she was on the plane once more, headed back to her New York life and the people who surrounded her in adulthood—people like Casey Whitcomb, former New York Giants-cheerleader-turned-activist and her closest friend in the city, who Elizabeth spent tons of time with, planning events and working out at the club together. Elizabeth had told herself then that the tension she'd felt with Naomi was because Elizabeth had changed. But she knew deep down that wasn't really the reason. She hadn't allowed herself to contemplate how different she and Naomi had been in their views on life in a long time, or to consider the fact that she'd left her best friend and hadn't bothered to keep in touch. She'd convinced herself over the years that they'd grown apart, and that was why she hadn't called, but the truth was that they'd always been different people.

"Why you wanna live anywhere else, Liz?" Naomi had asked her one day after school, their senior year, while Elizabeth had sorted her pressed flowers, locating each in one of her botany books, her brand-new acceptance letter from New York University open beside them on the floor.

Elizabeth had held up the yellow bloom of a sundrop that grew wild in the fields at Crestwood Farm, thinking about how her feet would tread a different landscape, somewhere new and exciting, by the end of the summer, and then slid the flower into the plastic pocket of her binder. "I want to change the world."

Naomi had crisscrossed her legs and propped her chin up on her hands, her long blonde ponytail cascading down her back as she lay on her belly next to Elizabeth. "That's a tall order. Don't you think you need to figure out who *you* are first?"

"I know enough about myself that I don't feel like this is the right place for me," Elizabeth had told her best friend.

"That's a shame," Naomi had said, the disappointment showing in her frown. "Because I think that the world can't get much better than this. It's God's country out here."

Elizabeth had shut her notebook and addressed Naomi, her friend's complete unwillingness to accept anything other than life in their insignificant little area of the world mystifying her. "So you think shoveling manure and running dirty plows is like Heaven?" she'd challenged.

Naomi had squinted at her and sat up. "Naw. That's just work. We all gotta work for what we want. And I want that clear fresh stream out back, all the fish in it, and my favorite people on the porch until the lightning bugs come out." Then she rolled over and she tackled Elizabeth, pinning her to the carpet. "You're my favorite people!" she'd squealed. "Don't go."

Naomi had always been the idealist of the two of them. Throughout their high school years, Elizabeth had tried to harness it and convince her best friend that there was more to the world than Mason's Ridge, but Naomi had been undeterred in her simple ideals. And when the day finally came for Elizabeth to leave, it had been the first and last time she'd ever seen tears in Naomi's disbelieving eyes.

"I also wanted to see if anyone had come to your door lookin' to buy your property," Travis said, bringing Elizabeth back to the present.

Mama's eyes rounded as she lowered herself slowly in the chair opposite them. "No one's come here. Why, do you think they will?"

Travis shook his head, his bushy eyebrows pulling together. "I don't know. Someone stopped by my house." He leaned forward, his elbows on the stained knees of his jeans. "He wanted to give me four million dollars for the farm so their company could develop it."

Mama gasped and then coughed as if the four million had literally been shoved down her throat. She grabbed her tea and took a drink of it.

First, the fancy coffee shop, then Elizabeth had met Paul who'd been talking about a 2.3 million-dollar Christmas miracle, and now someone was offering Travis four million for his little farm in the mountains? What was going on?

"I don't know why everyone has decided that Mason's Ridge is the new *It* spot for development..." Mama said, taking the words out of Elizabeth's mouth just as the idea had registered. Worry caused the lines in her mother's face to deepen. "I like things just the way they are."

"It wouldn't be the *It* spot if everyone quit sellin' off their land," Travis nearly barked.

"Four million, though?" Elizabeth asked, gripping her tea, considering how little they'd all had during her childhood. Farming wasn't an easy life. One bad season and they'd wonder how they'd put dinner on the table every night. Even in the good times, they weren't exactly comfortable financially. Four million dollars could be life-changing for them. Her mother wasn't getting any younger, and selling would allow her to finally rest after all her hard work. "That's incredible."

"An incredible joke." Travis looked at Elizabeth as if she'd just grown three heads.

"That's *a lot* of money," Elizabeth countered, amazed that he wouldn't have even considered it. Elizabeth knew from being friends with Naomi how every day for Travis was a grind. He spent from sun-up to sun-down working the fields. With four million dollars, he could buy a little house somewhere and retire, never working another day in his life.

"They can't put a price on my land. It's as much me as my right arm." He shook his arm between her and Mama. Then he gave Elizabeth that look that they'd all given her when she'd told them she was leaving Mason's Ridge: that incredulous expression that said, *If you need to leave, you never really belonged.*

"I just meant that you could do a lot with four million dollars," she told him, pushing down the unease that his look had caused her.

"I couldn't do nothin' with it," Travis said. "I get up every mornin' and have my coffee in the same metal cup I've had for the last thirty years and I like it that way. Ain't no money changin' that." He looked her up and down, as if assessing her, making her even more aware of how she stood out in her upmarket sweater and trendy jeans—the only outfit she owned that might have passed for something she could wear there.

"I agree," Mama said, offering a little smile of solidarity to Travis that only made Elizabeth feel more like an outcast.

"How are you going to manage the farm and everything that comes with it all by yourself?" Elizabeth asked Mama. Her mother had mentioned that money was tight this year. A buyout could certainly change that. They were sitting on a goldmine, from the sound of it.

"The older I get, the more I realize how important it is to slow down and do the things I really want to do." Mama's gaze went back to Travis.

He grinned at Mama as if they had some kind of insider information that had escaped Elizabeth her entire life, the two of them an obvious team in this debate.

"Well, I'd better go," Travis said, standing up. He grabbed his coat and peered out the window. "That snow's comin' down. If I don't get home, I might get stuck, and Dad and Naomi would be hungry without groceries for dinner."

Mama got up and followed him over to the door.

"Y'all got everything you need?" he asked, tipping his head down to address Mama, his broad body swallowing the tiny entryway.

"I think we're just fine," Mama replied. "Thanks for comin' over."

Travis nodded. "It's no problem."

Mama let him out and then locked the door behind him.

"So you want to live way out here among the farmhands?" Elizabeth asked, setting her tea on the coffee table and pulling the blanket from the arm of the sofa, draping it over her legs.

Her mother came back over and sat down next to her, thoughts clear on her face. "That's what it might seem like to you, but for me, I've been runnin' this farm with your nan and gramps my whole adult life, and it's all I know. I like to wake up to the orange sunrise every mornin', walk out on the old boards of the porch, and look out at nothing but pasture."

"But do you wonder if staying in your comfort zone is the best path for you?" Elizabeth asked. "I mean, what if there's something else you're great at?"

"Baby girl, when you've found what makes you perfectly happy, it doesn't matter what else you might be great at."

Elizabeth swallowed the lump that swelled in her throat as she took in the balled-up tissues sitting on the table, Mama's words hitting hard. Who was she to judge Mama or Travis? She certainly didn't have anything figured out.

"What gives me purpose is the life that surrounds us here at the farm," Mama continued, a mixture of nostalgia and sadness in her voice. She waved her hand through the air toward the window with the view of the fields. "Even after we're gone—your nan's gone, your grandpa, your dad—it continues. The birds keep goin', findin' food for their young; the trees bloom again in springtime; the water still babbles in the brook out back. Here, I'm reminded of *real* life. And without that reminder, I'll crumble."

Elizabeth nodded, her mother's wise words finally sinking in.

"Although a part of me could stand to make a little money," she said with a wink. "I'd love to rent out a room and have visitors to keep me company. I swear, sometimes I'd like to run into town and snatch up a few people, bring them back to the house, and make them a meal." Mama met Elizabeth's gaze, her eyes glistening. "It would be nice to have other people and their lives to take my mind off the fact that I'm alone."

Elizabeth reached over and put her arms around her mother, hoping to absorb the shock that still lingered, even a year later, from losing Nan. "Well, *I'm* here now," Elizabeth said in an attempt to soothe her, but she knew that nothing could take the pain away from them. Never again would she let Richard or anyone else keep her from giving her mother her full attention whenever she needed it. Elizabeth pulled back. "You were going to tell me what you'd called about last week before everything fell apart? Was it about selling the house?"

Her mother waved off her mention of it. “Let’s not talk about that right now.” She brightened. “You’re here! My baby is home and I want to enjoy the moment.” She went over to the thermostat, adjusting it. “I’m not sure this thing is workin’ right.”

The fact that what couldn’t wait a week ago, while Elizabeth had been standing in front of The Plaza, was now being brushed off made her very nervous. Her mother only avoided things when she was overwhelmed.

When Elizabeth had left to go to college, the whole week prior her mother had puttered around the house, ignoring the fact that Elizabeth was packing her bags. Whenever she’d mentioned her trip to New York, Mama had changed the subject. And when Nan had died, it had taken the whole week for Elizabeth to get her mother to talk about it on the phone, Elizabeth handling the funeral arrangements from New York.

She’d give her mother a little while to settle, but then Elizabeth planned to get to the bottom of it.

Chapter Three

"It's Casey. Sorry you missed me," Elizabeth's friend's voice came through the phone later that evening as she unpacked her things. "Leave me a message, darling, and I might call back."

"It's me again. I haven't heard from you in a week. Just checking in..." Elizabeth finished the message and hung up the phone, chewing on her lip. She hadn't heard from any of her New York friends since Richard had called it quits, and she wondered if her friendships had been a package deal with dating him. Casey, who lived in the apartment downstairs from them, had been one of the first people she'd met after moving in with Richard.

"I never thought I'd see the day you settled down," Casey had said to Richard that day, her perfectly toned body clad in the latest workout gear, as she pulled her dark glasses down her nose.

Richard's eyebrows had bobbed up and down playfully before he kissed Elizabeth. "This is Elizabeth," he'd said, introducing them. It had been the first time he'd ever referred to her by her full name. Until then, he'd seemed happy enough to call her Liz, but once he had begun fully incorporating her into his world, he'd made the change. That should've been a clue as to how the rest of their relationship would go—with him squeezing out every last trait of who she really was until she'd abandoned her own ambitions.

Early on, he'd swept her up in his lavish lifestyle, giving her little gifts at every turn, making her feel like a princess. Before she knew it, he'd groomed her. She was set up with an exercise trainer at "the club" as they called it, a massive campus of racquetball courts, weightlifting facilities, and indoor Olympic-sized pools; Richard had dressed her in designer clothes, had her hair cut and colored by the best stylists in New York; she attended dance classes on Monday nights as well as etiquette classes every Tuesday morning, and, in time, she could handle the most elegant of dinner parties with ease. Little by little, her old life was wiped away until it had disappeared entirely.

She'd originally started getting involved in the charity circuit as a way to give back. While she'd always wanted to travel and change the world, Richard's schedule for work and social events made it difficult to do.

"I need to get a job so that I can pay for my own plane tickets," she'd told him after explaining that she wanted to do mission work overseas.

Richard had given her a placating kiss on the lips. "Any job you'd get would be nothing more than a hobby, given our calendar, and it would look as if I couldn't support you."

"No it wouldn't," she'd said, but she knew the unwritten rules of their circles. Women weren't supposed to work, even though most of them were in their thirties or middle-aged. They were to spend their time grooming themselves to look great on their significant other's arm—an ideal that had never sat well with Elizabeth. She'd tried many times to protest, but was met with utter confusion and irritation every time.

"If you want a plane ticket somewhere, I think I can swing it," he'd said with a laugh, "but I'd prefer that we go to all these places together. You're not going to some third-world country without an escort."

"When then?" she'd pressed him.

He had expelled that annoyed exhale that she now knew so well, as if he were being forced to entertain her. "I'm busy. I'll have to find time in the schedule. Why don't you go to the club with Casey?"

To keep from going crazy, Elizabeth had found her passion in supporting charities, becoming the coordinator for an organization that provided outreach to women and children in need, something the other housewives found to be fashionable to support. She set up lavish events, worked with people who had real money to make a difference in the lives of others, and began to feel as if she had a purpose again. Until Richard began slowly encroaching on even that, suggesting, once he'd seen the guest lists, that they attend as a couple. Under the guise of good will, he was able to strike up conversations with various people, building relationships that benefited his diamond empire. All those wealthy men at the charities had wives and mistresses who loved diamonds…

Throwing her phone onto the old bed, Elizabeth sat down, the springs emitting a loud squeak in protest. She put her head in her hands, the tears returning. How could she have let it all go on for so long? But as she considered the answer, she realized that every change had happened very subtly until she had looked up and her life wasn't anything she'd planned it to be. Now her tears weren't because she'd lost Richard, but because she'd lost herself. She had no idea who she was supposed to be.

With a deep breath, she got up and smoothed the red satin dress she'd worn on that fateful night at The Plaza, which was now hanging in her bedroom at Nan's. She'd stuffed it into one of the boxes last week, not wanting to leave the Carolina Herrera gown in storage back in New York. So she'd packed it along with the other things that she'd express-shipped to the farm, although, of course, she'd never have any occasion to wear it there.

Still shocked by everything that had happened, Elizabeth sat back down on the tattered feather comforter that covered the wooden whitewashed bed in her room and stared at the dress under a beam of dim lamplight. Its red color screamed at her, crying out for a night of glamour that had never materialized. And now it was wedged into the small closet and would soon be hidden behind flimsy bifold doors, a remnant of a life Elizabeth certainly wouldn't be living.

Had she gotten it all wrong? She flopped onto her back and stared up at the yellowed ceiling, the old iron light fixture a far cry from the massive silver chandelier that hung above her bed back home. *Home.* For seven years that's what she'd called Richard's penthouse in New York. But now, as she lay there in her grandmother's house, the glamorous Upper West Side apartment didn't feel much like home anymore; she wasn't sure it ever had, if she were being honest.

Elizabeth found herself straddling her old life and her new one, wondering which side was more her, neither feeling as though it fit entirely. For the eleven years she'd been in New York, through college and then with Richard, she'd told herself that she was no longer the girl who'd grown up in Mason's Ridge. She'd matured, become more distinguished, she'd even begun to go by Elizabeth instead of Liz without a second thought, since her full name had sounded more like *her*. But had it? Here, she was just Liz, the girl who'd spent her days barefoot in the creek, searching for flowers and staying out until the crickets began to sing around her.

Nan, if you can hear me, show me what I'm supposed to do now…

Elizabeth closed her eyes and pictured the creek that ran through the woods out back. Nan had her hands on her hips, her gray curls pinned on the sides, and those strong green eyes they all had, looking as if they belonged to a twenty-five-year-old but peering out at Elizabeth from her lined, aging face.

"Good Lord, child, the entire bottom of your dress is wet," Nan remarked, affection in the twitch of her perfect bow-shaped lips. She slipped off her sandals and hoisted up her own skirt, stepping down into the creek, the clean water rushing around their ankles. "You have to grab hold of the hem like this," she said, pirouetting in the water. "That way it doesn't splash up on you when you dance..."

Nan had always been so sure of herself, so content in her skin. Elizabeth could only dream of being that confident and happy. She considered what could have given Nan that kind of self-assurance about life. Had she been born with it, or had it been created from an intangible recipe of life experiences, an elusive trait, built with time, that Elizabeth may never be able to grab hold of?

Movement at her bedroom door pulled Elizabeth's attention toward it.

"Hey." It was a voice, in a familiar southern accent, that Elizabeth hadn't heard at length in about a decade. "Your mama said you were back here."

Elizabeth rolled off the bed, stood up and faced her old best friend. "Aren't the roads getting bad?" she asked, not knowing what to say.

"They ain't that bad yet," Naomi replied, her gaze moving to the bed as if she were keeping herself from staring at Elizabeth.

"Your dad said…" Elizabeth peered out her bedroom window at the large Silverado in the drive out front, the snow no match for its colossal tires.

"He's always so worried about us. He went to the store and everything when he knows good and well that I can drive the truck just the same as he can." Naomi's light words seemed laced with disappointment and anger. Elizabeth was certain it was over her leaving all those years ago.

She turned back to her old friend, taking in the now mature features of the girl she used to catch lightning bugs with in the pastures until they'd hear the distant call of their parents from across the creek. Her cottontop-blonde hair had darkened to a sandy shade with age, but her features were just the same.

"It's good to see you," Elizabeth said carefully.

The woman shoved her hands into the pockets of her worn jeans, bunching up her oversized sweater at the waist. "Look, I'm not gonna beat around the bush. I'm not here to stir anything up. Dad sent me over to get a read on ya," Naomi replied, not allowing any relief for Elizabeth.

Elizabeth cocked her head to the side. "A read?"

"He's convinced the only reason you've come back is to try to buy out your mama."

"*What?*"

"My granddaddy told us you were here. He helped your mama decorate the tree outside, just for you, so Dad came to see for himself. Then he sent me."

That familiar shame over her mother's excitement at her coming home pelted Elizabeth, despite the fact that Elizabeth had neglected them all. Facing Naomi right then, Elizabeth's leaving without a word, and all the time she had spent away suddenly felt like a tragedy. Naomi had every right to be angry with her.

"So, is it true?" Naomi asked. "You plannin' to bulldoze this place for a shopping mall or somethin'?"

"No," she said, the word withering on her lips as she recalled having suggested that Travis might like to have the millions for his farm. "You can ask Mama," she added. "Where is she?"

"She let me in just before she ran outside."

"Oh?" Elizabeth peered through the window, past the truck, at the wide expanse of endless white snow. "Where in the world did she go?"

"She said she was goin' out to hang a head of cabbage in the chicken coop to keep 'em busy while they're all confined to the henhouse." Her friend paced into the room, neither of them acting like themselves. Naomi roamed around, her finger landing on one of Elizabeth's old botany books before she straightened and turned back to the door, heading toward the living room.

Elizabeth followed Naomi to the sofa, where Mama had set out her famous Christmas gingerbread cookies on the table by the fire, the gesture making Elizabeth feel worse. She picked up the plate and offered them to Naomi. "So, you still live in town?"

Her old friend pinched a cookie and plopped down in the chair where Nan had liked to sit, across from the Christmas tree Mama had decorated in the corner with all the ornaments Elizabeth had made at school over the years. "Yeah," she said. "I built a house next door, on Granddaddy's land, and I help him with the farm." Her chin lifted defiantly, as if she were proving some point from years ago about staying.

"You always did like being on the farm," Elizabeth said gently, hoping to make her feel more comfortable.

"I'm the *face* of Thistle Farms. That's what Granddaddy calls me, anyway," she said, humor in her voice.

Elizabeth sat down across from her. "So everything's going well?"

Naomi nodded, still clearly guarded. "I do all the sellin' at the farmer's market. It's gotten huge with the growth in the area."

"I've noticed."

"We've even expanded to Christmas trees. We're looking to hire more people, but it's tough when there aren't that many farmers around anymore." She took in an edgy breath, shifting in her seat.

Elizabeth pinched a gingerbread cookie in the shape of holly off the plate and snapped the corner of it, holding it in her fingers—more a nervous gesture than an urge to savor something sweet. "Things seem to be really developing around here. There's an actual coffee shop," she said, nibbling the green icing her mother had spread on it. "And every seat was full."

"I know. But the farms around here are going to be dinosaurs…"

"Maybe not all of them," Elizabeth replied, trying to appeal to Naomi.

Naomi shook her head. "The Hansons sold their horse farm to some bigwig developer who's gonna build a housing development. Thing's gonna have a golf course." That last word came out as if it were a curse word.

"You're kidding," was all Elizabeth could say at the mention of their old classmate's farm. They used to give tours to the kindergarten classes, letting them all ride their small pony. While she wasn't a stranger to the good life, and she couldn't deny that a million-dollar view like the ones in Mason's Ridge would be wonderful from across a golf course, she had to admit that there was something elusive about life through Nan's windows that no developer would be able to capture.

"We're holdin' on," Naomi said. "Granddaddy don't care if there are high-rises all around us. He said he might be the only farm left on the grid and ain't nobody takin' it from him."

Percy had always been one to dig in his heels and Elizabeth absolutely believed the fact that he wouldn't budge, even if the world grew up around him.

"So, what do *you* do now?" Naomi asked, appraisal in her gaze as she took a bite of her cookie.

It was a simple question and one that was logical in the flow of conversation, but Elizabeth held her breath. She could say how she'd met Richard in her senior year of college, moved in with him right away, and how after graduation she'd fallen into the busy life of dividing her time between charity lunches, social events, and workouts at the club. But she knew better than to try to explain that to Naomi.

"Cat got your tongue?" Naomi asked, finishing off her cookie. "Don't tell me you do something crazy. You're not some exotic dancer or somethin', are ya?" Naomi looked her up and down as if deciding.

Elizabeth laughed despite herself. "Definitely not."

Naomi blew out a puff of relief. "Thank God. With that body of yours and those perfect nails, I was wonderin'."

Elizabeth set her cookie on the edge of the plate and balled her fingers into a fist, suddenly self-conscious of her bright-red manicure. "I don't have a job," she admitted.

Naomi stared at her curiously.

"I swear, it gets colder every time I go outside," Mama said, interrupting them as she pushed through the front door, sending a wave of frigid air into the small room. She took off her coat and clapped her pink hands together, warming them.

"How'd Miss Maisy like her cabbage?" Naomi asked, her demeanor changing as she addressed Mama.

Mama shook the snow off her scarf and hung it up. "She was the first to start peckin' at it."

"Miss Maisy?" Elizabeth asked.

"She's our prized hen," Mama replied. "I bought her last month, and she's been making eggs for me ever since. In the winter!"

"Wow," Elizabeth said, feeling out of place in the conversation. She had no idea why making eggs in the winter was such a big deal; as a teenager, her sights already set on leaving, she'd stayed away whenever Nan had tried to teach her about the farm, and it had been so long that she couldn't even try to connect the dots now. This world seemed so different from hers back in New York, the pace slower, the concerns easier.

"Are y'all still comin' over to Beatrice Jennings's tomorrow for her ninety-ninth birthday?" Naomi asked Mama. "She's gettin' on in age, you know, and no one can come because of the snow. Her daughter-in-law has been makin' deviled eggs for days, and she needs someone to eat them all."

"Ray got married?" Elizabeth asked, the mention of Beatrice's daughter-in-law implying that her only son, Raymond Jennings, had finally found himself a wife.

"Miracles do exist," Naomi replied, finally chewing on a grin, causing the memory of Ray to float into Elizabeth's consciousness.

The shared recollection took Elizabeth back to better times with Naomi, releasing the tension between them, if only for a moment. "Remember when he professed his love to Mama at the market that day?" Elizabeth asked with a laugh, the feeling so wonderful after all she'd been through.

"Don't tease him, bless his heart," Mama said, wiggling her fingers in the air dismissively. "I've known him since we were kids, and he was just bein' nice."

The glimmer of humor in Naomi's eyes was clear, she and Elizabeth trying not to snigger at the memory for Mama's sake.

When Elizabeth and Naomi were kids, Ray—always trying to find his missus—had stopped Mama on her way to the car at the farmer's market one summer. He'd hitched up his denim bibbed overalls, removed his trucker's hat, and gotten down on one knee, right there in the middle of the gravel parking lot, and promised to take care of Mama. That was when he'd realized his knee was in a pile of horse doo and after some spitting and sputtering, he'd told her he'd have to take care of her later.

"Ray's gonna plow the roads from our farms to Beatrice's house, along with a few of the secondary roads," Naomi said, sobering as the moment passed. "But if we have to, I can get us there in the farm truck."

Beatrice had been Nan's best friend, and Elizabeth had only seen her very quickly at Nan's funeral. She and Nan had been joined at the hip their entire lives.

"The farmhands can help," Mama said, offering up her employees, the young men who Mama paid to live in the cottages on the property and work the fields. They usually did the plowing when it snowed.

Naomi nodded. "Thanks. Ray's gonna need all the help he can get."

"Gladys was worried about the storm putting a wrench in things for the party when I saw her in town last week," Mama said.

"Who's Gladys?" Elizabeth asked, trying to keep up, her mind still on her broken relationship with Naomi.

"Everyone knows Gladys," Naomi said.

The skin between Mama's eyes wrinkled. "Gladys," she said as if Elizabeth hadn't been able to catch who she'd been talking about, but Elizabeth could hear just fine. When she didn't say anything, Mama looked at her as if she'd lost her mind. "Gladys Adkins. Wow. I hadn't realized how long it's been since you've been back in town for any period of time."

"Oh," Elizabeth said uneasily, feeling ganged up on, although they had every right to.

"So can y'all come?" Naomi asked.

Her question hovered above the awkwardness, causing Elizabeth to choke up again. She swallowed it back down and tried not to think about how she'd been a terrible daughter and friend.

"Of course," Mama said. "I'd been plannin' to come the whole time. I bought her a new bakin' dish with a matchin' kitchen towel, since she still likes to bake."

"Hand me your phone," Naomi said, reaching out to Elizabeth, the gesture surprising her.

Elizabeth pulled her phone from her pocket, punched in her code, and held it out to her.

Naomi took it and tapped the screen. "I'll put my number in it and you can call me to come get you if the snow gets too bad." Her gaze remained on the phone as if it pained her to have to offer. "The party's at noon tomorrow."

"I don't have anything to bring her," Elizabeth worried aloud, wondering how she'd be able to cope with seeing everyone at once. She wasn't ready for that. And while Beatrice was sure to be the only one who was easy on her, there was no way she could show up to Beatrice's house emptyhanded.

Mama gave Elizabeth a knowing look. "I'm sure your presence is gift enough."

Elizabeth's heart fell into her stomach. She definitely didn't feel like much of a gift to anyone. But at least here, for better or worse, people seemed to acknowledge her, unlike her friends in New York. Her phone had stayed silent since the minute she'd left. Maybe coming home to the quiet place where she'd built her dreams the first time would give her enough hope to try to do it again.

Chapter Four

What's your story?

Nan's question floated into Elizabeth's mind as she stared at her old magic fortune-telling ball on the dresser in her bedroom where she'd retreated yet again for some alone time while Mama took a shower and got ready for bed. She lay down and opened her phone to her news app, scrolling absentmindedly through the articles that were curated "just for her" but not really paying attention, her mind on Nan's question. It had stayed with her since she'd first heard it at the age of thirteen.

"Will I marry Bo Atkins?" a young Liz asked her magic fortune-telling ball, while she sat on the wooden front step of Nan's house, her eyes closed. She pictured fourteen-year-old Bo swinging his baseball bat during his game the day before. A loud clack had buzzed in her ears when he'd made contact with the ball, Bo taking off, running to first base and then on to second, and blowing toward third before the other team had gotten the ball infield. He dove, reaching out to touch third, barely safe. When he got up, his silver cross necklace was swinging around his tanned neck as he unsuccessfully attempted to brush the red clay off his white uniform. Liz and Naomi had both given a swooning sigh.

Liz shook the ball and then opened her eyes, peering down at the answer that floated to the top of the glass window while Nan looked on from her rocking chair where the old woman sipped her sweet tea to combat the humid summer air.

"Outlook is not good," Liz said with a frown.

Nan chuckled, a loving look in her eyes. "He's not your story then," she said. "He's someone else's, that's all."

Liz set the toy down on the step, disappointed, and walked over to her grandmother, the wooden boards of the porch warm under her bare feet. "What do you mean?"

Nan offered Liz the other rocker and Liz sat down, the summer heat causing beads of sweat to roll down her back, even in her gauzy sundress.

"Your story can't be found over there," Nan said, tipping her chair and releasing it, gliding back and forth on the rails as she nodded toward the fortune-teller. "You have to pray first and then listen to your gut. Whatever you hear or feel is right—that's your story. That's your real little window of answers. Not the one over there."

"Do you ever hear answers?" Liz asked, sweeping her long chocolate waves into a ponytail on top of her head to allow the breeze to tickle her neck.

"All the time," Nan said, and the certainty in her voice assured Liz that it had to be true.

❄

When she swam out of her memories, Elizabeth looked away from the article on her phone screen, but not quickly enough for her to have missed the headline suggested for her. Her mouth gaping, she scanned the title: *Richard Oppenheim is Moving On.* She did a doubletake, reading the byline: *"The billionaire heir to the biggest diamond empire in the world has been spotted with twenty-seven-year-old model Tawny Ferguson."*

Elizabeth lay on her bed, staring at the words, her breath shallow. In shock, a tear meandered across her temple as if it were marching on its own, a lone leader before the flood. It slid along her skin and onto her pillow just as her lips began to quiver.

She'd meant nothing to him. All that time she'd given up, doing what Richard had wanted her to do, never able to explore her interests to any degree—it had all been wasted time.

Rolling over onto her pillow, she buried her face and screamed before breaking down into sobs.

Tawny had been a mutual friend; she'd hung around in their circles. A month ago, Richard had left a cocktail party early to take Tawny home after she'd had too many drinks. He'd told Elizabeth that he'd been late getting back because there had been a detour on his normal route, but now, through the absolute pain she felt at this news, she questioned everything.

Elizabeth was twenty-nine and she didn't have a story. She'd been living Tawny Ferguson's story, apparently. The girl she'd been, with all the big dreams to get out of that little mountain town and do something amazing, had just vanished into thin air. She knew now that the girl had vanished the very day Richard had come into her life.

That day and all its innocence was still vibrant in her mind. Elizabeth had met Richard at a bar. She'd caught his eye while she and her roommate were dancing to a local band. She could still remember it like it was yesterday: she'd had her hands over her head, the linen dress she'd bought on sale the day before billowing out as she spun around, and when she'd made that final twirl, she'd seen him. Richard had stuck out in the crowd, appearing slightly older than she was, more distinguished, with his designer-logoed shirt, high-dollar beer and perfect haircut. When he'd flashed her that smile, she'd fallen for him right then and there. Little did she know then how her life would turn out.

"Knock, knock," Mama said, rapping on the doorframe.

Hiding her sniffle with a little cough, Elizabeth turned over and faced her mother.

"You've got to be starvin'. I put a pizza in the oven, and I've thrown a couple of logs on the fire." She tucked her wet hair behind her ear, the creases in the corners of her eyes revealing the length of her day. She scrutinized Elizabeth's face but didn't ask any unwelcome questions. "Want to come out and sit with me?"

Elizabeth sat up, her head feeling as if it weighed a hundred pounds. Leaving her phone on the pillow, she followed Mama into the living room and settled on the sofa across from the fireplace. Two stockings hung from the mantle; Elizabeth recognized that they were hers and her mother's. For the first time since she'd arrived, she realized the third one for Nan was missing. With only five days until Christmas, and just the two of them now, she wondered what Christmas Day would bring.

Mama sat down next to Elizabeth and toyed with her wet hair. Since Elizabeth could remember, her mother had taken her showers at night, and her mother's skin had always glowed from the warmth of the water and the balms she put on. But tonight, she looked exhausted.

"Want to tell me about the phone call yet?" Elizabeth asked, her gut making her think that it had something to do with how tired her mother looked.

"Oh, I don't know." Mama shook her head as if it were nothing, but Elizabeth caught the fear in her eyes.

"Tell me," Elizabeth urged.

"Why don't we enjoy the night first," Mama said, getting back up. "We don't want to ruin dinner."

"Ruin?" Elizabeth got up and followed her mother into the kitchen. "I want to know, Mama. You said a week ago that it couldn't wait."

"I know, I just…" She sucked in a breath and turned toward the drawer by the oven, pulling out an oven mitt.

"Mama, the pizza isn't nearly ready yet." Elizabeth reached out and gently took her mother by the arm. "Tell me. What's going on?"

Gnawing at her bottom lip, Mama took a tri-folded letter from the drawer that held the old phone books, spreading it out on the counter.

Elizabeth leaned in to view it.

"Last week, I got a phone call… And then yesterday I got this letter from a lawyer, tellin' me the farm doesn't belong to us and we'd need to pack up our things."

"What?" Elizabeth took the paper from her mother and scanned it. "This doesn't make any sense…" She looked up at her mother. "It's saying we don't own the farm." Elizabeth flipped over the paper for any additional information, but the other side was blank. "Is this some sort of scam?"

"I don't think so. I was completin' the paperwork for Nan's estate and I had to get the deed for the farm. When I went to the title company's office so they could help me, they told me the deed was registered to Worsham Enterprises. Then I got this." Her mother tapped the name and address. "Pierce and Hughes. That's a real-estate attorney's office a couple towns over, in Riverbend. This Worsham Enterprises has decided to claim the land."

"Who in the world is that?"

"I've never heard of it," Mama said.

Elizabeth put down the letter and pulled out her phone. She did a quick search for the name, scrolling until she found an article of interest. She read an excerpt to Mama.

Worsham Enterprises is expanding. With new management stepping in, major restructuring has key investors wondering if the new entity will be a success. William Worsham, founder of Worsham Enterprises has no comment on the matter.

"This is definitely a mix-up," Elizabeth decided, relief flooding her once she'd come to her senses that Nan had to own the land. Anyone else owning it was absolutely preposterous. "There's no way the deed for Crestwood Farm belongs to anyone but Nan. Somehow wires got crossed or something, and they've recorded the wrong property." Thank goodness at least one of her issues could be resolved. "I'll call them first thing in the morning and we'll get it straight."

"You think so?" Mama asked, her shoulders falling, optimism showing in the creases of her forehead.

"Of course, Mama," Elizabeth assured her. "Nan and Granddaddy lived their whole adult lives in this house. They got married here. They raised *you* here. For what reason in the world would someone be able to suddenly take land that's been in our family for generations?" Elizabeth rubbed her mom's arm to comfort her. "Don't worry about a thing. Everything will be okay."

"It does seem outrageous now." Mama shook her head with a reassured smile, peering down at the official notice. "I just needed you to set my mind at ease."

"I'm glad I could," Elizabeth told her. With everything that was going on, the one silver lining was that she could spend time with her mother.

The buzzer went off on the oven, signaling that the pizza was ready to come out.

"Why don't we have some wine?" Elizabeth suggested, feeling suddenly festive with one hurdle behind her. She slipped on an oven mitt, took the pizza out of the oven, and set it on a trivet. "Got any in the fridge?"

Mama's eyes grew round with excitement. "Silly question," she said playfully. "You know I do." She pulled a bottle of Chardonnay out of the fridge and retrieved the corkscrew from the kitchen utensil drawer. "You bring the pizza to the table and I'll pour us each a glass."

Before she took two glasses from the cabinet, Mama clicked on the radio, turning the dial, the Christmassy sound of "Deck the Halls" filling the air. With the snow out the window, the fire crackling, and the twinkle of lights from their little tree, for the moment, Elizabeth relaxed.

Mama poured them each a glass and, with a little twirl, handed one to her. "I'm so happy you're home, baby girl."

Having not heard her mother's pet name for her regularly in so many years, emotion swelled in Elizabeth's throat, and she hid it with a crisp sip of wine, the buttery notes along with vanilla and spice settling on her tongue. "Me too," she said, and she meant it. Elizabeth put her wine down next to the plates Mama was setting on the table and walked into the kitchen to slice the pizza, carrying it over to their places when she'd finished.

"Nan used to fill this whole table with cookies every Christmas," she said, sliding a triangle slice of pizza onto her mother's plate. "She started baking weeks before."

"Yes, your nan loved to bake, didn't she? She made cookies for all the neighbors." Mama sat down and scooted her chair closer to the table, putting a paper napkin in her lap.

"She used to write a letter to each of them to go with the cookies, didn't she? Telling them the things she remembered about them from that year, and she tied the envelope to each tray of cookies with a red ribbon."

"She did that for as long as I can remember," Mama said, leaning on her hand with a nostalgic grin. "She called them her Christmas letters. She said once that she'd made it her life's work to spread joy on Christmas, and the red ribbon was a symbol of love."

Elizabeth took a bite of pizza, her gaze falling on the empty chair where Nan used to sit. "I wonder if anyone misses them."

Mama smiled at the question and took a sip of her wine. "I'd love to pick up where she left off, but I wouldn't have much to write."

As she fiddled with her slice of pizza, Elizabeth wondered what she'd include in her Christmas letter to someone like her friend Casey back in New York. She'd spent almost every day with the woman, so she'd surely have pages to say… She could mention their racquetball games or the polo matches that they'd gone to in the summers, but as she considered what she remembered about Casey specifically, she came up empty.

Yet, when she thought about Naomi, even with everything that had happened, there'd be loads to write. She could mention how she loved that Naomi was always direct, to the point that she'd even divulged her purpose for coming over, that Travis had sent her to get a read on Elizabeth. The idea of it made Elizabeth smile. Naomi had always been like that. Even now there was the fact that she was willing to help them all get to Beatrice's birthday party, offering to drive them in the farm truck if she had to, even though she was clearly still feeling hurt by Elizabeth's leaving all those years back.

Casey hadn't offered her a thing, not even a call to see how she was doing. And if she were being honest with herself, Richard hadn't given her anything to remember either.

"What are you thinking about?" Mama asked.

"Oh, nothing important," Elizabeth said, wondering how significant any of the last seven years had been to her. "I wish I could be like Nan and have tons to say about the people in my life, but I don't have anyone that I know that well anymore."

Mama's eyebrows shot up in surprise. "I thought you had a bunch of friends in New York. You were always running off with them to different events."

"Looking back on it now, I didn't really share a whole lot with them personally." She took in a slow breath, the revelation of it overwhelming. "I don't have anyone in my life who knows *me*," she said, her voice breaking on her words.

"Well, it sounds like we need to change that," Mama said, raising her glass. "Here's to the hunt for great friends who feel like family."

Elizabeth clinked her glass to her mother's, blinking away her tears, unsure if it could be that easy after the way she'd left Mason's Ridge.

Chapter Five

Elizabeth rolled under her covers and patted the side table blindly for her watch. Locating it, she pulled it toward her and opened one eye to view the time: almost 9 a.m. She couldn't remember the last time she'd slept past six. She was usually at the club by seven and having her after-workout protein drink with the ladies by eight.

She yawned, sitting up, the bed emitting its signature squeak under her to remind her where she was. She felt oddly refreshed instead of groggy, as if she'd slept off the last week and emerged from the fog.

She peered out the window. The snow was still falling outside, big downy flakes swirling in the air and disappearing against the white breadth of the fields that seemed to stretch all the way to the gray mountains on the horizon. The Christmas tree out on the porch was still lit from last night, the tiny bulbs offering a pale-yellow light, no contest for the bright white snow. With the blizzard outside and her fluffy blankets still wrapped around her, Elizabeth felt as though she were in a cocoon, protected from the entire world.

Reluctantly, she climbed out of bed and padded over to get a better look at the view outside, the cold air slithering through the seal, giving her a chill. She couldn't see a single person anywhere, making her feel very alone. Even though she'd been surrounded by people in New York, she might as well have been in the middle of a blizzard—the silence now was the same. The more she thought about her empty life, the more she wondered how Nan had done it. How had she made lasting relationships like she had with Beatrice and Percy, and all the people in town? Could Elizabeth manage to do the same? The idea of her and Mama making life-long friendships in the dead of winter seemed a bit far-fetched. At least they had Beatrice's party today. That would be a start.

But first she wanted to help Mama tend to the animals so she didn't have to do it by herself. Then she needed breakfast and coffee so she could think straight to call the lawyer's office and get the misunderstanding over the farm sorted out.

Elizabeth slipped on a pair of jeans and her thickest woolly sweater, twisted her hair into a clip, and opened the bedroom door, heading to the living room. Out the back window, Mama was already in her boots and long coat, lugging hay into the barn for the horses and goats, its doors wide open. Elizabeth watched her guiltily, guessing she'd probably been out there for hours.

Pulling on her coat and dropping her feet into a spare pair of boots, Elizabeth grabbed her gloves and scarf and went outside, going around the back of the house, and making her way into the barn. The old wooden floor was covered in soft hay, more bales of it stacked against the side. The fresh, sweet scent of the hay took her back to her childhood. If she squinted at Mama shoveling and tossing more onto the floor with the pitchfork, she could almost believe Nan had come back to them.

Elizabeth walked over to their chocolate-brown mare named Buttons and stroked her side. The horse's big eyes shifted, finding Elizabeth, the animal's jaw hanging slack the way it always had whenever she was happy.

Elizabeth smiled. "You glad to see me, girl?"

Buttons lightly stomped the ground and snorted. Elizabeth's delighted laugh pulled Mama's attention toward her.

"Mornin'," Mama called.

"Morning." Elizabeth patted Buttons on the side and headed over to see the other horse in the stall by Mama. "Who's this?" she asked, leaning over to find a young colt peering at her, his tail swishing.

"That's Buzz. He was born a few years back and is growin' like a weed."

"He's lovely."

"Yes, he is." Mama leaned on her pitchfork. "We need to take both the horses out to ride. They're goin' stir-crazy. I've been walkin' them around the barn and talkin' to 'em, but I can tell they're itchin' to get out."

"I wonder how hard the ground is," Elizabeth said, the rule about the horses needing a soft surface to run on coming back to her like a whisper from her past.

"I could still sink a shovel into it pretty easily, so they'll be okay. Maybe just a quick run around the rings out back so they can get their wiggles out and we don't freeze to death."

"I'll do it," Elizabeth offered.

"Think you can remember how to mount them?"

Elizabeth nodded. "It's like riding a bike, right?" she teased.

Mama laughed. "A bike that'll rear up and kick ya if you aren't careful."

Elizabeth grinned at her mother, but then sobered. "You could've asked me to help," she said, reaching out for the pitchfork.

"I've been doin' it all on my own so long, it didn't occur to me." Mama handed her the tool. "Spread this out here; that's all that's left," she said, waggling a finger at the piled hay at their feet. "When you're done, you can saddle up the horses and we'll take 'em for a quick ride. I'm gonna go milk the goats."

As Mama walked off, Elizabeth moved the large pile of hay into place, the pressure in her shoulder muscles a tiny reminder that she was alive. The farm seemed so far away from the rest of the world—like a safe haven, giving her time and space from everything but her family and the serene surroundings of her youth. The more she did within this place, the more she felt as though she'd been denying her soul its own existence, pushing it out until it had all but disappeared from her reality.

When she'd finished, Elizabeth set the pitchfork against the wall, pulled the saddle off the saddle rack, and took it over to Buttons. "Up for a ride?" she asked the horse.

Buttons tapped her hooves against the floor, the sound of it like music to Elizabeth's ears. She alerted the horse to the saddle pad, rubbing it against the animal's body. Then she slid it into place. She did the same with the saddle, rubbing the horse and tossing the saddle over the back of her, fastening the girth strap as Buttons snorted.

The horse's excitement hit her unexpectedly hard. She hadn't even realized until this moment how much she'd missed this. "Yes, we're going out, like old times," she said, rubbing the horse's cheek. "I know, I was gone way too long."

Those deep brown eyes found her and the horse snorted once more.

"I won't do it again," Elizabeth said. "I promise. No matter where I end up, I'll come back to you." She placed her foot in the stirrup and hoisted herself up, grabbing the reins. She squeezed her legs against Button's side gently to signal that she was ready. "Off we go."

Buttons snorted through her nostrils and let out a neigh that sent Elizabeth's heart soaring. The horse galloped toward the ring, allowing her to ride like she always had, the animal not tentative at all. It was if Buttons had been waiting for her all these years.

With a shiver, Elizabeth took another log off the hearth and tossed it into the fire, the flame protesting the new addition, sending sparks up the chimney. She'd ridden Buttons longer than she could stand it in the cold, but she'd wanted to let the horse run. Mama hadn't lasted nearly as long, having taken out the younger horse.

While Mama had run back to the barn to collect the buckets of goat's milk, Elizabeth—her hands numb from the cold—went over to the kitchen, making them each a mug of hot cocoa with marshmallows.

Feeling festive, Elizabeth filled the mugs and stirred the mixture, taking the hot chocolates and the lawyer's letter over to the living area just as her mom came in.

"Well, that looks delicious," Mama said, kicking off her snowy boots before shutting the door with her elbow, a silver bucket full of goat's milk in each hand. "It feels like it's below zero out there. I don't know how you rode Buttons for that long, but she seems very content now." She set the buckets down by her feet and shrugged off her coat, hanging it by the door.

Elizabeth nodded to the buckets as her mother picked them back up and took them into the kitchen, setting them on the counter. "Won't the farmhands milk the goats?"

Mama ran over to the fire and spread out her fingers, holding them toward the flames, her body still seizing in shivers. "Yes, but… that's not the point."

"What *is* the point?" Elizabeth asked, her hands wrapped around the warm mugs as she walked over and stood next to Mama, handing one of them to her, the heat from the flames tickling her skin.

Mama took the mug into the kitchen and Elizabeth lowered herself onto the sofa, tucking her legs under her body, pulling the blanket off the arm as she watched Mama working through Nan's ritual of preparing the goat's milk for making cheese.

"Well, I spent my whole childhood workin' this farm." Mama grabbed a pot, pouring the goat's milk into it and heating the burner. "And even though we had help, I still had chores." She moved the empty buckets over to the sink while the milk began to simmer.

Elizabeth snuggled under the blanket, feeling festive; the rich smell of the goat's milk mixed with the cinnamon and vanilla holiday scents in the house were uniquely theirs.

"Your nan used to say that our purpose in life is service to everyone and everything around us. She doesn't get to look after the animals anymore, but I do. I'm still here to do the work."

"Nan was so wise," Elizabeth said. It occurred to her that her own life might feel so empty because she hadn't really done a whole lot for anyone who she loved. Today she had, and she'd noticed how it had made her feel. "I'm glad I get to see Beatrice today. Maybe she'll tell us more stories about Nan. But I really don't want to show up without anything to give her."

"You only just got here," Mama said. She turned off the heat on the goat's milk and stirred in some lemon juice, sending a citrus flavor into the air. "And I already told you, Beatrice will understand. She'll be delighted to see you."

"It isn't that, though. I want to show her I care."

Mama turned around and gave her a warm look. "Ah, well that's a different story. You don't have to buy people things to show them you care."

Elizabeth nodded, pondering that fact. It had been quite a while since she'd had someone show her love without giving her anything. She recalled a time when she was about seven. She'd fallen, running through the fields of buttercups, and had scraped her knees on the rocky soil. Nan had jumped from her rocker and rushed over, scooping up Elizabeth and carrying her to the house. On the way, her grandmother had bent down and snatched a handful of buttercups. Then, carefully, Nan had set her down on the top step of the porch.

❄

"Let me see," Nan said gently as tears streaked Liz's cheeks. "I have just the thing. But while you wait for me to come back, smell these. It'll help." She handed Liz the handful of little yellow flowers.

Distracted by the sweet scent of the blooms, Liz touched their delicate petals, her fingers making prints on them. They were so vibrant and pretty that they'd kept her attention until Nan returned with a wet rag and a glass jar of honey with a small wooden stirrer inside.

"What's that for?" Liz asked, nervous that her grandmother would have to touch her wound.

"Hold out your finger," Nan told her.

When Liz did as she was told, Nan swirled the golden honey and then lifted out the stirrer, placing one drop of the nectar on Liz's finger. "Smell the flowers while you taste the honey and tell me what happens."

Liz put her finger in her mouth, the sugary taste exploding on her tongue. She sniffed the earthy, sweet scent of the flowers, the sun shining on her face, warming her.

"What did you notice?" Nan asked as she dipped the stirrer into the honey and released a single drop of the sticky substance onto Liz's knee, tapping it lightly with her finger.

"It made me feel like summer," Liz said, at a loss for words to explain at her age the absolute sensation of it.

"The honey will fix you on the inside and the outside. All better," Nan said, trailing her finger around Liz's leg. With the sugary taste and fragrant smell, she'd barely noticed that Nan had cleaned her knee.

❄

The only thing Nan had given her that day to show love had been her time and her kindness. Elizabeth hoped that one day she could be as great as Nan had been in that moment.

When she surfaced from the memory, the curds were draining in the cheesecloth and Mama was holding the lawyer's letter, her face turned down as she studied it.

"I was going to call them," Elizabeth said, waggling her finger at it.

"Let's call right now," Mama suggested, coming over to her and sitting down. "I'd like to go to Beatrice's and enjoy the day knowin' we've taken care of this."

Elizabeth pulled her phone from her pocket and sipped her hot cocoa before setting the mug down on the coffee table. "Yes, we'll find out once and for all that there's nothing to worry about."

She took the letter from Mama and dialed the number. The phone pulsed while she touched the speaker on the screen to allow Mama to hear the call. When the ringing stopped and there was a click, Elizabeth squared her shoulders in anticipation, but a recording answered instead.

"You've reached the law offices of Pierce and Hughes. We're currently closed, but if you'd like to leave us a detailed message…"

Elizabeth looked over at her mother. "I'll bet it's because of the snow." When the recording finished, she left a message with her number and asked if they'd call her back. She hung up the phone and twisted around toward Mama, who was wringing her hands in her lap, a frown on her lips. "We'll get it cleared up. I promise."

Mama nodded and, with a deep breath, lifted herself off the sofa. "I'm gonna finish preppin' the cheese and make us some breakfast. How does that sound?"

"I'll help." Elizabeth grabbed her mug and stood up. On her way to the kitchen, she gazed out the window at the rolling hills of white. "I wonder if Ray has been able to plow anything yet."

"I hope so. Otherwise, it'll be a long walk to Beatrice's…" Mama retrieved the basket of eggs that she'd gathered from the hens out back and pulled a large bowl from the cabinet. "Why don't you call Naomi and see how it's goin'?"

"I doubt she'd want me to bother her."

Mama washed her hands at the sink, drying them on a kitchen towel. "Nonsense. She gave you her number of her own free will."

"I don't think she's very happy with me for how I've behaved over the last decade," Elizabeth said honestly.

"Probably not," Mama agreed, turning to face her. "But you'll never patch things up by avoidin' her."

"I don't want to avoid her," Elizabeth said. "It's the opposite, actually. But I don't want to stir up unnecessary feelings for her either."

"When Travis asked her to come over, she didn't have to. She could've put her foot down." Mama gave her a knowing look.

"I didn't know you were aware that he'd sent her."

"It's not hard to guess." She wrinkled her nose at her daughter. "At least text her."

Elizabeth fired off a message to Naomi. "What's for breakfast?" she asked her mother as she put her phone down.

"I thought we'd have egg and sausage casserole. It used to be your favorite." Mama began cracking eggs into the bowl.

"Is it the one with the croissant topping and cheddar cheese?" Elizabeth asked. It would definitely be a departure from the usual matcha almond-milk superfood juice that she got on the way to the club every morning.

"Yes, ma'am," Mama said proudly, the bowl pressed against her bosom as she whisked the eggs. "I browned the sausage before you got here yesterday, so all we have to do is make the croissant dough. You up for it?" Mama waggled a finger at the cupboard door above her.

"If I can remember how," Elizabeth said, taking the flour from the cupboard at Mama's direction, stepping into the preparation tentatively.

Mama handed her the butter.

As they got going, it was easier than she'd thought, although the absence of Nan was hovering above them the whole time. But what gave Elizabeth happiness was the smile she saw on Mama's lips as the two of them worked side-by-side. With the glimmering lights of the tree and the stockings hung by the fire, it almost felt like a good Christmas already.

Chapter Six

"Ray's got the back lane already plowed, and he's takin' me into town for a minute," Naomi said through Elizabeth's flour-dusted phone speaker as it sat on the counter beside the croissant dough.

"We could do with some bakin' supplies—I'm down a few ingredients—and we need more milk," Mama said, reaching for the rolling pin in Elizabeth's hands. "You've done the hard part. I could take it from here if you wanted to catch a ride with Naomi."

"You sure?" Elizabeth asked, widening her eyes at Mama for vocalizing the suggestion while Naomi was on the line.

"Of course. Grab a quick snack to get you through and I'll have your plate full of steamin' casserole by the time you get home."

"Any for me?" Naomi's voice came through the phone, making her mother smile.

"There's always some for you, Naomi," Mama answered.

"Glad to hear that, Miss Loretta," Naomi said, addressing Mama like she had as a little girl.

"Are you all right if Liz comes?" Mama asked, leaning over toward the phone.

The line sat silent for a second, and Elizabeth held her breath.

"Liz, can you be ready in fifteen minutes? Ray's swingin' by and then we'll head your way."

"Yep." Elizabeth handed her mother the rolling pin, relief that she hadn't offended her old friend suddenly overpowered by the fact that she'd have to share a tractor ride with her into town. "See you in a few." Elizabeth ended the call and looked at her mother. "What if she hadn't wanted me to come?"

"Then she wouldn't have offered the fact that she was goin' into town."

Elizabeth nodded, still unsure. "I suppose you're right."

"I'm always right," Mama said with a wink.

"Well, I'd better get ready." As she rushed down the hallway, Elizabeth called over her shoulder for Mama to make a list of anything else she needed. From the look of the roads, this might be the only chance they'd have to get into town for a few days, so it was probably best that she did go.

Elizabeth hurried to her room, stripped off her sweater that was full of flour, and threw on a new one. She pulled out the old ball cap she used to wear in college and took a moment to assess the tattered brim. It had been a long time since she'd worn it… Not feeling much like putting a whole lot of effort into her appearance, she scooped her shiny waves into a ponytail and slid on the cap, then ran into the bathroom to splash a little water on her face and brush her teeth.

The sound of Ray's tractor clattering outside pulled Elizabeth's attention to the window. The massive John Deere treaded through the snowy field, the tires leaving a trail of giant Xs in the pristine landscape, a pine wreath with a red Christmas bow tied to the grill on the front just above the plow.

Elizabeth headed to the front door and put on her coat and boots, wrapping her neck with her woolly scarf.

"Here's the list of things to get at the market," Mama said, hurrying over to the door to hand her the piece of paper.

"These are all the cookie-baking ingredients you'll need?" Elizabeth teased as she studied the small list.

"You know I've already got most of it," Mama replied with a grin. "I'm always prepared for Christmas."

"Okay," she said. "I'll be back in a little while."

Elizabeth took the list and opened the door, a gust blowing sparkling snow into the house, the glittery flakes settling on the hardwoods at her feet. Shutting the door behind her, she ran out into the field, her boots crunching in the piled snow, sinking to her ankles. When she reached the tractor, the side door opened.

Ray leaned around Naomi, running a judging eye down her, making Elizabeth's shoulders tense. Naomi widened the door and beckoned her into the tractor.

Elizabeth put her boot on the metal step at the bottom and hoisted herself up, climbing into the cab next to Naomi and Ray. She greeted them both and then leaned across Naomi. "Nice to see you, Ray." She decided it was a good idea to start off on the right foot, even though she could tell he wasn't terribly thrilled to see her.

"Mornin'," Ray said, producing a forced smile, showing off the space between his front teeth. "Long time, no see…" He kept his eyes on the field in front of them.

Ray shifted gears, the tractor lurching slightly at the change, the engine growling against the pressure and tossing Elizabeth forward. She clutched the door to brace herself. Ray kept looking straight ahead as if nothing had happened. For an instant, she was frustrated, but then she realized that she'd been the only one to react to the jerk. As she sat back in the seat, Elizabeth wondered if he'd meant to toss her around or if it had just been so long since she'd been in a tractor that she wasn't used to the rhythm of it anymore.

When they got to the road, Ray lowered the plow, clearing the path and pushing up mounds of snow on either side of them as they made their way to town. Elizabeth grabbed on to the back of the seat to keep from bouncing into Naomi's lap. The tractor bumped along, snow falling into the drop-off down the mountain. Elizabeth closed her eyes, her knuckles white from her tight grip as if holding the seat would keep them from plummeting over the edge.

"We're stoppin' off at High Peak," Naomi said as they drove in to the nearly empty parking lot at the coffee shop, the entire area covered in snow. "Beatrice likes their coffee, so I'm gonna buy a bag of it for her birthday."

Elizabeth nodded, wishing again that she had something to bring Beatrice.

The idea of a warm cappuccino did sound enticing and Elizabeth welcomed the thought of heat from the fire that was probably roaring inside. She should've worn her beanie instead of the old ball cap to keep her ears from freezing and she couldn't feel her fingers.

When Ray pulled the tractor to a stop, they got out. Elizabeth hopped into the snow first, catching herself, her feet unsteady on the icy surface. Naomi stepped down without incident, and they trudged across the heavily covered parking lot in silence and went inside. Naomi walked straight over to the shelves of merchandise, while Ray waved to a man in bibbed overalls.

"Not really your kind of spot, Sid," he said, clapping the man on the back.

"Yours neither," the man said, eyeing Elizabeth. "I'm meeting my niece. She loves the place." He pressed his lips into a straight line. "That's the problem, though, isn't it? The next generation would rather have coffee shops than hold on to their birthright." He glared at Elizabeth as if she'd built the establishment herself. "How 'bout you?"

Ray turned Elizabeth's way. She twisted toward the coffee selection board to avoid gawking at the two men. "That's Loretta's daughter," she heard Ray say under his breath. "Ain't seen her in years until the land starts gettin' bought up. Then she magically appears..."

Elizabeth sucked in a quiet breath. Did *everyone* think that was why she was there?

"Well, I ain't sellin' mine," Sid said.

"Same. And if she thinks that bein' friendly with all of us'll make things easier if she decides to try to swallow up our land with her fancy New York bank account, she's got another thing comin'."

Elizabeth gritted her teeth and faced them, ready to stand up for herself. But her emotions got the better of her, because the truth of the matter was, she reminded herself, that she'd brought all this speculation on by her own behavior. Needing a minute to keep the tears from forming, she decided to head over to the fire.

The place was a far cry from before the storm had hit. There was only one person there, sitting by the fire, laptop in his lap. He turned around when Elizabeth walked closer, and her breath caught at the sight of those blue eyes. Paul Dawson, from yesterday.

"I can't do anything yet," he said into his phone, trying to keep his voice low. "There are a few... issues and I'm afraid it might take until after the holiday." He clicked keys on his computer, frowning at something on the screen. "I am fully aware of the timescale here." His jaw clenched and his chest filled with air. "How much time did they give us? ...You've got to be kidding me. Let me know what they say..."

He looked up, momentarily distracted by Elizabeth, but she turned toward the menu on the wall above the register once more so he wouldn't think she was spying on him. When she turned back around to face him, he'd ended his call. He got up and flashed her that smile of his, setting his phone on the table.

"So we did meet again," he said, pacing over to her, sending Ray's wary gaze their way.

Elizabeth tried to ignore it, focusing all her attention on Paul. The twitch of his lips as he took in her ball cap made her wish that she'd put on her woolly hat instead. Then she could yank it down over her face and sink into a chair.

"Those are pretty good odds for someone who said she doesn't come here much."

"We're getting a gift for someone." She nodded over to Naomi who was still browsing products at the counter.

Elizabeth sat down in the other chair by the fire, her heart fluttering at the sight of Paul's kind gaze. In the light of day, after a good night's sleep, he was even more handsome. Once upon a time, the sparkle in his eye when he looked at her would've had her flirting like crazy, but now she didn't feel confident in herself anymore. The universe was off-kilter, putting this nice guy in her path at the wrong time entirely.

She fixed her eyes on the small, framed map of Mason's Ridge that hung beside the fireplace. "I've always liked that map," she said, staring at it. "You can buy them at the general store… At least you used to be able to." She remembered finding Crestwood Farm on it when she and Nan saw them at the store.

"They should sell them here," Paul said, going over to it and inspecting it. He turned, those blue eyes settling upon her, nearly taking her breath away. "So, you're getting a gift in a blizzard?"

"Mm hm," she replied, not elaborating. "Were you working?"

He sat down across from her, leaning on his knees casually. "Yep," he said, and she could've sworn she saw slight tension in his shoulders when he replied. "Although, I'm trying to have a vacation from work."

"Everything okay?"

"Yeah," he said on an exhale. "I'm just a little burned-out, that's all. And there's always something to be done." He rubbed his shoulder and twisted his head around before straightening. "Maybe it's the call of the holidays. They're begging for me to take a break."

She smiled, trying not to make a comparison to Richard's constant drive to land that next deal…

"How'd it go with seeing your mom?" Paul asked, his gaze softening the way it had when she'd met him, giving her another flutter.

It was the first time someone had been interested in what she might be going through. Paul's reactions were such a stark contrast to what she was used to getting from Richard that she couldn't help but react to them. She pinched the side of her leg to make it stop.

"It was good," she said, feeling uncomfortable about having been so forward with her personal information, but at the same time relieved that someone could actually *see* her. In her exhaustion, she'd let her guard down, and now she had to face the fact that she'd offered up this little bit of herself to a random stranger. While Paul seemed so kind, she didn't know his motives. Just sitting there with him, she felt like she could tell him anything, and the idea of it was terrifying.

Ray shifted across the room, getting a bottle of water and settling at a table, while Sid went over and hugged his niece when she came in. They settled at a table with Ray. Naomi read the back of one of the bags of coffee before putting it back on the shelf and grabbing another.

"You sure?" Paul asked.

"Hm?" Elizabeth tore her eyes from Naomi.

"You seem uneasy."

She swallowed, her pulse racing at the fact that he could read her so easily yet again. "I'm not uneasy about my mom," she said. "She's great."

Paul tilted his head, that kind expression making it difficult to look at him for fear she'd spill her entire life story, and she was nearly certain he wouldn't want to hear that level of drama on his vacation.

"Then what are you apprehensive about?" he asked.

Elizabeth prayed he couldn't see the fire that spread over her cheeks when she considered how to tell him that *he* was the one making her edgy, with all his attention and compassion. "Nothing," she finally answered. "What are *you* doing working at the coffee shop in the middle of a blizzard?"

"I'm in the rental house next door," he said. "The Wi-Fi works better here. And it's either High Peak's homemade breakfast sandwiches or microwaved frozen spaghetti, which is all I had at the house before the snow began to fall. My car was stuck in the driveway long before you'd stopped in last night."

Despite what her head was telling her, Elizabeth couldn't just leave him there with his spaghetti. He'd been the only one except for Mama so far who hadn't judged her. "We're going to the market next. Would you like me to ask Ray if you can have a ride?"

"Really?" he asked, curiosity swimming in his deep-set eyes.

"Of course." She turned toward the table with the two men. "Ray, can we fit one more in the tractor?"

Ray perked up from across the room and then nodded suspiciously as he looked between Elizabeth and Paul. Naomi, who was checking out, turned around and peered over at them. Elizabeth shook her head infinitesimally at her friend to try to tell her that the offer wasn't anything more than that: an offer to give him a ride.

"Thank you," Paul said. He reached into his pocket and pulled out his wallet. "You haven't gotten a coffee. Let me buy one for you." Before she could answer, he was squinting at her. "Let me guess… Latte?"

Elizabeth cleared her throat, surprised that he'd presumed right, not letting him see the little thrill that pulsed through her. "You don't have to…"

"I know," he said.

"Cappuccino then." She wouldn't let him get off that easily, thinking he had her totally figured out. "Thank you. And could you get it to go, please?" she asked, not wanting to hold Ray up too long.

While Paul ordered Elizabeth a drink, Naomi came up to her, holding the bag of coffee against her chest like a baby, eyeing her suggestively and then nodding toward Paul. "Found yourself a *friend*, did ya?"

"I felt sorry for him, that's all," she whispered. "He's from out of town and, with the snow, he can't get out. He needs groceries."

"Call it whatever you want," Naomi said, "but he's not from here, and given the fact that he has no family to speak of in this coffee shop, I'd be careful. People'll start talkin'."

"Start?" Elizabeth asked. "I think they already have." She gazed over at Paul's broad shoulders, taking in the masculinity of his build as he stood at the counter. "Plus, I've got better things to do than to start rumors with a stranger."

"You sure about that?" Naomi asked.

Paul turned around and brought Elizabeth her coffee, nodding a cordial hello to Naomi. "Here ya go." He handed Elizabeth the cup and his fingers brushed hers.

She eyed Naomi self-consciously.

While Paul collected his laptop and phone, Ray hoisted himself out of his chair and tossed his water bottle in the trash. "Y'all ready?"

The four gathered in the center of the room.

"You in town for business or pleasure?" Ray asked Paul, without any introductions.

"Both," Paul replied.

Ray gave him a once-over. "You in real estate?"

Paul's eyebrows pulled together. "Sort of…"

"This is Ray," Elizabeth said, cutting in. "He's plowing all the streets and will probably do your drive if you'd like him to." She sent a please-be-nice frown his way, as if he'd listen to her anyway.

"It'd be no problem at all," Ray said through his teeth, shaking Paul's hand.

"And this is Naomi."

Naomi shuffled the coffee over to her other arm to offer her hand. A good sport, Paul shook it kindly.

"This is Paul Dawson."

"Well, Paul Dawson," Ray said, "wanna drop that somewhere?" He pointed to Paul's laptop. "You won't be needin' it around us, that's for sure."

"I'll just run it over to the house," Paul replied.

"I wouldn't be runnin' anywhere in this snow," Ray suggested. "We'll wait for ya."

Once they were outside, Ray was the first to get into the tractor, starting the engine, the loud hum ringing in Elizabeth's ears.

"It's gonna be a squeeze," Naomi whispered to Elizabeth as she opened the door on their side and slid in.

When she'd offered to give Paul a ride, Elizabeth hadn't thought this part through. She climbed up and scooted over to Naomi, allowing as much room as she could for Paul to get in, gripping her coffee cup. When he returned, he sat down next to her, his leg brushing hers as he shut the door. With nowhere else to put his arm, he stretched it behind her, and she found herself pressed against his side. She took in shallow breaths so as not to inhale his woodsy scent.

"Well, ain't this cozy," Ray said with an ironic chuckle, putting the tractor in gear and hitting the gas, chugging through the parking lot until they reached the road. Paul directed him to the little bungalow next door and Ray shoveled out the drive, clearing a path for the Mercedes that was parked at the end of it. Elizabeth stared at the rental car, wondering about Paul and who he was.

Just then, Paul's phone went off in his back pocket. "I'm terribly sorry," he said, leaning precariously toward her, the twisting motion he needed to get the phone putting his lips near her face.

Elizabeth held her breath.

"Mind if I get this? I'm waiting on some answers for work." Before she'd replied, he swiped the screen, the phone at his ear. "Hey, Jake. Whatcha got?"

As they bumped along the main road, the movement caused Paul's fingers to trail over her shoulder, sending a prickling sensation down Elizabeth's arm as he listened to whatever it was the caller was saying.

"I need three weeks at least," he said sharply, then resumed listening. "It's Christmas. There's nothing I can do. See if you can stall them." He finished the call and set the phone in his lap, staring forward, something clearly eating at him.

Elizabeth was glad when Ray started talking.

"You know, I met my wife in this here tractor," he said, with both hands on the wheel as they ground their way down a snowy road.

"You did?" Elizabeth asked, happy to hear that he hadn't gotten down on one knee that time.

"Yup. She lived a few towns over. She was gettin' her real-estate license and on her way home from takin' the test, she'd driven off the road in a helluva rainstorm. Her car was stuck in the ditch. I was drivin' between fields and I seen her cryin' on the side of the road, so I pulled over and hitched her up. That's what we country folk do when someone's in trouble." He flashed that gap-toothed grin of his at Paul. "I knew she was the one when she climbed in and sat up close to me on the way to the house. When she didn't leave to go back home, I figured that was my shot. Been with her ever since."

"I never knew how you two met, Ray," Naomi said. "This tractor must be good luck."

"Fingers crossed," Ray said, clenching his jaw in Paul's and Elizabeth's direction before they hit a bump.

Elizabeth flinched, leaning into Paul to avoid spilling her coffee all over them both. His breath at her ear, she gritted her teeth and straightened herself out. When she did, she caught a twitch of a smile from Paul out of the corner of her eye, and she was glad to take his mind off whatever he'd seemed to have been thinking about. She fixed her body toward the snow-covered road straight ahead.

Ray parked the tractor at the front of the market. Paul climbed down first and extended his hand to help Elizabeth. She didn't want to take it—she'd already endured enough touching on the way over there—but if she didn't, she and her cappuccino would be sure to fall face-first in the snow, which might be more mortifying than the touching. *Might.*

With a deep breath, Elizabeth took Paul's hand, keeping her coffee steady, and he guided her down, his grip gentle and solid. She let go the minute her feet hit the ground.

Then Paul reached up and offered to help Naomi down as well, but she declined.

"I do this every day," she said, grabbing hold of the side and hopping into the snow. "I should've been the one to help *you*, Mr. City." She squinted at him, her joke slightly cynical.

Paul seemed to be silently asking for an explanation as to why Naomi and Ray were being the way they were. Elizabeth shook her head, at a loss for how to explain it right then. Where did she begin?

"I'm gonna check to see if the manager wants me to clear his parkin' area," Ray said, striding across the lot ahead of them with purpose, his boots moving easily in the snow.

The three of them made their way toward the bright lights of the Ford's Corner Market. When she got inside, Elizabeth stopped. The whole place was decorated for the holiday, with twinkling trees at the checkout, wreaths hanging from the ends of every aisle, and Christmas tunes playing on the speakers.

"What happened to the old coffee pot?" she asked, astonished at how lovely the place was now.

"New owners." Naomi gave her a loaded look, and Elizabeth thought again about Travis's promise to keep his land. Her old friend grabbed a hand basket and walked over to the produce aisle, leaving Elizabeth and Paul staring at the only cart in the place.

"The others are out in the snow," the cashier said, looking over at them. "No one got them in before they left to go home last night."

Elizabeth couldn't help but think how Rodney Ford, the original owner, wouldn't have let that happen.

"We'll be fine," Paul called over to the woman. He grabbed the cart and turned to Elizabeth. "We can share this one. It works out—you can drink your coffee and chat with me while I push our groceries around the store."

"Thank you," she said, warming her cold fingers on the to-go cup and taking a sip.

"Where should I start?" he asked.

Still gawking at the gleaming wine displays and the rainbow of perfectly arranged produce, Elizabeth pulled her mother's list out of her pocket. "I need to get milk."

"No, I mean with the conversation." He gripped the handle of the cart, wheeling it around in front of them. "Are Ray and Naomi your *friends*?"

Elizabeth looked down at her coffee cup, deciding how to answer that. "They used to be."

"All right." Paul worked his way down to the dairy aisle. "And now?"

"They think I'm someone different from who I really am. And it's my job to show them they're wrong," Elizabeth said, scanning the lane signs to see if any of them would offer something she could buy for Beatrice. "Don't worry about them. They're good people."

Paul nodded, but he didn't seem convinced.

"I need to find a birthday present," Elizabeth said, changing the subject.

"Must be someone important if both you and your friend are getting gifts."

"My grandmother's best friend is turning ninety-nine."

Paul's eyebrows rose. "I hope I can get to my ninety-ninth birthday." He reached across her to grab a box of cereal. Whole-grain clusters. "What do you think you'll be doing at ninety-nine?"

As Elizabeth stood there, trying to find a good response for Paul's question, her mind was blank, making her suddenly anxious. She didn't have a clue what she'd be doing at ninety-nine because she wasn't even sure what her life held tomorrow. As a little girl, she'd had her whole future planned out. She'd imagined traveling with the Peace Corp all over the world, and one day she'd get married, live in a house out on a hill, just like Nan's… All of it now out of reach.

"I don't know," she said, shrugging to brush off the question and heading on down the aisle. When Paul didn't move, she turned around to find him squinting at her like he had when he'd guessed her coffee.

"What was that?" he asked.

Elizabeth looked around. "What?"

"The way you answered my question. I hadn't meant anything by it, but a cloud fell over you when I asked." He took a step closer to her. "I thought the reunion with your mom went well. You okay?"

"Of course I'm okay," she lied, but the look in his eyes that told her he didn't believe it sent fire racing across her cheeks. The fact that he could read her so easily was unnerving, and, without warning, her emotions swelled inside. She turned away and moved toward the back of the market.

Paul didn't say anything, but he pushed the cart up behind her, letting her take the lead. As she paced through the shiny aisle, Elizabeth's shoulders fell in surrender. None of this was Paul's fault. He'd only been trying to make conversation.

"I'm sorry," she said. "I'm sort of in limbo at the moment, and it's a touchy subject."

"What subject, exactly?" he asked.

"The what-am-I-doing-with-my-life subject." She took a bag of holiday coffee grounds claiming to have notes of cinnamon and nutmeg off the shelf and dropped it into the cart.

"Did you quit your job or something?" He reached for a can of soup, grinning at her.

But Elizabeth wasn't so lighthearted about it. She took a sip from her cup to buy herself a second, the liquid now cool, causing her to have to muscle it down. He was being kind and just trying to help, but she wasn't sure if she wanted to drag him through her mess of a life. Yet, whenever his gaze was directed at her with that adorable glimmer, she felt like, against all odds, he'd somehow understand.

"I've never had a job," she admitted. Saying it out loud only served to make her feel more awful about herself.

He stared at her, the can of soup still in his hand. "Ever?" he asked, placing the soup in the cart. There was no criticism in his voice, just curiosity, which eased her worry slightly.

"Not unless you count the stint at the Tasty Treat, serving ice cream the summer of my sophomore year."

"But you said you're in *limbo*," he pressed before taking a jar of tomato sauce into his hand, turning it around to view the label, reconsidering, and then grabbing another one.

"Limbo between two different lives," she said, wondering how he could, yet again, pull information out of her without even hardly trying. Perhaps she simply wanted to tell him her problems. It had been a long time since she'd had someone listen to her like he did. Although, she doubted he wanted to hear them. "One minute, I was all dressed up, hoping to do the waltz and the next minute I was on a plane here."

He gazed at her, something flickering subtly across his face that he didn't verbalize, and no matter the reason for it, it felt good to have his attention.

"I just got out of a seven-year relationship. It was pretty intense," she admitted.

His eyes widened in interest.

She shook her head, realizing the situation. "Why am I telling you all this in the middle of the canned foods aisle?"

He chuckled, that curiosity swimming in his gaze as if he wanted to know her entire life history right there, at the corner market.

"Sometimes I feel like the only one who doesn't have life figured out," she confessed.

That sparkle returned. "We all have things we're dealing with. And just to let you in on a little secret, none of us has it all figured out."

"What are *you* dealing with?" she challenged.

"Well, for one, overlooking the fact that I've been single for an entire year now and I have yet to learn how to cook for myself, there's the little detail that my wife left me for someone she said did 'more exciting things'." He put up air quotes.

"More exciting than comparing spaghetti sauces in the middle of nowhere during a blizzard?"

He laughed at her little joke, making her heart patter, and she had to fight the happiness that fizzled at the sound of it. She was so at ease around him that, for just an instant, she'd forgotten about her problems and said something funny. She couldn't remember the last time she'd said something to make someone else laugh. But then, as she thought about how Richard had probably felt the same about her as Paul's wife had about him, she sobered.

"Doing exciting things isn't all it's cracked up to be," Elizabeth said.

An earnestness came over him. "You don't have to tell *me* that. I'm not the one who thinks it is."

"I know. I was more telling myself." She peered up at him, that subtle smile of his starting to feel familiar.

"All right, then. *Not* exciting... So, you like doing boring things as well," he said, rounding the corner to the next grocery aisle. "That's a start in figuring out what to do with your life, right?"

Elizabeth grinned for his benefit, grabbing a red Christmas candle off the shelf, considering it for Beatrice. "I guess." She took the lid off the jar and inhaled the sweet scent of cinnamon and sugar.

"You're hardly in limbo now. We'll find you a nice spot where you can watch paint dry. Your future is secure."

His banter made her feel less worried about her life and more dedicated to the present moment. She liked how he did that. Holding back her smile, she capped the candle and put it into the cart for Beatrice.

"I have to admit that I was trying to do something exciting by coming to Mason's Ridge—venturing out into the wild unknown, relying on my instincts for my survival," he said, making her smile again. "Seriously, I came on the premise of work and was hoping for a vacation to get away from everything. But then the snow hit and I've been stuck between the little rental and the coffee shop. So thank you for letting me tag along with you all. It's a welcome diversion."

Naomi caught sight of them while putting a gallon of milk in her basket, her interest clear, but Elizabeth kept going, grabbing a tub of butter for Mama. She eyed the gift she'd gotten for Beatrice to avoid Naomi's curious look as if she and Paul were plotting the next big takeover. The thought of facing everyone at Beatrice's party suddenly swarmed Elizabeth and she didn't know if she was ready to face their scrutiny alone.

"I'm sure Beatrice wouldn't mind if you stopped by her party with us," Elizabeth said, wondering if that was actually true. What *was* true was that she'd feel a lot better with Paul there. He was an innocent party, certain to take some of the load off.

"Oh, no." He waved off her suggestion. "I wouldn't want to impose."

She nodded. He was probably right.

"But I would like to see *you* again. Maybe somewhere with less fluorescent lighting," he teased. "We could get a drink?"

Dates were different from tag-alongs to the market and birthday parties. While she liked being with him, Elizabeth wasn't sure she was ready for that just yet. There was no way she could be a good date for anyone in her state, so there was no need in stringing him along, even if she did find him incredibly charming.

"It's okay," he said, clearly misreading her silence. "I'll only be here a few more days anyway and then I go back to Chicago."

"Is that where you're from?" she asked, not bothering to set the record straight. It was easier to just let him think what he wanted.

"Yeah," he said, more words on his lips than just the one. But his phone rang, diverting their conversation. "Sorry," he said, frowning at the screen. "Mind if I get this?"

"Not at all," she replied, glad for the reprieve.

"Hello?" he answered, taking a couple of steps away from Elizabeth. "…I promise, it's getting done," he said, two lines forming between his eyes. "I told you that I've hit a tiny snag, but we'll get it cleared ASAP… Just put them off. Don't they stop for the holiday at all?"

His gaze met hers and she asked him silently if everything was all right.

He gave her a forced smile and nodded, but she wondered about the call. She pretended to look at a few items on the shelves as he kept talking.

"We can't move forward right now anyway," he said. "We won't even be able to break ground until spring. I don't know why they're forcing the issue. All I need is a few weeks, but I'm leaving soon anyway and I'll talk to them face-to-face…"

"Y'all almost done?" Naomi asked, stopping beside Elizabeth. "Ray's got the whole lot cleared outside and the engine's runnin'."

Elizabeth looked down at her list. "I just have a few things left to get." She motioned to Paul that she was taking the cart with her. He nodded once more, mouthing to her that he'd catch up.

As Elizabeth and Naomi made their way to the sections she needed, Elizabeth couldn't help but think about how easily Paul had been able to make her feel better about herself for the moment. Even though she shouldn't, she hoped that she'd run into him again before he left town.

Chapter Seven

Elizabeth arrived back at Crestwood Farm to find three young men sitting around Nan's table, immersed in lively conversation while they hung their heads over plates of Mama's breakfast casserole. A yellow lab rushed up to Elizabeth with his tail wagging furiously. She ran her hand through the dog's soft fur.

Mama waved Elizabeth over as she hung up her coat and brought the bags of groceries to the kitchen counter. The men's conversation slowed when she walked through the room, all of them turning their inquiring attention to Elizabeth. With every step, she felt as though they were assessing her, trying to figure out if the rumors about her returning to gobble up the farmland were actually true. She wanted to nip it in the bud right then, but it wasn't the time. Mama didn't need Elizabeth making her breakfast guests feel awkward.

"I thought the guys out back might be hungry, so I invited them over for a little holiday breakfast," Mama said when Elizabeth had reached the kitchen.

Elizabeth sank her hand into the grocery bag, pulling out a tub of butter and setting it onto the counter.

"Let me introduce you." Mama went over and stood next to a freckle-faced man with light-brown hair who barely looked eighteen. "This is Lenny," she said. "And that's Sabastian." The dark-haired man with a square jaw beside Lenny nodded in greeting. "And the one who's now on seconds of my casserole, his name is Harvey." Mama winked at the young man with ruddy cheeks and a big smile.

"And who's this?" Elizabeth asked, rubbing the dog's head while he pressed it against her leg lovingly as if he'd known her for years.

Lenny snapped his fingers and the dog came over and sat next to him. "It's my dog, ma'am," he said. "His name's Rosco."

Elizabeth smiled, wrinkling her nose playfully at the dog as she put a gallon of milk in the fridge. "So, you all take care of the farm?" she asked.

"Yes, ma'am," Harvey said. "We're the full-timers."

"Just the three of you? Weren't there more?" Elizabeth asked.

Lenny shot a glance over to Mama. "We've got about six of us all together if you count the hired help."

"Ah. What crops do you have planned for next season?" she asked. The idea of how Nan had supplemented her income from the apple orchard with rotating crops in two of the four fields returned to her. She continued unloading the groceries while she kept her eyes on the dark-haired young man named Sabastian.

"Well, because we had peanuts and cotton last year, in April we'll plant cotton and hay, ma'am," Sabastian answered.

"Did the crops do well last year?" Elizabeth asked, as she folded the grocery bags that she'd unpacked.

"Yep," Sabastian said, "but we still can't get the far eastern corner of the farm to grow. We'd always left it, but your mama was hopin' we could get a vegetable garden goin' out there."

"It might make for some good items to sell at the roadside stall," Mama said. She refilled the empty glasses on the table with orange juice, not bothering to ask if they needed any first. "I've been out there time and time again, and I can't, for the life of me, figure out why nothin' will grow in that little patch. Remember that, Liz? It's always been a square of dirt."

Elizabeth did remember. She'd played out there as if it were an enormous sandbox when she was young, scooping together piles of soil around little flowers she'd pulled up by the creek, thinking she'd know just how to make them grow. "I could take a look at it once the snow melts," she suggested. "Maybe we could get a few soil samples and have them tested."

Mama brightened. "Sounds like a good use of your time."

The idea of helping out around the farm was proving to feel more natural with every minute Elizabeth spent there. She could see how Nan and Mama had both felt fulfilled by doing it. "Well, it's nice to meet you all," she said, hopeful as she peered at their pleasant faces, realizing that maybe a few people in town weren't actually talking about her. "I didn't mean to interrupt. Please, finish your breakfast."

While she continued to put away the groceries, the men went back to their conversation. Once she'd finished, Elizabeth took the package of red tissue paper and spool of glittery ribbon that she'd gotten at the market over to an empty spot on the counter, opening up the paper. Then she reached into the drawer and pulled out the scissors.

"Whatcha got there?" Mama asked, leaning over her shoulder.

"Just a little something for Beatrice," Elizabeth replied, setting the candle in the center and pulling the tissue paper up around it. She snipped a piece of ribbon and secured the tissue with a bow.

"That's thoughtful of you." Mama gave her a pat on the arm. "You can put it under the tree for safekeeping until the party."

Elizabeth caught sight of the little Christmas tree in the living room, realizing suddenly that there were no gifts under it. In her haste to get out of New York, she hadn't brought any presents at all, and unless she got her mother a candle at the market like the one in her hand, there wasn't a lot in the way of gift options available in town. Seeing how much time and effort her mother was putting in at the farm and how she'd prepared for Elizabeth's arrival, she wished she could do more.

But then their earlier conversation swam through her mind. Perhaps she could do something nice for Mama instead of buying her things. She might see if she could keep the house tidied for her or find out one of the farm tasks that Mama didn't love and do it for her. One thing was for sure: Elizabeth had all she wanted just being there with Mama. Maybe being with each other *was* gift enough.

Later that day, when Elizabeth and Mama arrived at Beatrice's house for her party, the door opened, and instead of the warm, arm-stretched hello Elizabeth had gotten as a child, a middle-aged woman stood in front of them. The woman had mousy hair swept into an updo, eyes that almost disappeared when she smiled, and a hunter-green corduroy dress with Christmas trees printed all over it. Her gaze fluttering over to Elizabeth, she beckoned them inside. "I'm Ella, Ray's wife," she told Elizabeth.

"Nice to meet you," Elizabeth said as Ella beamed at her over her shoulder, while her mother swung the gift bag with the kitchen dish and towel set she'd gotten for Beatrice by her side.

Ella ushered them down the narrow hallway of the house to the kitchen that smelled of sugar and butter. The long rectangular farmhouse table was covered in Christmas cupcakes on pedestals, all of them decorated with different green and red icing shapes, assortments of holiday cookies, and platters of food. Ray was perusing the fare, pinching a few crackers with cheese, a paper plate in his weathered hand. Lenny, Sabastian, and Harvey had gathered in the corner, holding overflowing plates of food and talking about harvest schedules with Travis, and there were a couple of strangers chatting with Percy that Elizabeth didn't recognize. They all quieted to a hush when Elizabeth walked in.

She looked around helplessly for Beatrice, wondering when she'd make an appearance and take the pressure off.

"Y'all want some deviled eggs? I've got plenty," Ella asked, ladling cider from a silver warmer into a porcelain teacup with painted holly on the sides. She handed one to Mama and then grabbed another cup, filling it.

Elizabeth spotted Naomi, who was leaning against the olive-green Formica counter. Her friend grinned at her for the first time, their earlier conversation about all the eggs playing out between them. She held up her hand, an egg-half pinched between her fingers. The tiny olive branch was enough to bring tears to Elizabeth's eyes.

"Maybe in a bit," Elizabeth replied to Ella. She held out the wrapped candle. "I brought something for Beatrice."

"Oh, how nice," Ella said, putting the cider onto the counter, taking it from her, and placing the tissue-wrapped candle beside the smattering of other gifts in the corner of the kitchen. Mama followed her over, set down her gift bag, and began talking to Ray.

Taking a moment, Elizabeth looked around, meeting Travis's suspicious gaze. She smiled at him, hoping to lighten the mood. His face softened a little, and he turned back to the farmhands.

"Where's Beatrice?" Elizabeth finally asked Ella. "I'd love to see her."

"She's in the living room. You can go on in."

Elizabeth followed Ella into the small room where Beatrice was sitting in one of two blue upholstered recliners with crocheted doilies on the arms of them, an afghan over legs that were crossed at the ankles. Her body was smaller than it had been; a shrunken, hunched version of herself. Her gnarled hands rested in her lap.

Elizabeth swallowed, the sight surprising her, but it shouldn't have. At Nan's funeral, the old woman had had to have help walking up to the front row of the church, and she hadn't stayed very long at the reception. Even as bright a star as Beatrice had been, Elizabeth couldn't have expected her not to age over the years.

Elizabeth took another step toward her and the old woman lit up.

"I'll be in the kitchen," Ella said, breezing out of the room.

"Liz, my sweet girl," Beatrice said, holding her arms out as Elizabeth walked over, leaning down to embrace the old woman. The lines on her cheeks deepened with her smile. When she pulled back to look at Elizabeth, her eyes glassed over with emotion. "Your nan *knew* you'd come back. She used to say, 'I know Elizabeth. One day, she'll realize that she'd rather be sitting on the porch swing overlooking the fields with her mama beside her, bare feet, and a glass of lemonade in her hand.'"

Beatrice's words crashed into Elizabeth. Was that what Nan had wanted for her? She'd never said… Could it be why Elizabeth was feeling so comfortable on the farm with Mama?

Her old friend squeezed her loosely, her arms not as strong as they once were. Beatrice's lavender scent brought Elizabeth back to the summer days that seemed to stretch on forever, nibbling homemade apple pie out on her porch while Beatrice and Nan laughed about old times.

"I thought I'd never see your lovely face again after the funeral," the woman said in her ear before letting go.

Elizabeth sat down in the twin recliner next to Beatrice, trying not to allow the ever-present remorse from the woman's last comment to surface. "Happy birthday."

Beatrice grabbed a tissue and dabbed her eye. "Thank you." Then she took in a long breath as if she were drawing the very essence of Elizabeth into her lungs. "Tell me everything you've been doing since you left."

"Oh, gosh," Elizabeth said, shaking her head. "That's a lot." She hadn't meant she'd done a lot, but, rather, that the idea of what she hadn't done was a lot.

"I'll bet your nan would be proud of you," Beatrice said, reaching over and taking Elizabeth's hand.

The mention of Nan and what her grandmother might think of her failed adult life stung Elizabeth unexpectedly, and tears brimmed in her eyes. Mortified to take the attention off Beatrice's special day with her own baggage, she pulled away and pretended to cough into her sleeve, but the fall of the old woman's lips into a frown revealed that she'd noticed. The last thing Elizabeth had meant to do was to upset one of her favorite people from childhood. This was Beatrice's day and Elizabeth couldn't even get through the first few minutes of it without ruining it.

"What y'all talkin' about?" Naomi said, coming into the room.

Elizabeth pushed a friendly expression across her face, blinking away her tears, thankful for the distraction, although Beatrice's attention was still on her.

"I'd just sat down," Elizabeth replied.

"We were actually talking about Elizabeth's grandmother, Harriet," Beatrice interjected.

Naomi brightened. "I miss her," she said. "Remember how she used to bake us Christmas treats and write us all letters at Christmastime?"

A plume of fondness swelled in Elizabeth's chest at the thought that they did remember. "Mama and I were talking about that," she said, the subject of Nan's Christmas traditions bringing a little calm to her storm.

"Ah, yes," Beatrice said with a nostalgic nod. "I remember when you two girls used to stand on the kitchen chairs at the counter and help her with the cookies. Naomi always wanted to make the shapes and, Elizabeth, you wanted to decorate them. You two were a perfect pair." Beatrice gave both of them a knowing look.

"Yes, we were," Elizabeth agreed.

Naomi turned her gaze toward the Christmas tree in the corner of the room, thoughts behind her eyes.

"I have quite a few of those letters that she wrote." The old woman pursed her lips, tapping them with her withered finger. "Wonder where I've put them. It sure would be nice to hear her voice today, if only in my head."

"I could find them for you, if you tell me where to look," Naomi offered.

Beatrice gave Naomi a grateful smile but continued her thought. "You know, when we were girls, it felt as though life would never expire, our days like grains of sand on an endless beach. But before I knew it, I was aware of the clear domed walls surrounding my life, the hourglass was emptying out, and there were unsaid words and unfinished stories…"

"What unfinished stories?" Elizabeth asked.

Beatrice's attention landed on her, a yearning showing behind it, as if she had something important to say. But just then Ella came into the room with a cheery flutter, clapping her hands.

"It's time to get this party started. We need to sing to the birthday girl!" She floated over to Beatrice and leaned down to address her. "Do you want everyone to come in here, or would you rather me help you up so you can go into the kitchen to blow out your candles?"

"I can get up," Beatrice replied, grabbing onto the doily-covered arms of the chair and struggling to stand.

Elizabeth jumped to her feet and offered assistance to the old woman, but Beatrice shooed her off. However, when she stumbled, Elizabeth put an arm around the woman's back, keeping her steady until she could manage on her own.

Beatrice leaned into Elizabeth. "Promise me you'll come back tomorrow so I can talk to you," she whispered urgently.

"Of course," Elizabeth said under her breath, her curiosity piqued.

Beatrice lifted her head and put on a smile, taking labored steps into the kitchen. "Where's the birthday cake you speak of?" she asked. "I'm dying for a big, sugary plate of it."

When they got into the kitchen, Ella pulled a dining chair into the middle of the room for Beatrice, while Ray lit the crimson candles on the massive cake that had waves of white icing and little red polka dots trailing around the top of it. Mama and Naomi came over and stood next to Elizabeth.

As they began to sing, Elizabeth wondered about the message the woman had for her. No matter what it was, Elizabeth was glad that she would get to see Nan's best friend again.

"Beatrice seemed really happy to get her presents," Mama said, sliding the paper plate full of cake—that Ella had insisted they take home—into the fridge.

Elizabeth slipped off her boots. "Yes. It was good to see her." She paced over to the hearth and threw a couple of logs into the fireplace, while Mama grabbed the matches from the kitchen drawer, coming in to light the fire. "She wants me to come back tomorrow."

"Oh?" Mama struck the match and leaned in to ignite the small piece of paper under the log, getting the fire going. "What for? Just to chat?"

"I'm not sure. It seemed like she wanted to tell me something. But I have no idea what."

Mama fanned the fire as it took hold. "She might just want to see you. She's always loved you."

"She told me today that Nan would be proud of me and I almost lost it, right in the middle of her birthday party," Elizabeth admitted as she sat down on the raised brick hearth next to Mama, the heat at her back. "I feel so ashamed."

"Ashamed?" Mama took her hand. "Why?"

"You and Nan took care of an entire farm *and* raised a family, and I've never made anything of myself. Nan wouldn't be proud..." She trailed off, her words catching on the lump in her throat.

"What about all the charity work you've done? That's important," Mama said, those green eyes of hers full of unconditional love.

The heat had intensified at her back, so Elizabeth went over and plopped down on the sofa. "I did it with Richard's money," she replied, the idea of it now making her feel like a fake. She didn't even want to mention how Richard's ulterior motives had cheapened it for her anyway.

"But it's still work," Mama countered, following her. "You were givin' of your time."

"Writing a check from someone else's bank account at a nice dinner doesn't really feel like *work*. I want to make Nan proud, but most of all, I want to feel like I'm contributing something to the world. I just lost sight of my goals for a while."

"Okay," Mama said, snuggling under the blanket on the sofa next to Elizabeth. "What are your goals?"

Elizabeth tucked her feet under her legs. "Sit in my jammies and eat tubs of ice cream?" She wrinkled her face in misery, trying not to allow the wobble in her voice. "I haven't really figured them out yet."

"Before you met Richard, you wanted to do something with the Peace Corps, to help people. And you really loved botany. Are you still interested in either of those topics?"

"I do still love learning about people and helping those in need, but it's been years since college. What do I put on a job application—'been shacking up with a guy and haven't worked'?" Elizabeth hung her head. "What was I thinking?"

Mama leaned into her view. "You were in love," she said. "Swept off your feet, like in the movies. You're not alone; love happens to a lot of people."

"But it didn't end like the movies," Elizabeth said.

"All that means is that God's got another journey for you."

Elizabeth smiled at her mother. "You sound like Nan."

Mama laughed. "I feel more like her every day." She leaned back, kicking her socked feet up on the coffee table. "After your father died, it took me a while to find myself too. I didn't know who I was without him."

Elizabeth twisted around to give Mama her full attention. Her mother didn't look as tired today, but there was a sadness to her now.

"I took a long look at the things that bring me joy, and what I realized was that I missed bein' *here*, working the fields and tending to the animals." She turned to the view out the window that was now draped in a deep purple as darkness fell upon them. "Somethin' about this place makes all the other things fade away. Life is slower, people take time to notice you…"

"I know what you mean," Elizabeth said.

"You do?" Mama asked.

"The more time I spend here at the farm, the more natural it feels. The idea of staying has actually crossed my mind. I'm just not sure of my place in it."

"You can only do what makes you happy, Liz. Follow your intuition. It'll lead you and you'll find your place."

Without warning, Elizabeth pictured Paul's eyes and how they creased at the corners when he smiled at her. Her instinct was telling her to be smitten by him, and that was definitely not what she wanted. If she let her intuition lead her, she might find herself making more wrong life choices because she'd decided to follow a man. She needed to be able to stand on her own two feet first this time.

Mama fluttered her hands in the air as if she were clearing it. "What do you say we put on our warmest pajamas, cuddle up, pop some popcorn, and watch a Christmas movie together tonight? Your nan's got a ton of DVDs in the closet."

A few hours' break from her troubles? "I like the sound of that."

Chapter Eight

The next morning, before Elizabeth had even made the holiday coffee that she'd picked up as an impulse buy at the market yesterday, Mama met her in the living room and held her coat out to her.

"What's this for?" Elizabeth asked.

"Finding your place."

Elizabeth yawned while trying to make the connection through the blur of just waking up, but when it came to understanding what her mother was talking about, she hadn't a clue.

"You wanna get your life straight? The only way to hash out your plan is to start doin' somethin'." Mama dangled Elizabeth's coat from her index finger. "Get a pair of jeans on and you'll want your scarf. It's cold this mornin'. Plus, Travis might stop by later to check on the thermostat, so I need to get the chores done."

Before she knew it, Elizabeth was standing in the frigid field out back of the house, unloading wood chips into a bucket of hay. The sun was just coming up from behind the mountain, turning the peaks purple, the yellow rays making the layer of frost on the fields sparkle as if they were covered in diamonds. The sun had melted some of the snow, but the low overnight temperatures had refrozen it into a compacted, hardened surface that crunched beneath her boots when she walked.

"Bring the bucket over here," Mama called from the green-and-white clapboard chicken coop, beckoning Elizabeth with a wave.

With gloved hands, Elizabeth picked up the bucket, lugging the heavy thing through the snow and setting it down with a thud. "How is this helping me move my life forward?"

"That answer's up to you," Mama said. "But, I promise, you won't find the answer sittin' like a lump on the sofa inside." She checked the heating to make sure the chicken coop was warm enough and cooed at Miss Maisy, who clucked back at her.

Elizabeth studied the hay and wood chips, internalizing what Mama had told her, and trying to figure out what this exercise had to do with her life.

"Just spread that along the bottom of the coop while I check on the horses and the goats in the barn next door," Mama instructed. "Back in a second."

Elizabeth lifted the heavy bucket, tipping it, the contents sliding onto the floor of the coop. But the weight was too much for her thin frame and she was unable to keep the bucket steady. She shifted it in her arms in an attempt to regain control, her feet slipping on the ice under them. While she wrestled with the bucket, still dumping its contents, the chickens clucked in protest. Before she could react, she was suddenly aware that the ground was no longer under her feet. The chickens clucking and flapping their wings at her, she fell backward onto the snow below, the hay and wood chips burying her. The bucket rolled away on the hard surface of the ground.

"Good Lord, child," Mama said, marching over and grabbing Elizabeth's hands to pull her up, the two of them wobbling on the ice before they managed a standing position. "I leave you for a second and you're spreadin' hay all over yourself."

"Sorry," Elizabeth said. "I'm not very good at this."

Mama laughed. "Not good at what—ice skating? You slipped."

"*You* don't slip," Elizabeth said, brushing the hay off her coat, straightening her shoulders and trying not to feel sorry for herself, but failing miserably.

"No, I let my daughter do it, apparently." Mama shook her head, still clearly amused. "Just gather it back up and put it in the coop by the handful instead of using the bucket."

Reining herself in, Elizabeth bent down and scooped up the hay mixture. Then she reached inside the wooden structure, dropping in clumps and smoothing it out to give the chickens a warm bed on that cold morning. The smell of the fields and cedar filling the air took her mind off the fact that she'd struggled to even do a simple farm task well. She ducked inside the coop again to make sure she'd covered the entire bottom and the interior felt incredibly cozy.

She wondered what it would be like to wake up on the farm every morning, maybe have a family like her mother and Nan had… But it all seemed like a far-off dream, none of it attainable.

Then, as if the universe had sent her a little lift in spirit, she spotted the most adorable thing. "Oh, look," she told Mama, sliding her hands under their newest chick's delicate little body, pulling it from the coop, and slipping it inside her coat. The yellow ball of feathery fluff snuggled down against her, cheeping quietly.

"Well, look at that," Mama said with pride. "We've got ourselves another chick." She reached over and rubbed its head with her gloved finger. "The brooder plate must have worked, and the warmth from it allowed this little one to hatch. What should we call it?"

"Let's name her Holly—in honor of Christmas," Elizabeth said.

Mama cooed at the tiny being. "Hello, Holly."

Elizabeth took off one of her gloves and placed her hand on the down of the chick, its sides expanding and releasing as it breathed. And just like that, a little life had formed like a Christmas surprise.

Mama was right. Being out there made all her troubles seem so far away…

"I've never known you to be a tomboy," Mama said, after meeting Elizabeth in the hallway.

Elizabeth tucked her wet hair behind her ears.

"You've been wearin' dresses by choice from the time you could walk. But you haven't curled your hair or done your makeup even once since you've been here. How come?"

Her question caught Elizabeth off guard. "I don't really feel very glamorous anymore," she said honestly.

"You are a stunnin' young lady no matter what. And you're welcome to be more natural if that's what you feel like doin', but if you're lettin' your mood dictate what you do, it might be better to get yourself together." She rubbed Elizabeth's arm warmly.

"So, you think curling my hair will make me feel like a better person?" Elizabeth asked.

"If all you can do to feel better is start with the outside, then so be it. It's a step." Mama fluffed her gray curls. "And I was hopin' you'd show me all those beauty secrets you learned in the big city. Got any tricks to erase twenty years?"

Elizabeth laughed. "Who are you trying to impress? Travis?"

Mama's cheeks flushed. "I'd just like to see what you can do with this canvas." She ran her fingers playfully under her chin.

"You didn't answer my question," Elizabeth said, still half joking. But when Mama remained silent, coupled with her pink cheeks, Elizabeth sucked in a breath, her eyes rounding. "He's coming over today, too. Is something going on between you and Travis?"

Mama clasped her hands together, twisting her fingers nervously. "He's never given me any reason to think..."

Mama had a crush on Travis. Who'd have ever thought... "Want me to do your hair and makeup then?" Elizabeth asked softly.

Mama smiled bashfully. "Remember when you used to paint my nails sparkly colors when you were in elementary school?"

Elizabeth had almost forgotten. "I do," she said, recalling her childhood beauty kits. Mama and Nan had let her paint their nails different shades of glittery pink. Neither of them ever took it off for weeks.

She walked into her bedroom and opened the bifold doors of the closet, browsing her boxes for the one containing her beauty products and dragging it into the open space in the room. She reached in, scooping up an armful of lotions and skincare items. With all the bottles gathered in her hands, one of them tumbled to the carpet and she picked it up, seeing it with new eyes.

The etched glass bottle with the gold top had sat on her penthouse's marble bathroom counter every day. She'd slathered her skin with its contents without a thought each morning, while she ran through her digital schedule for the day and sipped her collagen protein smoothie, but now it seemed out of place in her new surroundings, the contents costing more than what Mama could make at the produce stand in a month.

Elizabeth took everything into the bathroom and set the products in a line on the sink.

Mama came in and picked up one of the bottles. "Wow, it looks like a fancy beauty parlor in here." She set the bottle back down, handling it as if it might break by her touch.

Elizabeth grinned, giving Mama the face wash and then showing her how to use each one. When she'd finished, she went back into the bedroom and got her makeup.

"You went through all this every mornin'?" Mama asked as Elizabeth applied foundation and powder to Mama's skin and then dragged a blush brush across her cheeks, making them rosy.

"It all seems pointless to me now," Elizabeth replied. "I mean, who's gonna look at my face? Miss Maisy?"

Mama laughed. "That never bothered you when you were young. You were you for yourself and no one else."

Elizabeth's hands stilled, the end of the eyeshadow brush powdered with her favorite shade: Metallic Cashmere. "I don't feel like myself," she admitted. "I think that's the problem. Close your eyes." She applied the shadow to Mama's outer rims and lid.

Mama opened her eyes. "What makes you feel the most alive?"

The way Paul listened to her floated into Elizabeth's consciousness. She realized then that while she was with Richard she'd been an accessory for him, a vehicle to propel his business forward, and the reason she didn't know herself was because she hadn't actually been seen. But Paul saw her. He wanted to know how *her* day had gone and who *she* was. He'd made her laugh with his comment about watching paint dry, both of their mundane lives not feeling so mundane together.

"Being around good people makes me feel alive."

"I like that," Mama said.

"I think I'd like to see more of Paul Dawson. *He* makes me feel alive."

Mama's newly made-up face filled with light. "I'm glad to hear that."

"Well, we'll see how it goes," she said, still cautious. "But it's a step, right?"

Mama smiled. "It's definitely a step."

Elizabeth turned her mother around to face the mirror.

"Oh, my goodness," she said, leaning forward as if she were trying to make sure the reflection was actually her. "I look like a new woman." She regarded Elizabeth. "You have a way of seeing things that not everyone does. You should use that talent." She patted her daughter on the shoulder. "I'll get out of your hair now and let *you* get ready."

Once alone, Elizabeth picked up one of the high-dollar bottles, thinking over what her mother had told her. Maybe it was time to see things differently, both about herself as a person and her future.

Naomi and Travis stood on the porch, the afternoon sun that had fought its way out from behind the winter cloud cover casting a long shadow down the boards at their feet. The massive four-wheel-drive Silverado with farm-use plates sat in the snow-filled driveway behind her.

"I'm here to check the thermostat for your mama," Travis said.

"Yes, come in." Elizabeth ushered them into the house and shut the door, surprised but genuinely pleased to see Naomi again.

"And I brought you this." Naomi held out a yellowed envelope tied in an old red ribbon, the ends fraying.

"What's that?" Mama asked, draping the dishtowel that she'd used to dry the breakfast dishes over her shoulder as she came into the living room to greet them.

Travis did a double take at Mama's makeup and Elizabeth chewed on a smile to keep it from surfacing.

"Beatrice asked me to bring it over to Liz," Naomi said.

"This looks like Nan's handwriting." Elizabeth ran her finger over the loopy script with Beatrice's name inscribed on the outside of the envelope.

"I was goin' stir-crazy, bein' stuck in the house." Naomi slipped off her coat and draped it over the back of one of the chairs next to the fire, while Travis got right to work, tinkering with the thermostat, popping the cover off and assessing the wiring. "So I walked over to Beatrice's to see if she needed anything, and she told me to get it out of her bedside drawer and bring it to Liz."

Mama patted the sofa. "Have a seat. I'll bring in some nibbles."

"I'm supposed to see Beatrice today," Elizabeth said, lowering herself next to Naomi on the sofa when her old friend sat down. "She asked me to come over."

"Yeah, I know. She said you'd want to read this before your visit."

Curious, Elizabeth asked, "Mind if I read it now?"

"Up to you. I'm just the messenger," Naomi said, but her curiosity was clear.

Elizabeth consulted Mama, who urged her with wide eyes to find out what was inside as she took the cellophane off the plate of cookies and set it onto the table, grabbing the crackers that they always ate with the homemade cheese made from their fresh goat's milk.

Tentatively, Elizabeth pulled at one of the tails of the bow, the ribbon falling loosely around the envelope. She slipped it off, running a finger under the flap and lifting it, as Mama hovered.

"Why don't we scoot in together so we can all read it?" Elizabeth said, preparing herself for the opportunity to read what Nan had penned and needing their support. Just the idea of it caused her hands to tremble.

Loretta sat down and Naomi shuffled in closer on either side of her, looking on as Elizabeth pulled the paper from the envelope and smoothed it out flat on her lap. Her breath caught at the sight of her nan's signature "Harriet" at the bottom. With a deep breath, she read the letter:

December 24, 1940

Merry Christmas, my darling Beatrice,

Just calling you "darling" has me singing Dinah Shore's "Yes, My Darling Daughter." I can't get that lovely song out of my head ever since I heard it on Mr. Cantor's radio program. I think about the day when I have my own daughter to dote on. Am I rushing things? It's easy to do when a girl's in love.

How I've adored our year together, you and me. I must say that this year has been one of the best. You and I became fast friends, and you met Tony and I met Jimmy—what a gas!

We are incredibly lucky gals… I just love the way Jimmy looks at me. I feel like a princess when he reaches for my hand to help me out of his car. And when he kissed my cheek the other day, I almost fainted right in the park. I had no idea that love could feel like this. So, this letter is all about love—the only truly untainted thing left in this world.

Elizabeth looked up, addressing Mama, "Who's Jimmy?"

"I have no idea," Mama said, leaning over and inspecting the letter.

"Maybe a friend of Beatrice's?" Naomi suggested. "Beatrice's husband was Tony, so that makes sense."

"Ever heard of anyone named Jimmy, Travis?" Mama called over.

Travis turned her way, only to stare at her face as if she were stealing his words. "Nope," he said, turning back to the task.

Still clearly thinking, Mama counted on her fingers quietly. "Nan was in her teens when she wrote this. Maybe an early boyfriend?"

Elizabeth waggled her eyebrows. "Oooh, I'll bet Gramps wouldn't like that," she teased.

Mama grinned fondly. "Ah, she didn't marry your granddaddy until she was in her twenties."

"How did she meet Gramps?" Elizabeth asked.

"She told me once that she'd met him when he'd come home from World War Two, after he'd moved here for a slower pace," Mama said.

"Aw, sweet Gramps." Elizabeth remembered how he used to click on the radio and then pick her up under her arms and set her on his feet, dancing around the kitchen wildly. It would make her laugh so hard that she'd stumble off his shoes.

"Hello?" Naomi said, waving a hand between Elizabeth and her mother. "You're leavin' me hangin'. Read!"

"Oh, yes! Of course." Elizabeth cleared her throat, straightened out the paper, and began again, the sound of Nan's voice in her head like music to her ears.

So, what have I loved—no, adored—about this year with you, my beautiful friend? I loved traveling into town and sneaking out of the picture show to get ice cream with you and then rushing back before Daddy picked us up.

I will never forget horseback riding through the fields, only for you to jump off and do your Greta Garbo impersonation with your hair windblown out on the sides just like hers. It still has me doubling over in fits of laughter.

I will always hold dear the night you and Tony walked the mountain trails with Jimmy and me, the four of us making a pact to all grow old together and never leave one another. Oh, my dear friend, how blessed we are!

I've made you an assortment of cookies this year: peanut wafers, butterscotch and chocolate icebox cookies, and a Lazy Daisy cake, cut into little squares just perfect for Christmas. I do hope you enjoy them.

All my love,
Harriet

"That's lovely that Beatrice still had this," Mama said, taking the envelope off the table and turning it over in her hand like a rare diamond.

"I wonder why she wanted me to read it before I went to see her instead of waiting to give it to me then?" Elizabeth asked, scanning it for any clue but coming up empty.

Mama shook her head. "No idea. Maybe she's hopin' you'll make the Lazy Daisy cake before you come," she teased.

"I'm searchin' for the recipe right now to find out what's in it," Naomi said, tapping on her phone. She gasped, scrolling up. "It's vanilla cake with broiled brown sugar and coconut icing. Oh, my gosh. That sounds delicious."

"Maybe we could try to make it this Christmas," Elizabeth suggested. She'd never heard of it either, and certainly never known her nan to make it.

Naomi eyed her, the corners of her mouth twitching upward just enough to give Elizabeth a little optimism.

"We'd need a party full of people to eat it," Mama said. "Wouldn't it be so wonderful to have a house full of people?" Mama looked up at the ceiling dreamily, as if she could see it.

Travis snapped the box closed, drawing their attention to him. "I'm going to go shut off the power for a quick sec," he said.

Just then, Elizabeth's phone rang in her back pocket. She wondered if it might finally be Casey returning her call, or if Paul had somehow gotten her number, so she pulled it out to check. But the number was local. Slightly disappointed but not surprised, she asked, "Do you mind if I get this?" wondering who in this area would be calling her.

Both Mama and Naomi shook their heads.

"Hello?" Elizabeth answered, setting the letter onto the table.

"Hello, my name is Shirley Clark with Pierce and Hughes Law Firm. Sorry to have taken a little while to get back to you. I'm returning your call regarding our notice of eviction."

Elizabeth mouthed, "The lawyer."

"Put it on speaker," Mama whispered.

Elizabeth eyed Naomi, but Mama insisted.

She clicked the screen and set the phone on the coffee table. She and Mama huddled over it while Naomi looked on.

"Yes, thank you for calling me back," Elizabeth said. "There seems to be a misunderstanding with who owns our farm, and we wanted to get it cleared up so that we can transfer ownership to my mother, Loretta Holloway, who currently lives here."

"Are you speaking of Crestwood Farm in Polk County?"

Elizabeth bent forward a little more to speak into the phone. "Yes, that's right."

"Our client, the landowner, is actually requesting that the property be vacated… immediately," the woman said, her voice gentler than the message she was conveying.

Mama's mouth fell open and Elizabeth took her hand to tell her it would be okay, Naomi's face crumpling in confusion.

"But we *are* the landowners. That's why I'm calling. This farm has been in our family for generations," Elizabeth explained.

"I'm sorry, but I have public record here that says it's, in fact, owned by Worsham Enterprises, who are requesting that the property be cleared."

"Yes, I understand, but what I'm saying is the deed has been recorded incorrectly." Elizabeth patted Mama's hand. "And we're attempting to pass it to the daughter of the original owners that should be recorded on the deed: Roger and Harriet Sloan."

"Is there a time when you could come down to the office to discuss this?" Shirley asked. "I'm about to leave for the day, so you'd have to come tomorrow, which is the last day before the offices are closing for Christmas."

Mama turned to Naomi and covered the phone. "Could you drive Liz to Riverbend in the truck tomorrow?" she whispered.

Naomi nodded.

"I can come first thing tomorrow," Elizabeth confirmed.

"How about ten o'clock?"

She peered over at Naomi, who gave her a thumbs up. "Yes, I can be there at ten."

"I'll see you tomorrow, then," Ms. Clark said.

"All right. Thank you for calling." They said their goodbyes.

"What was all that about?" Naomi asked.

Mama filled Naomi in on everything, while Elizabeth set Nan's letter in her lap. There was no way she would let anyone take Nan's favorite place in all the world. If she had anything to do with it, they would have big Christmases there with all the people Mama wanted to invite for years to come.

Travis came back in with some wire cutters and tampered with a few more wires behind the panel, snipping the end of one of them and reattaching it to one of the screws inside.

"Hey, Dad," Naomi said. "Have you ever heard of Worsham Enterprises?"

Travis turned around. "No, why?"

"Some lawyer says that company owns Crestwood Farm."

Travis slipped the wire cutters into his pocket. "What's she talking about?" he asked Mama.

Mama brought him the letter. Travis snapped the front of the thermostat back on and then took the paper. When he'd finished reading, he folded it and handed it back to Mama.

"I don't see how they can own something that's been in your family since you were a little girl."

"We'll get it figured out," Elizabeth said. Clearly something was amiss in the paperwork. She'd have it all cleared up and then maybe, while they were in town in Riverbend, she could convince Naomi to take her shopping after, so she could fill the space below the Christmas tree with presents. The trip would be a great cover for surprising Mama.

Chapter Nine

Elizabeth knocked on the door and pulled her coat tighter as she shivered on Beatrice's front porch, rethinking her decision to walk there. While she waited, she moved a few steps over and then back to keep the blood flowing, admiring the bundles of holly that adorned each of the windows.

Ray answered the door, wearing his signature overalls. "You here to see my mama?"

"I am," she replied. He stepped aside to allow her to enter and the warmth of the house felt like a soft embrace. "She asked me to come." Elizabeth unwound her scarf and took the beanie off her head, gripping Nan's letter tightly in her other hand.

"Yeah, she told me you might be comin'," he said over his shoulder, beckoning her down the long hallway to the back of the house, where they'd gathered in the kitchen during Beatrice's party. "She can't get to the door these days, so Ella and I've been on greetin' duty. Luckily ain't nobody comin' round too often."

Ray led Elizabeth into the living room, where Beatrice was in the same chair that she'd been in last time, her head tilted back, her eyes shut, dozing by the fire.

"Mama," Ray said, giving her arm a gentle shake.

The woman snorted and came to life.

"I've got Miss Liz here to see you."

"Ah, yes. Hello, my sweet girl," she said, blinking and wriggling in her chair as Ray left. Her socked feet were barely able to keep her steady as she attempted to stand.

"You don't have to get up," Elizabeth said, coming over to her. "I'll sit beside you."

Beatrice lowered herself back down, and, without the buzz of the party to give the old woman energy, she looked even more frail than she had before. Her hands unsteady, Beatrice gripped the arm of the chair, her transparent skin showing off the blue veins underneath.

"I brought this back." Elizabeth handed Beatrice the envelope.

Beatrice's face filled with life as she took it. "Have you read it?"

"Yes," Elizabeth replied.

The old woman held the letter to her chest. "After you'd left the party, I remembered saving this one in my dresser drawer because those memories your nan mentioned in it were some of my favorites. When Naomi came over, I made her go up and get it for you."

"Thank you," Elizabeth said, genuinely glad to have a little more insight into who her grandmother was as a young girl. "So, who's Jimmy?" The question had been going around in her head since she'd read the letter.

From the softness in Beatrice's breath and the faraway look in her wise eyes, it was clear that Jimmy had been someone important in Nan's life. "That's why I wanted you to read the letter. I wanted your nan to introduce him to you first. You needed to hear her excitement when she spoke about him."

"She seemed to love him," Elizabeth said.

Beatrice nodded slowly. "Yes, she did. Very much. And he loved her. It was a whirlwind romance." Beatrice's expression darkened. "Then he went off to war."

Elizabeth cocked her head to the side, captivated, but already expecting the worst.

"He never came home."

As they sat there in the silence that followed from a statement like that, a mixture of emotions swirled through Elizabeth: the fact that had the man come home, Elizabeth might not be sitting there beside Beatrice, and the loss of someone Nan had cared so deeply about making Elizabeth wonder why she'd never even had an inkling about him. "What was Jimmy's last name?" Elizabeth asked, wanting to give full respect to a fallen soldier who had been in her nan's life before he'd given his own for their country.

The creases between Beatrice's eyes deepened, and she shook her head. "I can't remember. It's been about eighty years and I only knew him a short time now that it's all said and done. I'd only just moved to the area myself when he'd left for war." Her gaze roamed the blanket in her lap as she attempted to place it.

Disappointed, Elizabeth said, "Maybe I can research and find out."

Beatrice looked up. "Perhaps you can. But his name isn't what's important to me. His presence in your nan's life was more important. I'm hoping that by showing you how it changed your grandmother, I can help you with whatever it is that's causing that storm cloud to fall over the vibrant girl who left this town headed for great things."

Elizabeth's cheeks heated with Beatrice's observation. Despite her attempts to hide it, the older woman had noticed her turmoil.

Elizabeth recalled the last day she'd spent in Mason's Ridge before leaving for college at New York University. She'd wanted to do important, life-changing work, and in order to do that she'd felt she needed to expand her horizons, to get out into the world. And New York had seemed the perfect place. That day, Nan had made her a cake and they'd all had slices of it with glasses of sweet tea as they sat around a bonfire outside until the lightning bugs had come out.

"I gave Liz an envelope with cash for emergencies," Mama had said to Nan while busying herself with making sure they all had napkins for the cake. "Liz, you know you can come home any time."

"You're fussing over her," Nan had pointed out lovingly.

Mama had rung her hands. "It's such a busy city. I just worry about sendin' my only little girl into it unequipped."

"What do you mean by that?" Liz had asked.

"You've never lived anywhere like that before—none of us have."

"I'm strong, Mama. I'll be fine," Liz had insisted.

She certainly was a shadow of that young girl now. And if Beatrice could see that fact, all Elizabeth could think about was whether it was evident to everyone.

"Your nan wrote Jimmy letters during the short time he was overseas," Beatrice continued, and Elizabeth shifted her focus back to the woman. "I have them right here." Beatrice fiddled with a pile of letters on the side table next to her, also tied in a red bow.

"Why did Nan give you the letters?" Elizabeth asked, trying not to think of those blissful days when she was younger and small-town life was all she had known.

"Your nan gave them to me for safekeeping when she'd received them right after the war because she knew that I was the only one of her friends who understood how she'd felt for Jimmy. She said she didn't know what to do with them, because they were from a time that caused her so much pain, but she couldn't bear to discard them."

"I'd love to read them," Elizabeth said.

"I'll let you take them home."

"Do you think Nan would approve of that?" Elizabeth wondered aloud. After all, she had never once mentioned them.

Beatrice nodded. "If it's to help you, I think so." She reached over and took Elizabeth's hand into her cold fingers. "Want to tell me what's going on with you?"

Elizabeth sucked in a breath, not wanting to unload her issues onto the ninety-nine-year-old.

When she didn't answer, Beatrice said, as crystal clear in her thoughts as she'd been Elizabeth's whole life, "I don't know what you're dealing with, but I saw the anguish in your eyes when I asked you about yourself at the party." She pursed her lips and studied Elizabeth for a moment. "Tell me."

Elizabeth took another deep breath. "My whole life I've wanted to get out of this town, to see the world and to help people," Elizabeth admitted. "I was the only one, it seemed like, who had those kinds of ambitions. I always felt different because, for me, where I grew up felt as if it were closing in on me instead of making me feel free like it did for Naomi."

"And you got out," Beatrice said.

"I did. And my life still wasn't what I thought it would be. I didn't follow any of the dreams I'd set for myself, instead I got sidetracked by my ex. I broke up with my boyfriend after seven years, and I feel like I've lost myself." She swallowed, unable to get any more out for fear the tears would begin to fall.

Beatrice nodded, narrowing her eyes at Elizabeth. "I figured." She let go of Elizabeth's hand and patted the back of it.

"Why did you figure?"

"Life can go haywire every now and again—and love can definitely do it. Sometimes it's less to do with where we are and more with what's up here." Beatrice tapped her temple. "I'd heard about your breakup. And that's exactly why I brought you here today. To tell you that you aren't the only one to have a relationship ripped from you. Your nan hit a point in life where she truly didn't know if she could go on."

"Really?" Elizabeth asked, surprised. Nan had always seemed to be the one solidly grounded person in her life who'd had it all together without a single crack.

"Yes. It's all in the letters."

"You said she'd received them after the war. Those are the letters Nan sent to Jimmy?"

"Mm hm." Beatrice picked them up, the large size of the bundle causing her to fumble, letting them thump into her lap.

"If they were sent to this Jimmy person, how did Nan get them back? Were they returned to sender?"

The corners of Beatrice's mouth turned upward, her fondness for Nan showing as she peered down at the stack of letters. "All the answers are in there." She handed the stack to Elizabeth. "Merry Christmas."

Elizabeth held the envelopes, feeling that Nan had something she wanted to say. And if her words also had answers for Elizabeth, she couldn't wait to find out what they were.

Holding the stack of letters against her chest, Elizabeth made her way back to Nan's, taking careful steps in the two tracks that had melted along the icy road. She tipped her face up to the warm sun that had peeked out after the storm, relishing the warmth and the orange glow between gusts of icy wind, the next round of snow predicted to move in within the next day or so. Gold beams of light shone down onto the ice, reflecting off it in a nearly blinding light.

I don't know what to do with myself, Nan, she thought as she walked, hoping holding the letters would help her to reach her grandmother. *I feel so lost. Tell me what to do.* But her inner dialogue was cut short when she heard the shushing of tires coming down the road through the snow. She took a large step to get out of the way, her boots sinking into the snow-filled ditch.

The sound slowed behind her until it came to a stop. Elizabeth turned around to find a Mercedes with the passenger window sliding down, those blue eyes that she would recognize in a second on her.

"Fancy seeing you here," Paul said.

"It's easy to do in this town," she said, trying to rationalize the fact that Paul had shown up right when she'd asked Nan what to do.

He reached over and opened the car door. "It's freezing. Hop in."

"It's not safe to drive these roads in this." Elizabeth waggled a finger at the Mercedes before grabbing hold of the door and opening it wider. "What are you doing out here?" She climbed into the warm leather seat, kicking snow off her boots before placing her feet inside.

"I had cabin fever," he said, flashing that warm smile of his. "And the reason I traveled to Mason's Ridge in the first place was to see the sights outside of town, but then the snow hit."

Elizabeth closed the door, cocooning them in the purring vehicle, placing the letters in her lap.

"How about you?" he asked, pulling off in the direction of the farm, his attention flitting over to the letters and then back to the road.

"I was visiting Beatrice, the woman I bought the candle for."

"Ah," he said. "And what are those?" He nodded toward the pile of envelopes.

"They're letters from my grandmother. Beatrice wanted me to have them."

His eyes remained on the road, but they creased at the corners, that kindheartedness radiating from them. He glanced over at the farm a few times as they passed it, and she considered pointing out that it was her stop, but then decided against it. While she'd told Mama that she wanted to see him again, it might be better if she didn't tell him where he could find her just yet, leaving the ball in her court. The last thing she needed was him showing up on the front porch when she was in a fit of tears over something. Her resolve wavering, she suddenly wasn't even entirely sure why she'd gotten into his car, apart from the fact that it was warm and he was so darned handsome. Was she doing the right thing?

"So, where are we going?" she asked as the eastern corner of the farm slid past her.

Interest swam around Paul's face. "I was just out for a drive. But now that *you're* here, want to get that drink?"

She chewed on her lip, unsure. She wanted to have a drink with him, but doing what she'd wanted hadn't really turned out very well for her in the past, and she second-guessed her intuition.

"No pressure at all. Just a drink."

Chapter Ten

When Elizabeth considered her answer to Paul's question, she asked herself how one drink would hurt. And it wasn't any different from sharing a coffee with him. "I know a place," she said. "But it's more cinnamon and sugar, and less martinis and Chardonnay."

He chuckled. "Sounds perfect."

As they drove along silently, she turned to the view out the window, a memory of Richard floating into her mind. Last Christmas, they'd decided to walk the two blocks to his favorite Italian restaurant. He hadn't wanted to walk, but he'd humored her.

"It's so festive," she'd said to him, taking his arm as they had strolled down the sidewalk in the freezing New York winter, the lights from the storefronts twinkling in front of them.

"You're making me earn our dinner," he'd mumbled.

"We have forty minutes until the table's ready anyway," she'd said, taking in the aroma of fresh popcorn and funnel cakes from the street vendors. "Oh, look!" She had pointed to a pop-up Christmas shop. "Let's get a hot chocolate," she'd suggested.

"I was more hoping for a brandy at a heated table in Francesco's."

Her good mood had slid away. "We don't have to stop," she'd said, hoping he'd reconsider, grin down at her, tell her that he was sorry for being a grouch, and they could absolutely get a hot chocolate, that it was the holidays after all.

"Thank God for that," he'd said instead, breezing past the shop.

"Take a right at the next intersection," Elizabeth said to Paul as she fired off a text to Mama so she wouldn't worry.

They drove along until Paul pulled the car to a stop in front of the quaint log cabin that sat nestled into the side of the mountain, the vines that usually held bright-purple flowers over the doorway now had a holiday garland with white lights woven through it. The only place in the area for really great southern cooking, Mama Jane's had been the place Nan had taken them whenever she'd wanted to celebrate. They'd gone to Mama Jane's for birthdays, anniversaries, and after Elizabeth's high school graduation. At the off-hour of four o'clock, it wasn't terribly busy, but by dinner time, the charming cabin would fill up to the brim.

The Mercedes's tires spun wildly when Paul attempted to straighten out his parking in the slushy snow. He put the car in reverse once more and hit the gas, fishtailing slightly until he got the vehicle into a straighter position.

"Don't move." He got out, went around to her side, and opened the passenger door, his chivalry giving her a plume of fondness for him.

Grasping the letters, she got out and walked up to the door with Paul, welcoming the cozy atmosphere that was visible through the holiday-pine-draped beveled glass panes on the front window. Paul opened the door and let her enter first, classical Christmas music playing softly throughout the dining area.

The place was nearly empty, but it was just as she remembered, with colorful mismatched chairs and tables dotting the distressed wood floor, every tabletop adorned with tea-light candles and little pots of flowering rosemary. The faint smell of cinnamon and apple pie combined with the scent of burning hickory in the fireplace floated throughout the space, taking her back to the days when her family would gather around one of the largest tables, her tummy rumbling for their chicken and dumplings with a side of blueberry cobbler.

Paul pulled out a chair at a table with a view of the snowy hills, and Elizabeth sat down, placing the letters on the table, next to the frosty window.

Paul eyed them, having a seat across from her. "You didn't want to leave those in the car?" he asked.

Elizabeth shook her head. "I don't want to let them out of my sight," she said. "They're the last chance I have to hear my grandmother."

"You were close with her?"

"Yes."

She had to admit that she liked the way Paul wanted to know her thoughts on things. And, if she were being honest with herself, she wanted to know more about him, too. What was his story?

The waitress came up, handing them a menu and filling their water glasses as she offered the specials. But all Elizabeth could think about was how easily she'd found herself there, across from this man. She'd only just met him, yet she'd climbed into his car without even a thought otherwise. Was she clouded by some sort of rebound haze?

"What are you thinking about?" he asked after the waitress had left them to look over the choices.

"How you could be a kidnapper or a murderer," she said.

Leaning on his elbow, his fist covering the huff of a laugh that escaped his lips at her comment, he asked, "What?"

"I got right into your car and I still don't know anything about you. Tell me something interesting about yourself."

He pouted, thinking. Then, he looked at her with those sapphire eyes. "You'd said earlier that you'd hoped to do the waltz."

"Yes," she replied, stunned that he'd remembered.

"And did you not get to?"

"No. I broke up with my boyfriend instead." She tipped her head back wistfully, remembering the bright-red ball gown she'd been wearing. "I was hoping to dance that night." She straightened up. "But what am I doing talking about me again? I asked to know something about *you*."

"Well, I can dance the waltz."

She grinned, surprised by his admission. "You can? I don't believe it."

"I can," he insisted.

"Oh, really?" She eyed him skeptically. "You just happen to know the waltz—the one dance that I love to do."

"Yes." He looked around the room and then stood up, offering her his hand. "I'll prove it. Dance with me?"

Elizabeth laughed at the spontaneity of his suggestion. "In the middle of the dining room at Mama Jane's?" She assessed the empty room.

"Is there a better place that you can think of?" He grinned at her, so comfortable with his suggestion.

"Not in Mason's Ridge," she said with another laugh.

He stood there, his hand outstretched, while a few of the waitresses gathered to see what was going on. She couldn't just leave him hanging… Elizabeth took his hand and followed him to a spot between the tables. "Silver Bells" played overhead.

"We'll start with the basic box step so I can warm up," he said lightly, taking her into his arms.

With his strong hand at her back, it made it difficult for Elizabeth to breathe as he moved her through the room with grace. The two of them glided between tables, the waitresses clapping when he spun her out and then back in. They nearly floated together, Paul turning her in circles whenever they found an empty space.

He pulled her in again, his woodsy scent tickling her senses as he locked eyes with her, making her pulse quicken. In his arms, she felt incredibly vulnerable yet free at the same time, it was as if the intimacy of the dance had opened up something in her that had been closed off, making her feel again. Then, unexpectedly, he dipped her, the shock of it making her laugh. The waitstaff cheered and whooped. Paul righted Elizabeth and then gave a little bow in their direction before walking her back to their table.

"What else do you want to know?" he asked after they'd both taken their seats once more.

Still reeling from the dance, Elizabeth tried to empty her mind to contemplate the question. She cleared her throat, trying to calm her pulse. "Have you always lived in Chicago?"

"Yep." He took a sip of his water. "I grew up about thirty miles west of Chicago in a little town called Naperville, but after college I moved to the city to take a job in urban planning."

"Is that what you do now?"

"Sort of. I run the family business."

She inwardly flinched, having not fared well with Richard's family business, but those were old wounds, she reminded herself. Paul was clearly a totally different person. "And what is the business?"

"Corporate property assessment and development."

"So are you one of the people buying up all the land around here?" she asked.

He shook his head. "With all the growth in the area, the idea did occur to me. And, I have to admit, I tried to delve into it a little, but no, I'm not buying anything." Swirling the ice in his glass, his thoughts seemed to float away from the conversation.

"What is it?" she asked.

He looked back at her as if deciding whether to say what was on his mind. "This talk about work brought to mind the fact that my grandfather isn't very happy with me."

"Why's that?"

"He didn't want to expand the company, but the board believed it was for the best."

She folded her hands on the table. "And you did want to expand?"

"I adore my grandfather, but he was getting too old to run the company, making decisions that weren't optimal in this day and age. The board wanted to try to force him to retire to keep the business afloat and to keep the board members from losing their jobs if the company went under. They wanted me to run it. I told my grandfather their ideas and he was so upset with me and his board that he stepped down on his own." Paul took in an unsteady breath, the weight of the decision clear. "My grandfather hasn't spoken to me since, and I've put a lot of pressure on myself to make it a success to prove to him that I wasn't out to hurt him and that I have the best interests of the company at heart."

The sincerity in his face struck her.

"The early years of throwing myself into the business is what caused my wife to leave me. I wanted to prove myself to my grandfather and I worked way too many hours. After she left, it took me some time to get used to being just *me* again."

His openness made her feel as though somehow everything would be okay. The way he looked at her—so honest—she believed every word. "I understand."

"How so?" he asked.

"The seven-year relationship I'd told you about at Ford's… I met a guy in college and moved in with him right after graduation. When our relationship fell apart, it wasn't as easy as picking myself back up. It's as if my life in New York disappeared without a trace. My old friends haven't called, I don't have the same experiences here that I had in the city, and the longer I spend in Mason's Ridge, the more I realize that my life in New York was a complete façade. But the slower pace of life now is cleansing in a way. I just need to figure out who I am here. It's hard to know."

"That is difficult," he said with an empathetic frown. "But it also means that your life can literally be anything you want it to be."

"I've thought about that a lot." She leaned on her elbow, the new little chick in the henhouse and riding Buttons coming to mind. "There's something about this place… My whole life, I'd wanted to escape it, but now it feels more like me than anything else has."

Fondness for her comment showed in the rise at the corners of his mouth. "I definitely know what you mean."

His eyes locked with hers and there was nowhere else she wanted to be than right there, in his gaze. There they were, the two of them coming together, lifting each other's spirits on the wings of fate. Neither of them were supposed to be at Mama Jane's, but that was how the chips had fallen, and she couldn't be happier about it.

"Y'all ready to order?" the waitress said, interrupting them.

"I haven't even looked," Paul said, clearing his throat and peering down at his menu. "We'd agreed to drinks, but I'm actually a little hungry. Mind if I get an early dinner?"

"That sounds perfect," Elizabeth said. "Do you still have the all-day chicken and dumplings?" she asked the waitress, scanning the menu for the dish.

"Yes, ma'am."

"I'll have that." Elizabeth handed the waitress her menu and addressed Paul. "I'd definitely go for their chicken and dumplings. They're incredible."

"Done." Paul handed his menu to the woman.

"They're also known for their hot chocolates," Elizabeth said, recalling the thick sweetness of them and the impressive display of chocolate on top. "Want to get one as an appetizer?"

"Of course," Paul said, bobbing his eyebrows up in a dramatic display of excitement.

"All right. I'll get those orders in for you," the woman confirmed before leaving them alone again.

"I've extended my stay," Paul said suddenly, his entire attention on Elizabeth as if he were waiting for a verdict.

Without warning, hope bubbled up that he'd actually stayed for her, sending her mentally scrambling to think rationally, but the way he was looking at her was making it difficult.

"The snow's made it nearly impossible to leave town, and with more on the way, it makes sense to ride it out," he added. "It's really nice here in Mason's Ridge." His gaze lingered on her as if he were trying to decipher some sort of invisible code to unlock her. "It's a great place to spend a holiday."

"And you're okay spending Christmas by yourself?" she asked.

Paul shrugged, rearranging the salt and pepper shakers, moving them like chess pieces. "It's always been the plan."

"What will you do on Christmas all alone? Do you have any decorations at all? Any gifts?" In the years she'd been in New York, the holidays a huge opportunity for her charities, Elizabeth hadn't been able to come home for Christmas, but now she was reminded of how much she'd missed, and she couldn't imagine being alone for the holiday.

"Maybe I'll get a little tree at the tree lot down the road."

The thought that he'd shop at Percy's tree lot filled her with happiness. "And what will you decorate it with?"

He set the pepper shaker down. "I'm not sure. Where do I get decorations in Mason's Ridge?"

"Probably the general store on the edge of town."

"That's a good idea. I'd like to check it out anyway to see more of Mason's Ridge."

"There's not much here to see," Elizabeth warned.

He looked around the restaurant, his attention moving to the stone fireplace. "I've barely even seen any of it yet, with the storm having halted everything." He looked back at her. "There's something about this place that feels like home, even though it's nothing like any home I've ever lived in."

Nan's voice drifted into her memory as Elizabeth pictured her grandmother standing in the yard, pushing her on the rope swing. *All the love I've ever known has been right here. There's nowhere else I'd rather be…* "I know what you mean." She eyed the letters beside her.

"So, tell me more about those," Paul said, following her line of sight to the stack of envelopes.

Elizabeth fiddled with the red bow that encircled them. "My grandmother's best friend, Beatrice, thought I should have them." She explained about the young man named Jimmy and how Beatrice had thought they may help Elizabeth.

Paul glanced over at them again, his interest clear.

Nan's words were very personal, and Paul was a near-stranger, but he'd been so easy to talk to that Elizabeth felt she wanted to let him in just a little to test the waters, even though it went against her resolve. But perhaps there was something in the letters that could help him too.

"Would you like to read one with me?" she asked.

His eyes widened, that little smile showing at the edges of his lips. "I'd love to."

Tentatively, Elizabeth slid the top letter out of the stack and opened it, pulling the single page from inside and flattening it out on the table between them so they could both read the words.

May 4, 1942

My dearest Jimmy,

Sometimes I feel like I'm drowning in my tears. I cannot believe you've gone off to fight. What a senseless act, this war. It's tearing us all apart. My heart aches for your safety. I don't know what I'll do with myself until you come home. I worry all day. While I play Bridge with the other ladies in town, while we get sodas at the corner market, in the evenings when I'm having dinner—all I do is fret. But we need to keep our spirits up, don't we?

Beatrice is taking me out to the cinema tomorrow night to start our weekend. I'm hoping that it'll take my mind off wondering about where you are and what you're doing for a few hours. I know you promised me that you'd keep yourself safe, but it doesn't ease my fears about you being in harm's way. My nights without you are very long indeed.

You are my whole life. I miss you, my love.

Until my arms are around you again,
Harriet

When Elizabeth looked up from the letter, Paul seemed to be deep in thought, two lines having formed between his eyes, his lips turned downward. "That's incredible," he said. "She truly loved your grandfather."

"Yes. Except Jimmy isn't my grandfather," she told him.

"Oh? I'm sorry. I'd just assumed…"

"I had no idea my nan ever loved someone other than my grandfather." She folded the letter slowly, placing it back into its envelope and slipping it under the ribbon. "It's such a strange revelation."

"I have to admit that I've never felt that kind of love, or fear for that matter," he said. "And she was able to feel it twice, I'm assuming, if she later married your grandfather."

Elizabeth thought back to her early days with Richard, knowing that she hadn't felt that level of love either. "Do you think *everyone* finds that kind of emotional connection, though?"

"I don't know. But everyone deserves it."

They shared a moment between them, as if they both wondered what could be. The intensity of it scared Elizabeth just a little bit. She wouldn't want anything to ruin this gorgeous thing they'd started. Could life inch its way in and mess up everything? Would Paul go back to Chicago and forget all about her? But she was probably getting ahead of herself…

The waitress returned, setting two overflowing red mugs in front of them. Each one was adorned with little Christmas trees circling the rim that were barely visible under the massive pile of whipped cream with green and red sprinkles, chocolate syrup and full-sized chocolate bars protruding from the top.

"I see why this is so popular," Paul said, clearing his throat and pinching the candy-cane-striped straw, swirling the contents around. "It looks delicious."

Glad for the distraction, Elizabeth scooted her mug toward her. "You can't drink from the straw," she told him, reciting Nan's rule.

"I can't?"

Elizabeth chewed on a grin. "Nope. You have to tip it up so you get the whipped cream, the toppings, and the hot chocolate in one sip."

"Right..." He ran his finger up the mug to catch the drip of whipped cream that had begun to slide down the side, licking it. "Tasty."

Elizabeth lifted hers to her mouth, the nutty, sugary scent tickling her nose. "If you drink it correctly, there should be a hole in the whipped cream when you're done. Ready?"

Paul threaded his fingers through the handle. "Ready."

Elizabeth sank her lip into the enormous pile of whipped cream as she attempted to take a sip, the thick malted hazelnut-infused chocolate mixing with the milky cream, the chocolate bar slipping forward, bumping into her lips. She swallowed.

Paul set his mug down. "How did I do?"

Elizabeth laughed. "I don't know. How *did* you do?" she asked, not alerting him right away to the dollop of whipped cream on his nose. "Did you get a good drink of it?"

"Yes. It was very chocolatey."

"Lean in," she said as she wrapped a napkin around her finger.

Paul put his hands on the table and came toward her. It was then that she noticed the silver flecks in his blue eyes as they locked with hers.

"You have whipped cream on your nose," she said, wiping it with the napkin, the two of them face-to-face, inches from each other. It would've been so easy to lean in and kiss him, the way he was looking at her, the thought taking her by surprise. With everything she'd been through, she hadn't expected this. She pushed back, breathless.

Paul reached for the napkin that was in his lap, balling it into his hand and holding it up to let her know it was at the ready, evidently trying to let her off the hook because she was certain he'd felt that moment too. He took another sip, getting more on his nose.

Another laugh burst from Elizabeth's lips, unexpectedly, given her nerves over the electricity between them. She couldn't remember the last time she'd enjoyed someone the way she was enjoying Paul right then.

"I did it again, didn't I?" He dabbed at his nose, inspecting the napkin to see if he'd gotten the whipped cream. "This is clearly a skill I haven't mastered. How are you drinking that?"

Elizabeth couldn't hide her enjoyment, the lightheartedness between them soaking into her shattered soul. "Tip your head back a little when you drink it."

"Or I could do this." He removed the chocolate bars and then leaned down, and with a giant bite, gulped a mouthful of the whipped cream, leaving only a tiny layer on the surface.

Elizabeth gasped and clapped a hand over her mouth to stifle her amusement.

Paul blotted the cream that had escaped at the corners of his mouth and swallowed. "There."

"How will you get all the flavors now that you've decimated the toppings?" she teased, still attempting not to let him affect her like he was, but failing miserably.

He grew serious. "Ah, but sometimes it's better to focus on one thing at a time so you can really experience it without distraction."

She contemplated his answer, and as she looked into his eyes, she wondered if there'd been a suggestiveness in his tone and maybe she should apply that logic to more than just the hot chocolate. Just then, his phone rang. His face falling to a more serious expression, his jaw clenching as if he were wrestling with whether to check it or not.

"Feel free to get that," Elizabeth said. After all, this had already turned into more than just a drink and that was all it was supposed to be.

Reluctantly, he answered the call. "Hey, Jake." His shoulders rose as his attention returned to Elizabeth and then away again, his eyes rounding. "What do you mean, he's going to pull out?" Paul pushed back from the table and stood up. "The contractors have already been paid. I can't lose his investment now."

Flashing her an apologetic glance, he walked across the dining area and went outside, leaving her pondering whether divine intervention had put a stop to the moment before it had gone too far.

Chapter Eleven

"Sorry about that," Paul said, returning to the table. "Has the food been here long?"

"It just came." Elizabeth draped her napkin in her lap. "Is everything okay?"

"Just work," he said, shaking his head. "One of my investors is giving me a hard time. He wants me to hurry, threatening to pull out of the deal, but it's Christmas and the timing is out of my hands."

"Would it be the end of the world if he left?"

Paul's chest filled with an anxious inhale, giving her the answer before he'd even said anything. "Yes. A whole lot of people would lose their jobs and the family business would probably fold. This is our big chance to keep it going."

"Oh, gosh," she said, feeling awful for him.

"But why am I worrying you with it?" he asked with a smile as he picked up his fork and knife. "It's the holidays and I get to have dinner with an amazing woman I've just met."

Elizabeth couldn't deny the delightful feeling she got from the compliment. "I'm glad you drove by today," she said.

He smiled. "Do you live around here?"

"Not too far," she said, not feeling as uneasy now about bringing him back to Nan's.

"It's beautiful country out here."

"It certainly is." As she sat there in the small dining room at Mama June's next to Nan's letters, with this wonderful surprise of a man, Elizabeth felt that, somehow, she might just get the answers she was looking for.

"How did we even have an appetite for dinner after those enormous hot chocolates?" Paul asked, patting his belly as he opened the car door for Elizabeth.

Big, soft flakes had begun to fall from the gray sky above, and the icy wind cut right through Elizabeth, her coat doing nothing to keep her warm as she slid onto the cold seat of the Mercedes, holding the letters. "It doesn't matter. Mama Jane's food is so good that you'll eat it anyway—whether you're full or not."

Paul shut her door and went around to his side, getting in and starting the engine, the vehicle coming to life with a soft purr.

The heater blew in a cold burst of air at her face, giving Elizabeth a shiver. She blew into her hands before slipping on her gloves. "That front is coming in already," she said, wishing they could take a long drive so that she could have more time with him.

He started the engine, the windshield wipers sliding back and forth to clear the newly fallen snow. "We'd better get you home," he said. Putting the car in gear and adjusting his mirror, Paul pressed the gas to pull out of the parking space. The car didn't move, its tires instead spinning in place. He looked over at Elizabeth and both of them, having lived in northern climates, knew exactly what was happening.

He turned the wheel and tried again, the car growling in disapproval. Moving the wheel back and forth, his foot switching between the gas and the brake, the car wouldn't budge.

"We're completely stuck," Elizabeth said.

"The melted slush turned to ice while we were eating." Paul put the car in park and got back out, walking around it and then getting back in. "The front tires are pretty impacted," he said. "But we might be able to jostle it out. Would you come over to the driver's seat and put the car in reverse while I push?"

Elizabeth got out of the car, setting Nan's letters on the passenger seat and going around to the driver's side. She wound down the window so she could communicate with Paul. Then, she placed her foot on the brake, both hands on the wheel.

Paul slid on his leather gloves and spread out his fingers on the snowy hood of the Mercedes. "Okay," he called. "Put it in reverse and I'll count to three. Ready?"

She shifted gears. "Ready."

"One, two, three," he said with a grunt as she hit the gas, his face turning red, the tires spinning madly. The car didn't move.

Elizabeth took her foot off the gas.

"Let's try again," Paul said. "Hit it."

Elizabeth pressed the gas once more, with the same result. Paul let out an exhale and shook his head, his attention on the unmoving tires.

She stuck her head out the window. "Ray can pull us out with the tractor and tow you home." Elizabeth took her phone from her pocket. "My friend Naomi has his number. Let me just text her." She typed a quick text, but it failed. The signal wasn't terribly strong, so she held her phone out the window and tried to send the text again. When it still wouldn't go through, Elizabeth got out of the car. She danced around, shivering as she attempted to text Naomi once more, to no avail. She tried to call, but the call was unsuccessful as well.

When she looked up from her phone, Paul was grinning down at her.

"You're cold," he said.

Elizabeth pulled her coat tighter. "Freezing."

She turned around again, her back to him, typing the text again, hitting send, and trying to get a signal. Taking a step forward, the bars on her phone stubbornly stayed in the same position. She stepped back, as if it would help, and collided with Paul, sliding on the icy surface. He grabbed the top of her arms, steadying them both.

Once they were standing, he didn't let go, his gentle grip and breath at her ear while her back grazed his chest made it difficult for her to catch her breath. His touch felt as if she'd been meant to experience it her whole life and the universe had been holding out on her. Slowly, Elizabeth turned around to face him, looking up into his kind face.

He swallowed as if he felt the same undeniable energy that she did buzzing between them. He gently rubbed the tops of her arms to keep her warm, although she didn't care about the cold anymore. Trying to answer the questions in his eyes, her phone sounded with the alert that her text had gone through.

Her phone rang then, tearing through the moment.

Paul silently surrendered to reality, pulling away, and she put the phone to her ear. "Hello," Elizabeth answered.

"What's up?" Naomi asked, as Paul walked back over to the Mercedes.

"We've got a car stuck in the snow at Mama Jane's," she said, following Paul back to the vehicle, seeing him differently now and wondering if the moment would stick once she'd ended her call. "I was wondering if you could give me Ray's number so I can see if he can tow us out?"

Paul opened her car door for her and then climbed into the driver's side. As they got back into the car, he put up the window, immediately shutting out the cold.

"I can, but Ray's gone into town to help plow the side streets. With the storm comin' in earlier than expected, we had to have all men on deck. The county sure ain't gonna have enough people to get it done in time way out here."

Elizabeth chewed on the inside of her lip as she took in Paul's hopeful stare.

"... *I'm* headin' that way, though," Naomi added. "I can swing by and pick y'all up in the truck."

"Oh, Naomi, that would be awesome," Elizabeth said, relieved. "Thank you."

Paul eyed her expectantly.

Elizabeth ended the call. "Ray's busy, but Naomi's coming to get us," she said. "We'll leave your car for now. I'll try to catch up with Ray to get it unstuck tonight, but given the storm, it might be tomorrow. He's out clearing roads."

"All right," Paul said.

They waited in the running car for Naomi, both of them silent as the buzz radiated between them, the snow falling down at a record pace, covering everything in a blanket of white.

"I keep thinking I should take you back inside and offer you another hot chocolate while we wait for your friend to arrive, but I'm not sure either of us have room after all we ate," Paul said.

"Definitely not." Elizabeth gave him a little chuckle, meeting his gaze, both of them clearly wondering what this was they were both feeling. He had to leave for Chicago soon. The very last thing she was ready to do was to chase someone to another state. But she couldn't deny the tug at her heart that she didn't want to let him go.

"Should we read another letter to pass the time?" Elizabeth asked, waving Nan's stack in the air, trying to change her thoughts to something lighter.

"If you'd like to," Paul said with interest.

Elizabeth pulled the second letter from the stack. "Oh," she said, looking down at the boxy, unfamiliar writing. "This one's from Jimmy."

She smoothed the letter and read the message aloud, tingles spreading over her skin.

June 5, 1944

My dearest Harriet,

I asked you to marry me before leaving because…

"Wait, what?" Elizabeth said with a gasp. She looked over at Paul, dumbfounded. "*Marry?*"

"You didn't know?" Paul leaned in to view the letter.

"I had no idea," she replied, everything she'd just accepted about Nan over the years going through her mind at once.

"What a shock," he said, empathy oozing from his features, making her suddenly glad he was there with her to receive this news.

"I wonder why she never told us he'd proposed to her." She peered back down at the sentence to make sure she hadn't misread it, but knowing she hadn't.

"Maybe it was too difficult. It's pretty clear how this turns out, right?"

"Yeah…" She held up the letter, the gray light from outside illuminating it, still stunned. Nan had never given her any indication that she'd been engaged before. She'd always seemed so content with everything, never letting even the tiniest crack show. "Sorry," Elizabeth said, coming back to the present moment. "Want me to finish reading?"

"If you feel ready to," Paul replied.

Her mind still reeling, she took in a steadying breath and resumed.

I asked you to marry me before leaving because I want us to be together forever. Don't worry yourself with this war. It is only one season of our lives together. I will have you in my arms again soon.

I keep your photo in the breast pocket of my coat, and you are with me every minute of this conflict.

I do have to tell you that we're boarding boats tomorrow, headed across the English Channel, after this terrible storm that is upon us passes. If my letters are delayed, please don't fret. I'll be able to respond once I return to my post in Great Britain.

Sending you all my love across the sea,
Jimmy

Elizabeth stared at the words, processing how an entire future had simply evaporated into thin air. All the motivations, dreams, and feelings that were present in that one letter were just… gone. She could definitely understand what it was like to face a future that was unrecognizable.

A knock on the car window caused Elizabeth to jump with a start. Naomi stood on the other side of the glass, crossing her arms and shivering.

"Looks like our ride is here," Paul said, cutting the engine.

Elizabeth waved to Naomi and folded the letter, putting it back under the ribbon and opening the door.

"Thanks for coming to get us," she said on autopilot, still trying to climb out of her contemplations.

"When you said 'we,' I figured it was you and your mama," Naomi said, her eyebrows pulling together warily.

"Paul and I had an early dinner," she replied, trying to be casual.

"Well, well, well…" Naomi said under her breath, before she sucked in her cheeks, ushering the two of them over to the Silverado. "I needed to get to the Feed 'n' Seed for some chicken feed before it closes for the day. Hey, Paul," she added in greeting.

Paul lifted a hand in friendly response and Elizabeth opened the door, climbing into the crew cab of the truck. Paul followed, inching nearer to Elizabeth so they could both fit on the backseat bench.

"Does your mama need any feed, or are y'all good?" Naomi asked, putting the truck in gear and reversing over the snow with ease.

"I think she's got plenty, but I'll text her to be sure." Elizabeth wiggled, attempting to pull her phone from her back pocket while keeping the letters from sliding off her lap.

Naomi eyed Elizabeth in the rearview mirror, clearly still suspicious of her and Paul's motives. Then she steered toward a bump, purposely driving over it, causing Elizabeth to bounce in her seat. Elizabeth offered a questioning look toward her friend.

"The snow is treacherous, ain't it?" Naomi said.

"Definitely," Elizabeth replied through her teeth.

Another bump.

Elizabeth tried to focus on something other than her old friend's wavering trust of her, reading the response from her mother that she didn't need anything at the Feed 'n' Seed. She put the phone into her pocket and stared through the two front seats at the snow-covered road before them for the duration of the drive.

"You can let me off here," Paul said as they neared the coffee shop. "I'll walk over."

Naomi pulled the truck to the side of the road and put it in park.

Elizabeth held out her phone to Paul. "Put your number in so I can text you tomorrow when Ray is able to get your car."

Paul typed in his number, handing it back to her. "I'll see you soon," he said, letting himself out the truck, his attention lingering on her, that hint of a smile emerging. "Thank you for the ride, Naomi."

"No problem," she said, giving Elizabeth a sideways glance.

After a quiet ride home, Elizabeth arrived back at the farmhouse. If Naomi wasn't going to be open enough to ask the nature of her visit with Paul, Elizabeth certainly wasn't going to explain.

Mama was at the kitchen table, scribbling notes on a legal pad while the kettle warmed on the stove. "When this ground thaws out, I'm gettin' serious about that section at the edge of the property."

Elizabeth stripped off her coat.

"I want to know why crops aren't growin' there," Mama continued. "We could make more money if we expand our fields into that area. We're barely breaking even and I've got to figure out what to do to increase our income."

Elizabeth walked over and sat down across from her mother, setting the stack of letters on the table. "I'll help you figure it out."

"Whatcha got there?" Mama asked, noticing the letters.

"Beatrice gave them to me."

"Oh?" Mama moved the legal pad out of the way.

"She thought they might help me."

Mama leaned on her hand, her forehead creased in interest, a pencil still poised between her fingers.

"I think you might want to know what I've read in them so far."

Mama set down the pencil and gave Elizabeth her full attention. "Tell me."

"Why don't we have some tea and cookies?" Elizabeth suggested, attempting to soften the blow of what she was about to tell Mama.

Mama's eyes widened before she got up to tend to the tea, mixing her Christmas blend of cinnamon and cloves with orange spice tea leaves. "It must be pretty interestin' if we need tea and cookies," she said, clearly not understanding the gravity of the subject matter. She pulled a plate from the cabinet and loaded cookies onto it, bringing it over to the table. Back at the counter, she poured water over the tea leaves, a festive scent rising into the air. "So what do the letters say?"

"Well, for starters, Nan, it seems, was engaged before Gramps."

Mama's face contorted into a look of disbelief. "What? That's not possible." She brought the mugs over to the table and handed one to Elizabeth.

"Oh, yes, it is," Elizabeth said, pulling out the first two letters. She slid them over to Mama.

While Elizabeth took a bite of a gingerbread cookie, Mama opened the letters and scanned them, her eyes bulging with every new line.

"This doesn't make sense," Mama said, when she'd finished.

"I'm not worried at all about her having loved someone before Gramps. I'm more concerned that she never told us about it. Did she ever mention anything at all about this Jimmy person that you can remember? *Anything?*"

Mama shook her head. "No. I've never heard of him."

"Doesn't that seem odd, since she clearly loved him? So much that she almost *married* him?"

"Indeed," Mama said, still staring at the letter, confusion showing in the lines between her eyes as her brows pulled together. "Do you know if Beatrice is aware of this? She's never divulged such a thing."

"She knows."

Mama produced a confused frown. "What do the other letters say?"

"I've only read the first two."

"Open the next one," Mama said, picking up her steaming mug.

Elizabeth pulled out the third letter, this one in Nan's swirling handwriting. She settled back in the kitchen chair and began to read.

July 8, 1944

Hello, my dear,

I haven't heard from you since you told me you were headed to France, and I know that so much transpires in your days and nights, so I'm not offended by your silence. I fully believe that you will set my burdened mind at ease as soon as you get the chance.

I had started to listen to the news on the radio each night, but turned it off after hearing about the Battle of Normandy that began on June 6, the day you'd said you were leaving on boats. Almost 30,000 soldiers were killed in that battle and I cannot bear to imagine what you might be encountering. If I do, I wake in the night in terror.

I want you to know that I'm utterly in love with you and I wait here with my heart open and my hopes high for your swift return.

All my love,
Harriet

"What happened to him?" Mama whispered, her tone giving away that it was more a question of *how* he'd died rather than if. Her gaze was on the holiday-draped mantle in the living room, but her mind seemingly on events nearly eighty years ago and an ocean away that may have led to Jimmy's death.

"I can only guess what happened." With a heavy heart, Elizabeth took a warm sip of her tea, the spicy sweetness of it feeling like a blessing in itself.

"There are so many more letters," Mama noted, dragging her finger along the edges of the envelopes. "How many had she written before she knew?"

Elizabeth couldn't imagine how it must have felt for Nan to sit there in the farmhouse day in and day out with no word from the man she loved, wondering about whether he was dead or alive. It must have been excruciating.

"Read the next letter," Mama urged her.

Her curiosity consuming her, Elizabeth grabbed another envelope and opened it. When she saw the signature, she sucked in a breath, the hairs on her arms standing up. Elizabeth turned the paper around to show her mother. "It's from Gramps."

September 20, 1944

Dear Harriet,

My name is Roger Sloan. I have had the immense pleasure of serving with Jimmy over the last few months in the same platoon before his squad was sent on their next mission. I have to tell you that he has an excellent Donald Duck impression! A few of the children in the town of Le Havre were upset by the bombing and they were fearful of us in our uniforms; Jimmy bent down and did his impression of the cartoon character, making them giggle. It was such a delightful sound—the giggles, not Jimmy.

Elizabeth laughed. "'The giggles, not Jimmy.' Gramps was always so funny," she said, her heart squeezing at the humor that lingered there on the page. Elizabeth could still recall the strength in his tenderhearted embrace and the way he bent down to be at her level when she ran through the fields toward him.

"The grass is tall," he'd noted when she'd run through the wildflowers to greet him once when she was about six, the long weeds tickling her bare legs in her shorts. He'd scooped her up into his arms. "How about if we cut it?" he'd teased, holding her upside down by her ankles, swinging her and making her squeal with laughter. "I'll run you around and you eat the dandelions. Think you can get them all?" He had zoomed in a circle, the movement tickling her tummy like a fair ride. Then he'd reached down, slipping a strong arm under her back, righting her, and she had wrapped her arms around his neck still giggling.

Elizabeth surfaced from her memory to find Mama nodding in agreement. "He was the best father and grandfather. All my memories of him are happy ones. I can't recall a single time he got upset. Given the things that life can throw at a person, that's really sayin' somethin'."

"I know."

"What else does the letter say?" Mama asked.

Elizabeth began to read again.

Jimmy has told me all about you. He absolutely adores you. He left me your picture for safekeeping, telling me that by leaving it with me, he guaranteed that he would come back to get it, since he promised you that he'd keep it with him. He was convinced that knowing I had it would propel him through battle and he'd return more quickly.

I wanted to reach out because I've seen your letters piling up, and I didn't want you to worry. Jimmy is on the front lines and he's unable to respond. However, you should know that he is the epitome of valor and he represents you and our country well.

I do hope you welcome this response and if you have any other queries or if you feel anxious about Jimmy, you are always free to send a note to me and I'll do my best to find out anything I can.

Sincerely,
Roger

"So *that's* how Nan met Gramps," Elizabeth said, laying the letter on the table.

"It still doesn't explain why we've never heard about Jimmy," Mama said. "Especially if Dad knew all about him."

Mama was right; it didn't make sense at all why Nan would never have given Jimmy his place in their family and honored his memory by telling them about him. "Why don't we ditch the tea, pour some wine, get comfy by the fire, and dig in to the rest of the letters?" Elizabeth suggested. "Maybe we'll find out."

Chapter Twelve

Elizabeth took in her first conscious breath of the day, inhaling a buttery, sweet aroma, the cloudy view of Nan's letters strewn over the living-room floor, alerting her that she was on the sofa, covered in one of her grandmother's quilts. The wine had taken over her will last night, and she'd lost the battle with keeping her eyes open. But today was a busy day, so she needed to get going.

"Mornin' sunshine," Mama said from the kitchen when Elizabeth sat up. She flipped a pancake in the cast-iron skillet and turned down the heat before making a cup of coffee and bringing it over to Elizabeth.

"What time is it?" Elizabeth croaked, throwing the quilt off her legs and yawning.

"I reckon it's about six, why?" Mama held out the mug.

"I've gotta call Ray to get Paul's car out today and then Naomi's taking me to the lawyer's at ten." She reached out, accepting her mother's offer of a steaming cup of Joe.

"Well, the good news is that the storm came quicker than it was supposed to and it's leavin' just as fast. The high today is forty-two, so I'm hopin' it'll melt some of this so we can get back to life as usual."

Elizabeth understood what her mother meant after their earlier conversation about the farm. With the snow covering everything, Mama couldn't get out in nature and fulfill her purpose. As Elizabeth considered this, she took in Mama's stance, the gray of her hair, and the way she wore Nan's apron, wondering how much of Nan's blood ran through Mama's veins. Had Nan thought the same way as Mama about the farm after Jimmy had died? Had that been why Nan had been so full of life whenever they were outside in the fields and why she had always chosen the rocker on the front porch over the chair inside?

They hadn't gotten any more answers in the letters they'd been able to read last night, which made her doubtful she'd find anything else in the rest of them. They'd learned more about the budding relationship between Gramps and Nan. In the letters, Gramps was kind, always setting Nan's troubled mind at ease. And he defused the weight of the situation with humor—something Nan was clearly appreciative of. Through their letters, they'd built a friendship as the two of them waited for Jimmy's return, which had never come. Elizabeth had drifted off at that point, and questions still remained, but this morning there was much to do.

"Yes, it would be nice to be able to come and go, wouldn't it?" Elizabeth said, wishing for the weather to turn for her mother. But as she thought about it, she had to wonder if her wish had been for her as well. Would she be the third generation of women in her family to find solace there at the farm? Taking in the quaint little space that wrapped around her like a warm hug, the idea didn't feel that far off…

"It certainly would." Mama looked out the kitchen window with the view of the orchard, her hands on her hips. "I need to check the vole guards around the apple trees to be sure they're all still intact. I meant to do it before the first snow and I got too busy. And I have to feed the animals." She turned and faced Elizabeth. "After your coffee, wanna help? I'll pay you in sausage and egg casserole."

"Done," Elizabeth said lightheartedly, the cool morning air snaking around her ankles despite the flickering fire across from her. "Anything for your casserole."

"Good girl." Mama slipped off her apron and hung it on the hook by the refrigerator. "I'm gonna go make my bed and pick up in the bedroom and then we can head outside."

"Okay. I'm excited to see little Holly the chick again."

"Me too," Mama said.

Elizabeth paced across the living area with her coffee, gathering up Nan's letters that she and Mama had opened last night, folding them and placing each one back into its envelope. She couldn't wait to read more of them, but they would have to hold off. The farm called her like a beacon of hope, and she had apple trees to inspect.

Elizabeth's breath puffed out in front of her as she bent down and rattled the circular fencing at the bottom of one of the tree trunks. Certain the vole guard was secure, she righted herself and tightened the collar of her coat to keep the cold from sneaking down her neck, while she took a seat on one of the hay bales they put out every year.

❄

"Why do you have hay in the tree fields, Nan? For chairs?" Elizabeth could remember asking when she was a child. She was probably seven, running through the orchard barefoot, her gauzy sundress blowing in the summer breeze. Out of breath, she went to sit down and Nan yanked her back up by the elbow.

"Careful," Nan said, drawing Elizabeth into her arms protectively and then releasing her to explain. "Bees nest in them."

"Bees?" Elizabeth took a wide step back from the bale of hay. "Why do you keep them here if bees are in them?"

"They pollinate the flowers," Nan told her, picking a white bloom from one of the trees and threading it through Elizabeth's dark locks above her ear. "In the winter, we put them out for the mice and, when the mice leave in the spring, the bees follow their scent and move in."

"Like a hotel," Elizabeth said, seeing the rectangular stacks in a different light.

Nan laughed, the sound like windchimes. "Yes. Like a hotel."

"There are more trees than I remember," Elizabeth said to Mama at the other end of the row.

"We're tryin' to maximize revenue," Mama explained, as she came toward her. Mama rattled one of the guards, fiddling with it. "That's why I want to use that barren spot at the end of the far field. I want to plant on it come spring."

"Why don't we take a look at it when we finish up here?" Elizabeth suggested, considering whether the botany classes she'd taken in college would come back to her.

"Sounds like a plan," Mama said. The glimmer in her eyes revealed how happy she was to have Elizabeth working the farm with her, and Elizabeth was glad to help, feeling the same sense of joy that it gave Mama. Suddenly, she couldn't wait to see the blooms come spring.

They finished the last three rows of trees and then grabbed a shovel from the old shed out back before they made their way across the fields. Elizabeth's boots sank in the mix of sloshy snow and mud left behind after the clipper storm yesterday. It had come in like a lion and then hurried out, leaving a bright-blue sky in its wake.

"It's just a giant patch of soil," Mama said, bending down and scooping up a gloveful of dirt in the empty area once they'd arrived.

For as long as Elizabeth could remember, nothing had grown there, but Nan had never seemed too worried about it. "The ground's still pretty frozen, but let's try to dig up a sample."

She plunged the pointed end of the shovel into the hard earth, jumping on either side of the blade, using her weight to push it down, but it barely budged. Confused, she tried another spot with the same result.

"I've hit rock or something," she said, walking further inward. While Tennessee was known for its rocky soil, this seemed to be an enormous rock bed. Elizabeth found a new spot and tried again, with no luck.

"I've never seen anything like it," Mama said from under her scarf, crossing her arms. "The roots can't get deep enough to take hold."

"We might have to get a professional in to break it all up."

"I don't have that kind of money," Mama worried aloud. "One of the harvesters stopped workin' and I had to sink everything I made on the sale of our house on a new one. I'm barely makin' it."

"Could Travis or Percy help?"

Mama shook her head. "They wouldn't have anything strong enough to break this up."

"I could pay for it," Elizabeth offered, Richard's ten thousand dollars sitting in her account coming to mind. She couldn't think of a better use for it.

Mama brightened but immediately dismissed it. "Oh, no. I couldn't make you do that."

"I can pay for it," Elizabeth insisted.

But Mama waved away the offer with her gloved hands. "Just like your nan, this is my destiny. I want to take care of it myself, because struggle is what makes a person whole on the other side. And maybe it's the Christmas spirit in me, but I know, somehow, it'll all be okay—with or without crops on this spot." She looked out at the field. "I'll see if I can get the farmhands to dig a little deeper to find out what kind of rock it is so we can take a guess as to how difficult it will be to till it."

Elizabeth tucked the shovel under her arm, her visit to the lawyer's office tickling her consciousness. She was sure it was just a misunderstanding that could be ironed out, but she hesitated… "Why don't we wait until the ground warms up. We can come back and take a look again."

"All right," Mama said, stepping up beside her.

"But for now, we can still see what's going on with it. I'd like to dig down to the rock and figure out what kind it is, too. I'm curious."

Mama's affection for Elizabeth showed in the curve of her lips. "You were always interested in things like that. It's good to see it comin' back." She put her hands on her hips and looked out at the empty spot. "Let's go feed Holly and Maisy. Travis wants to take me to brunch."

"Brunch?"

"Yes," Mama said with a big smile, as she patted her hair. "I have to get ready."

"I can help you if you'd like."

"I'd love that," Mama said.

They both stood together, facing the vast fields. As Elizabeth took in the view in front of her and the little green farmhouse at the end, her destiny seemed to be shaping up right in front of her eyes.

"Got stuck, did he?" Ray asked, his gapped-tooth grin on display. He bent down in front of the Mercedes at Mama Jane's, the tractor rumbling behind them, and inspected the front tires. "Mr. City ground himself right on in…"

"He sure did." Elizabeth leaned down beside him. "Think you can pull it?"

"I can get him out. You drivin' it to him?"

"He's got the keys. Could we maybe tow it to the coffee shop?" Elizabeth asked, rubbing her hands together for warmth, the sun not quite strong enough yet to keep the wind's chill at bay. "He said he could meet us there. Would that work?"

"All right," Ray replied in his slow southern drawl. "Hop in the tractor and I'll get him hitched up."

"Okay." Elizabeth climbed into the warm cab and brushed the dust off the seat with her glove. While Ray hooked a chain to the bottom of the car with skilled precision, she texted Paul to let him know they'd meet him in a few minutes.

Paul came right back to her, his words floating onto the screen: *I'll thank you with a coffee. What kind would you like?*

A flurry of happiness prickled her insides. She texted back: *You don't have to do that.*

Her screen lit up once more with: *I know I don't have to. I want to. Do you like caramel or vanilla?*

She grinned down at her phone just as Ray got up into the cab, eyeing her. "Why you got that look on your face?" he asked, wriggling into a comfortable position and placing his hand on the gearshift.

"What look?" she asked before typing "Vanilla" and hitting send.

"That dreamy look." He leaned over the phone to see what she was texting and she pulled it back.

"I have no idea what you're talking about."

He shook his head with a chuckle and put the tractor in gear, heaving forward, the car's tires protesting. The engine roared, lurching and tugging until the car broke free of its snowy confines. Slowly, Ray rolled down the icy street, the Mercedes trailing behind them.

Elizabeth turned around protectively to view the car. "It won't hurt it to drag it like that?" she asked.

"Naw, it's just rollin'," Ray said, not taking his eyes off the road. "That phone of yours sure was pingin' a lot. You chattin' up Mr. City?"

Elizabeth twisted forward again. "Definitely not," she replied, her face heating up. "He offered to get me a coffee as a thank-you for bringing his car back."

Ray laughed—one loud guffaw—making her jump. "You ain't done nothin' but sit in the passenger side and look pretty. Did he ask *my* coffee order?" He nodded toward the phone and her face flamed.

"You like vanilla? You can have mine," she said.

"I'm just teasin' ya," he said. "I ain't drinkin' that frou-frou drink. I'll take a black coffee from my own kitchen over that stuff any day." He turned the wheel of the tractor, eyeing the Mercedes in the oversized side-view mirror. Then he pushed the gas, pulling them out of the turn.

Elizabeth held her breath as the luxury car swung around the corner on the icy street, until it had straightened out again. They bumped along quietly after that until Ray pulled to a stop in the parking lot of the coffee shop. He parked the massive vehicle and got out, unhooking the Mercedes just as Paul paced across the lot to greet them.

"Thank you so much," he said to Ray, shaking his hand. "Would you like a coffee? The line's probably died down by now."

"Don't ask him," Elizabeth interjected with a wink at Ray.

"Naw, y'all two enjoy your drinks," Ray said, with a loaded look back to Elizabeth, their little moment of humor hanging between them. With a wave, he hopped back into the tractor and drove away.

Paul regarded Elizabeth, the two of them standing in the now quiet parking lot. "There was a line," he said, throwing his thumb over his shoulder, his words casual, but his thoughts clearly deeper, making her wish he'd say more about what was on his mind. "So we can order our drinks together."

"While you get the car into a parking spot, why don't I order for us and grab us a couple of seats by the fire?" she asked, the current that buzzed around inside her more frequent now whenever those blue eyes met hers. "What would you like?"

"Surprise me," he replied and offered that adorable look of contentment before turning away and walking to his car.

Elizabeth turned away from his broad shoulders and rugged walk, and opened the coffee shop's wooden doors, heading into the festive space. The Christmas tree in the corner was lit, along with the fire, and Christmas carols played over the loudspeaker. The spiky-haired barista wasn't there today; another woman with jade earrings and wispy blonde tendrils tied up into a ponytail sat behind the register.

As a few customers before her put in their orders, Elizabeth peered up at the menu, wondering what Paul would like. Feeling cheerful, she decided she'd convert him to a hazelnut mocha drinker after the hot chocolates they'd had yesterday, so she ordered them both one. She put in the order with the barista and the woman rang up the drinks.

"What did you get me?" Paul asked, sending a tingle down her limbs. She turned to face him.

"I got you a hazelnut mocha."

"Sounds good." He handed the barista his credit card before Elizabeth could protest.

When their mugs were ready, they took them over to one of the sofas next to the fire. Elizabeth sat down beside the tree, the gold star shining at the top.

"I'm glad I got to see you again," Paul said. The look of vulnerability on his face made it hard to focus on his words. He sat down beside her. "I've been hoping I would." The fire flickered in his blue eyes, making her want to stay there in them and never leave, against her better judgment. It was as if everyone there had faded away and it was just the two of them. He leaned toward her, his woodsy scent tickling her nose. "I didn't expect this."

"What didn't you expect, exactly?" she asked, her heart racing.

He licked his lips before he spoke, pausing as if he were trying to define it. She hoped he would, because she certainly didn't know how to explain what she felt when she was around him. It was a different feeling than the one she'd initially had with Richard. It was as if both she and Paul had been through the hard parts of their lives and come out on the other side fully aware of their brokenness and finding each other despite it.

"The moment I first saw you, you looked like your world had been turned upside down," he said with a gentle smile. He shook his head. "I came here for work. I thought I'd get some peace and quiet to complete the business deal I'm working on and have a chance to unwind. I didn't want to see anyone. But then you walked through that door…" He trailed off, but the meaning was clear.

His admission both terrified her and thrilled her.

"I don't want to worry you," he said. "I know you've got things you're dealing with, and I'm headed back to Chicago, but I just wanted you to know. I'm glad I met you this Christmas."

"I'm glad too," she said, wanting to put her hands on his face and kiss him. The thought completely took her off guard. But the more the idea settled upon her, the less crazy it seemed, somehow. "Christmas is in two days. I can't imagine you sitting alone in your rental house all by yourself. Don't you have family you want to be with?"

He shook his head, that smile falling for the first time. "My parents both passed away a while back—cancer for my mother and my father had a stroke. I lost them within a year of each other."

"I'm so sorry," she said, the grief from her own father's death swimming its way to the front of her mind. She couldn't imagine losing both parents close together. "Do you have any other family? You mentioned your grandfather…" While Paul seemed so capable of being kind to others, she hoped he had someone to look after him.

He shook his head. "Just my grandfather. He taught me everything I know about life. And the business. But he won't speak to me, remember?"

"Sounds like you had a good bond with him before the big change with the company," she said.

"Yes, I used to." His expression fell into one of contemplation, the pain from their rift clear. "I feel like the clock is ticking on our relationship. I wouldn't be able to live with myself if anything happened and I lost him before I could show him how much I love him. And, right now, the only way to show him is to do right by the business he built."

She offered an empathetic nod, the idea of being at odds with family unimaginable.

"Have Christmas Eve with *us*," she suggested. She wanted to at least offer. He'd been nothing but kind to her. It was the least she could do.

He looked at her questioningly. "I wouldn't want to ruin your family time."

"You wouldn't," she assured him. "I'm nearly certain of it. It's just my mama and me. It would be nice to have a full house. And entertaining is my mother's favorite thing to do—I swear, if she had enough rooms, she'd rent them out like a bed and breakfast just to have people to talk to. She'll have you full on cookies and casserole the entire time."

"I'd love to," Paul said, the corners of his eyes creasing in that adorable way of his.

Right then, as his expression filled with fondness for her, she knew she'd made the right decision and that this Christmas might be one of her most memorable yet.

Chapter Thirteen

"Your mama told me you were here when she popped over to see my dad," Naomi said through the open window of her truck as she pulled up at the coffee shop after Elizabeth had accepted her text offer to pick her up. Naomi gave her a guarded look. "They're goin' to brunch. Did you know this?"

"Yes," Elizabeth said, climbing into the truck. "I helped her get ready for it." The excitement on her mother's face had been lovelier than the makeover. She'd practically glowed.

Naomi rolled up her window while Elizabeth shut the door and fastened her seatbelt. "Never saw that comin'," her friend said, their mutual connection making conversation a little easier for the both of them.

"Neither did I."

"Dad put on cologne." Naomi made a face, giving Elizabeth a little punch of humor. Her friend cranked up the heat and looked over at Elizabeth, her expression slightly friendlier than it had been. "I guess if you think about it, they're kinda perfect for each other."

Elizabeth had known Travis her whole life and adored him, but she'd always thought of him as only her best friend's dad. "You think so?"

"Yeah. They both love workin' on their farms. They talk about everything from crop schedules to expansion options. It was Dad's idea to plant more apple trees. He actually helped the farmhands put 'em in."

"Oh, wow. Mama hadn't told me that." It gave her reassurance to know that her mother had someone to lean on.

"I think she's still a little shy over it all." Naomi pulled off and steered the truck around the corner. "Speakin' of matchmakin', Ray mentioned helpin' you get your city boy's car out of the snow at Mama Jane's." She eyed Elizabeth. "And your mama told Dad when your text came in that your new beau is stayin' for Christmas."

"He's nice, that's all. And he's by himself this holiday." But Elizabeth worried that her friend could see through her. "He'll leave in a few days and that will be that," she added.

"I'm only kiddin'," Naomi said, shaking her head, her golden braid swinging from under her baseball cap.

"You and Ray both," Elizabeth said as Naomi drove out of Mason's Ridge, headed for the law offices of Pierce and Hughes in the neighboring town of Riverbend.

"Whatcha mean?" she asked, her focus darting over to Elizabeth and then back to the route in front of them.

"Giving me a hard time about Paul," she replied. "I feel like everyone's talking about it…"

"Because they are." Naomi made a turn onto the street leading to the main road.

"Really?" Elizabeth asked.

"The two of you are city folks and lots of city folks've been lurkin' around here these days," Naomi said. "Did you know that some guy stopped Granddaddy the other day when he overheard him talkin' about the farm? He actually asked if Granddaddy wanted to sell it, sight unseen. He wanted to subdivide land for retail and he heard that our farm was just off the main road."

"That's crazy," Elizabeth said.

"And then the minute *you* come back from the big city after so long, you're all heart-eyes for the first out-of-towner you meet. People are chattin' about it, and they're not too thrilled. They were hopin' to get their golden girl back, but it looks like you'd still rather be anywhere but here."

She hadn't known what she would do when she'd first returned to Mason's Ridge, but now the idea of leaving seemed unfeasible. "That's not what's happening at all," Elizabeth said, defensive. "I've really enjoyed being back in Mason's Ridge. So much so that I've been thinking how I'd like to stay here. For good."

Naomi gawked at her, a glimmer of hope showing behind her cautious eyes, but then that wall she'd put up to avoid getting hurt slid back into place. "You don't have to convince *me*. You know what they say: Don't tell 'em they're wrong; show 'em."

Elizabeth looked out the window, pondering the situation. She would. *If* she could ever win them back over. After all, she'd walked out on this town over a decade ago, and until now hadn't really looked back. They saw her as an outsider, but they didn't know that since she'd returned she'd felt more and more like this was where she belonged.

Naomi turned up the radio just a bit, a country music version of "We Wish You a Merry Christmas" that Elizabeth didn't recognize playing in the background.

"I can sense it's a sore subject," Naomi said, "but if I can say one thing before we move on, it's that you can be anyone you wanna be and fall for anyone you wanna fall for. It's no one else's business but yours. As long as it's what *you* want." She shifted gears like a pro, navigating the hills. "*I'm* still here in Mason's Ridge because I'm happy here."

Elizabeth's conscience took another direct hit at Naomi's connection of the situation to herself. Her absence had affected people who cared about her. Naomi had clearly felt left behind. But what about her friends from New York? They certainly weren't feeling the way Naomi felt.

"I'm sorry I left you and didn't keep in touch," she said, looking over at her friend who'd been there for her for all those years. "I… don't know why I let myself get so wrapped up in that life that I left literally everything behind, including the people I love. I'll never do it again."

Naomi pulled to a halt at a stop sign and turned to Elizabeth. "I believe you," she said. "I did keep waitin' for you to call. I thought surely you'd want to fill me in on what it was like to live in a mansion and wear all those diamonds…" She allowed a smile, but then it fell. "You were a princess in my eyes, and my best friend."

Tears pricked Elizabeth's eyes and she nodded, unable to speak for fear she'd sob all over her friend. Finally, when she could muster it, she said, "You didn't deserve to be left in silence like that. There aren't any words that do it justice."

Naomi put the truck in park, reached over, and put her arms around Elizabeth. And then the tears came.

"I'm so sorry," Elizabeth sobbed into her best friend's shoulder.

"We can make up for it, right?" Naomi said with her infallible grace.

"I'll make up for it every single day."

While Elizabeth got a napkin out of her handbag, wiped her eyes, and collected herself, they drove through the hills until they reached the town of Riverbend, where Naomi pulled over to the curb. The law office was nestled on the main street, full of Christmas shoppers maneuvering around the snowy walks. Santa Claus was taking photos at one end.

"Once I get this misunderstanding with the farm settled, we should do a little Christmas shopping. I need to get something for Mama," Elizabeth said, testing the waters with her friend.

To her relief and utter happiness, Naomi replied hesitantly, "I'll scope out the shops and find the best ones while you're in there. Text me when you're done."

"I should be back out in just a sec."

Elizabeth walked over to the law firm and went inside, alerting the receptionist that she was there to see Shirley Clark.

The woman called through to Ms. Clark's office to let her know she was there.

"Good to see you," the dark-haired woman in a stylish two-piece suit said, coming around the corner and offering her hand in greeting. "Elizabeth?"

Elizabeth shook her hand.

"Shirley Clark," she said, introducing herself. "Come on back."

Elizabeth followed her down the hallway to a small office, where Elizabeth settled into a wooden chair across from Ms. Clark's desk.

"So, you're here to discuss ownership of Crestwood Farm in Mason's Ridge, is that correct?" Ms. Clark asked, sliding on a pair of bright-red readers and shuffling her papers around.

"Yes, ma'am. There's been some sort of mix-up. My family's owned that land for generations."

Ms. Clark pursed her lips as she read the paperwork in her hand. "I have the deed right here that states the property belongs to Worsham Enterprises, and I've spoken again to the company representative to confirm the address of the property in question: 247 Pinetop Lane."

That was Nan's farm. "How can that be?" Elizabeth asked.

"Is your mother Loretta Holloway?"

"Yes," Elizabeth replied.

Ms. Clark looked over her glasses to address Elizabeth. "The existence of the land is a recent development for Worsham. When your mother reached out to complete the paperwork to inherit the land, the county office alerted Worsham's representative that someone was claiming to be the owner. The spokesperson for the company hadn't even known they'd owned it until then. That was when they called us." She handed the copy of the deed to Elizabeth.

Elizabeth scanned the legal jargon, running over the address once more. There were no other houses that faced Pinetop Lane. Percy's was on Magnolia and Beatrice lived on Putnam Road. No other numbers matched up. She took in the seal on the document. "Could this be a fake?" she wondered aloud, grasping for some understanding of the situation.

Ms. Clark shook her head. "It's officially registered, and there are no other documents showing an ownership change."

"How would my grandmother have paid taxes on it if she didn't own it?"

Ms. Clark clicked a few keys on her computer. "Well, it looks like it's tax-exempt since the land is being used for agricultural purposes, but taxes have been paid in the past, it seems, by Mr. William Worsham."

Elizabeth struggled to make sense of it all. "Wouldn't my grandfather have noticed if someone else were paying taxes on his land?"

Ms. Clark shrugged. "I can't answer that."

"Well, whether he knew or not, clearly if Mr. Worsham paid taxes on the land, then he had to know someone was living on it. Why, now, does he want everyone off it?" she asked, rattled.

"I can't speak to that either," the lawyer said. "But my guess is that he has other plans for it. The rezoning has been approved, so he needs the land cleared."

"Rezoning?"

"Yes, it's been rezoned from rural to commercial," Ms. Clark clarified.

"This makes absolutely no sense at all." Elizabeth handed the paper back to Ms. Clark, her stomach plummeting. "It belongs to *us*—it has to."

The lawyer clicked a few more keys on her computer. "If the deed is in the company's name, and there's a tax history, the land is legally Worsham Enterprises'. You'll need to see if you have any documents stating otherwise, and I'd also suggest getting your own legal counsel if you do find anything, because plans are moving forward with the land."

Elizabeth's mind whirred. "I'm sure we have something…"

Ms. Clark gave her an empathetic nod. "I feel for you," she said. "I grew up around here, and I'm aware of what's happening too." She folded her hands. "Maybe go home and see what you can find as a first step."

Elizabeth sat still, speechless.

"With the growth in the area, land prices are soaring, and these sorts of things have been coming across my desk more than usual," the lawyer continued. "It's prime real estate."

"How long do we have?" Elizabeth asked, still wrestling with the reality of the news.

Ms. Clark offered a compassionate pout. "They're giving you all the holiday and then they're going to start pushing."

Elizabeth lost her breath and had to force herself to take in the perfumy air of the office. "Do you know what they're rezoning for?" she asked, feeling suddenly strangled.

"I was told they're planning something in the resort market." She leaned forward, less lawyer and more small-town woman to small-town woman. "You'll need to find something stating this property is yours so you can attempt to contest it, or, I'm afraid, you'll need to find another residence."

The gravity of the situation was overwhelming. Surely, there was a way to resolve this. "Is there a contact person who I can call to find out what's going on?"

"I can't give you the number without permission, since it would violate our client policy," Ms. Clark said. "But I could certainly pass along a message to either get in touch or permit us to relay a response to you. Can I reach you at the number you used to call us?"

"Yes, thank you," Elizabeth said.

"It'll be after the holiday," Ms. Clark warned her. "Their offices are already closed."

Elizabeth nodded and then saw herself out, leaving the lawyer's office in a daze. She walked along the busy sidewalk not noticing the passers-by, her thoughts consumed with whether to tell Mama this news two days before Christmas. How could they ever celebrate or have any kind of normal holiday with something this massive hanging over their heads?

If, by some unknown reason, this William Worsham did actually own the land, the farmhands would lose their jobs. Everyone she knew in Mason's Ridge would face living around the corner from a busy resort. She and Mama would have nowhere to go. Mama didn't know how to do anything else, and she said herself that she'd crumble. She didn't have the money to buy another piece of property, and Elizabeth didn't have enough savings to help her with anything that involved.

She'd yet to see any paperwork around the house. Mama had been calling to get the deed in the first place, so she probably didn't have what she needed to claim it…

"Hey," Naomi's voice coming toward her distracted her momentarily. "I found a great little shop with lotions and stuff," she said. "Your mama would love it." Then she stopped, honing in on Elizabeth's demeanor. "Hang on. You don't look too good."

"It doesn't fit in any scenario I play out in my head," Elizabeth said, continuing the thoughts that were tumbling around in her brain, "but our land might not actually belong to us."

"What do you mean it 'might not actually belong to us'?"

Elizabeth recapped what the lawyer had said.

Naomi crossed her arms. "That doesn't make any sense at all." She pulled out her phone. "Let me see if Granddaddy has heard of any of these people." She dialed his number, the two of them stepping to the side to avoid the holiday shoppers. "Hey, Granddaddy," she said, cupping her hand over her exposed ear and tilting her head down. "Do you know anyone named—" She peered over at Elizabeth.

"William Worsham," Elizabeth said.

Naomi repeated the name, her gaze moving along the sidewalk by their feet as she listened. "You sure? Never?" she asked. "All right… It's nothin'. I'll tell you when I get home. Thanks, Granddaddy." She ended the call and looked back at Elizabeth. "He says he's never heard of him."

"Who in the world is he?" Elizabeth asked, shaking her head. But she knew there was nothing she could do until the holiday was over. The lawyer herself had told her they weren't coming for the farm until after Christmas. Given the news, Elizabeth was determined to make it the best holiday her mother had ever had. "I don't want Mama to spend Christmas with nothing to unwrap."

"I agree," Naomi said, still clearly worried. "What are you gonna tell your mama?"

"Nothing," Elizabeth replied. "We'll tell her nothing. And then I'll find a way to fix it."

Elizabeth and Naomi made their way through the crowds while Elizabeth tried not to dwell on the fact that this could be their final Christmas at the farm.

"I'm home," Elizabeth called as she entered the farmhouse, a group of shopping bags hanging from each arm.

"How did the meeting go at the lawyer's?" Mama called from her room as Elizabeth set the bags down by the tree.

"They won't be able to give us any information until after the holiday." Elizabeth just didn't have the heart to tell her about the farm. Not yet. She and her mother deserved this holiday together.

"Good Lord, child," Mama said, coming down the hallway. "What in the world is all that?"

"Christmas presents," Elizabeth replied, as she pulled the brightly wrapped packages from the bags, arranging them under the tree.

"Did somebody win the lottery?" she asked, wide-eyed, inspecting the gifts, flipping the little paper tags that hung by ribbons on each one. "These are all for me?"

"Yes." Elizabeth continued unpacking the bags, filling the tree skirt completely. "I wanted us to have the best Christmas this year." She righted herself and put her hands on her hips, admiring her handiwork.

Mama eyed the gifts lovingly.

"Speaking of the best Christmas ever, I know how much you enjoy hosting people, and Paul doesn't have any family to celebrate with. That's why I asked him over—it's sort of an extra gift for each of you."

Mama's eyebrows rose. "And what about you? Are you gettin' a single present this year?"

"I don't need any. I already got the greatest gift: being able to spend the holiday here with you."

Mama gave her an affectionate squeeze. "And Paul," she added after pulling back.

"I thought you wouldn't mind having him, since you'd mentioned wanting people in the house."

"Of course I don't mind. And it will be nice to meet the person you've spent time with." Mama set the gift she'd been inspecting under the tree. "We should do more decoratin' before he comes. What else needs to be done...?"

Elizabeth grabbed her mother's hands. "Right now, let's go to Percy's tree lot and see if we can find some greenery for the porch outside—my treat."

Mama spun her around. "And mistletoe!"

Elizabeth stopped spinning. "Mistletoe? Who's going to use that?"

"It's just so... festive," she said with a laugh. "There's a whole display of it at the lot. I want to have Christmas from top to bottom in the house!" She danced around the room. "Let's blare the Christmas carols, wear nothin' but red sweaters, and bake all of your nan's cookie recipes. We'll have everyone we know over, and make it the most memorable Christmas ever."

That certainly sounded great to Elizabeth. "Let's head to the tree lot then, shall we?"

Mama grabbed her coat. "Absolutely. I have a feelin' this will be a Christmas we'll never forget."

"I hope so," Elizabeth said. "I hope so."

Chapter Fourteen

Across the aisles of Christmas trees, Percy threw up a hand from inside a small red building. It had a cut-out window and a register on the ledge. His lanky frame was hidden by a giant coat to protect him from the winter cold.

"Hey, Percy!" Mama called, waving madly.

"Well, hello there," he said, his attention on Elizabeth. "Naomi sure is glad you're back."

Affection for her friend gave her a burst of cheer. "I'm so glad to hear that."

"So what can I do for you two?" he asked.

"We're here to buy up all your Christmas greenery," Mama replied.

"Sounds like a plan," he said with a chuckle that started in his chest before exiting his lips. He came out the door and met them next to one of the stout fir trees. "Whatcha in the market for?"

"I want to drape the porch railin's in greenery and put big red bows at every post," Mama said. "And I want wreaths for all the windows…" She counted on her fingers. "Ten of them. And I'd like, say, six of your biggest bundles of mistletoe!"

"You been eatin' too many of Beatrice's Christmas cupcakes or somethin'?" He eyed Elizabeth. "She on some kinda sugar high?"

Mama jumped between them. "I'm just wrapped up in the Christmas spirit," she said, doing a little twirl around Percy and sending another chuckle bursting from him.

"Can't argue with that," he said, shuffling over to the mistletoe. "Wanna pick out your favorites and I'll get 'em wrapped up?"

He shouted over to Naomi, who had just appeared across the lot getting into her truck, the headlights like two yellow sunbeams on the snow as she drove toward them.

"You called, Granddaddy?" Naomi asked out the window, pulling up.

"Yep. Help these two get half the lot over to Loretta's, would ya?"

Naomi put the truck in park and hopped out. "I'm not even gonna ask," she said, eyeing the bundles of mistletoe Elizabeth was gathering. "I take that back. I'm totally gonna ask. Is all that for Mr. City?"

"Definitely not," Elizabeth said, lumping the bundles onto the counter of the little red shop. "Mama wanted them."

Naomi whirled around to face Mama. "You and Daddy got plans I didn't know about?"

Mama laughed, blushing. "They're just so beautiful with those cascading ribbons." She picked one up and let the silver ribbons fall, admiring them. "For the first time in a long time, I feel like everything is going to be okay."

Elizabeth smiled at her, but she caught Naomi's eye and, deep down, she feared that it certainly wouldn't be. However, she wouldn't think about that right then. Instead, she sent a silent prayer up to Nan to help her figure this out.

"Hold that end for me," Mama said, her breath puffing out in front of her as Elizabeth and Naomi held the greenery in place on the railing of the farmhouse's front porch. Mama secured it with wire. Naomi had stayed with them to help unload all their purchases and had offered to lend a hand to decorate.

"This looks beautiful," Naomi said, hopping onto the snowy ground and admiring the swags of fresh greenery with red bows at the peaks.

Mama climbed the ladder and hung a bundle of mistletoe over the front door, its ribbons dangling down overhead like party streamers. She stepped down the rungs. "I'm feelin' so Christmassy. And frozen. Let's go inside and find more places for all this mistletoe."

As they entered the house, Elizabeth couldn't ignore the fact that the excitement of the season seemed to be lifting Mama's spirits and Elizabeth was glad for that.

Once they'd placed mistletoe above every doorway, Naomi put her hands on her hips and said, "Well, it looks like the house is pretty well booby-trapped for smooches. Now, who are we bringin' in to test it out?"

"We don't have time to test it out," Mama said. "We've got Christmas cookies and a Lazy Daisy cake to bake." She clicked on the radio and, with Christmas music playing, set out opening cupboards.

Elizabeth assessed the ingredients, getting more excited by the minute. "Wait, peanut butter?" she asked, licking her lips. "Are you making your world-famous peanut-butter chocolate truffles?"

"You know it!" Mama said excitedly.

"Oooh, I remember those!" Naomi said with a twinkle in her eye. "We ate them until our bellies hurt, remember, Liz?"

"I do," she replied, making a conscious effort to savor this moment with two of her favorite people.

As she and Naomi fell into the task, both of them by Mama's side, it all came back to Elizabeth and she sifted flour, scooped sugar, and stirred chocolate like she hadn't spent the last eleven years away from it. And the more time she spent doing it, the more she wondered how she'd ever been able to go so long without it.

The kitchen table was completely covered in trays of cookies, the sky pitch-black outside. Chocolate balls, sugar cookies iced in Mama's homemade royal icing, creamy shortbread cookies with raspberry preserves, gingerbread men, pecan snowball cookies, Snickerdoodles, cranberry orange cookies, peppermint balls, and cranberry blossoms filled every inch of the table's surface. Elizabeth, Mama, and Naomi fell onto the sofa.

"I can't believe we made all those," Naomi said with a yawn, as she tipped her head against the back of the sofa, flour on her cheek. "What time is it?"

Elizabeth checked her watch. "It's nearly midnight."

"Mind if I stay over?" Naomi asked.

"Of course you can stay," Mama said, brightening despite her obvious exhaustion. "I'll pump up the old air mattresses and we can all sleep in the living room just like old times."

"You don't have to go to all that trouble pumping up mattresses." Elizabeth remembered the nights the two girls had spent in their nightgowns, cuddled by the fire. Mama had braided their hair, fluffing up all the quilts they had in the house and tucking them in. Those had been some of the best times of her life, she realized now, and having Naomi there today had felt as wonderful as those nights so long ago.

"It'll be fun," Mama said, already in the hall closet, pulling out blankets.

When they'd moved the coffee table to one side, thrown a few more logs onto the fire, and gotten the air mattress blown up and dressed with sheets and blankets, Mama snuggled in on the sofa, while Elizabeth wiggled down under the blankets next to Naomi.

"I feel like we need a bedtime story," Naomi teased. "Anybody got a good one?"

Elizabeth sat back up and reached over to the coffee table, grabbing the stack of envelopes. "We've got Nan's letters," she suggested.

Naomi propped herself up on her elbow. "Oh, yes. Let's read one or two."

Elizabeth filled her friend in on Nan's budding friendship with Gramps, and what had been going on in the last few letters. Then she opened up the next one. "Oh, this one's from Gramps," she said.

Mama and Naomi scooted close, and Elizabeth began to read.

December 10, 1944

My dear Harriet,

This war has made me question my choices in life, and the more I think about it, the more I want a slower pace. You say how much you love the Smoky Mountains, so I was wondering if, when I get home, you'd like to show me around the area to see if it might be a good place for me to settle down.

I'd enjoy seeing all the wonderful things you talk about: the rolling fields of apple trees, the babbling brooks, and the endless sunshine—how I miss the sunshine… The bombs have clouded the sky to a deep gray, and, coupled with the winter weather, Europe has been dark and dreary.

I hope to hear from Jimmy soon. The minute I do, I'll tell him you miss him, and I know he misses you.

Roger

"We know where this is going," Naomi said, her eyebrows bouncing up and down. "Ol' Gramps is moving in on Jimmy's girl."

Elizabeth grinned as she folded the letter and returned it to the stack. "Gramps would never... I'm sure their courtship was completely innocent."

"Well, let's wait to find out," Mama said. "It's late, and we need our beauty rest."

"*Beauty* rest?" Elizabeth teased her.

Mama folded her arms playfully. "The farm isn't going to tend to itself and we have cookie deliveries tomorrow." She clicked off the lamp, sending the room into darkness, the only light the glow of the fire.

As Elizabeth's eyes began to feel heavy, she thought about how she couldn't have had a better night. Pushing all the worries out of her mind, by the flicker of the flames and the scents of sugar and cinnamon, she slipped into dreamland back in her family home, next to her favorite people.

Chapter Fifteen

"Tell Percy that we said merry Christmas," Mama said, getting up from the table and handing Naomi a plate of cookies over their empty breakfast dishes. "I'll be over to see Travis later."

Naomi walked through the living room, taking the assortment with her. "I'll tell them," she said, giving Mama a side-hug as she balanced the plate in her arm.

Elizabeth opened the door and the icy air gave her a shiver as she addressed Naomi. "I'm glad you stayed."

"Me too," Naomi said. Then she reached out and embraced Elizabeth.

Elizabeth gave her friend a big squeeze, so thankful for their reunion. "See ya later," she said with a happy heart.

Naomi threw up a hand to Elizabeth and then headed down the steps with the cookies.

"Well, that was fun." Mama came over as Elizabeth closed the door behind Naomi.

Elizabeth walked back into the center of the room and ran her hand along the folded blankets. "It was just like when we were girls."

"Want to have another cup of coffee while we pack gift bags for the neighbors?"

"I'd like that," Elizabeth said, wanting to savor the moment. She followed her mother into the kitchen and washed her hands before grabbing the stack of plastic bags that Nan still had in the drawer and the spool of ribbon Elizabeth had bought the other night to wrap Beatrice's gift. She scooted the chair up to the table in front of the plates of Christmas cookies, unwrapping them while Mama made the coffee.

"Naomi had some luck at the farmer's market last fall," Mama said, peering out at the orchard while filling the coffee maker with grounds, the rich aroma floating over to Elizabeth. "I'm wondering if we should get a truck so we can take more apples over there." She pulled two mugs from the cabinet, the cups dangling from her fingers as she stared at the ceiling in thought. "But the cost of the truck would probably be more than any extra profit we'd get… It's all so hard to figure out, and now I'm over my head."

"What about cotton sales?" Elizabeth asked, dropping a shortbread cookie in each bag. "You always make a good amount from that."

"Not enough," Mama replied. "And hay is worse. Especially with the development."

The name on the deed floated into Elizabeth's consciousness, but she wouldn't allow it to worry her. Sitting at that table, surrounded by all the cookies and warm memories, there was no way she would let them take the farm from her and Mama. She'd lie down in the floor and refuse to leave if she had to.

"There aren't as many farms buyin' from us anymore," Mama continued. "I've been tryin' to come up with an idea to make us more money."

"When do you have to order the seed for next season?" Elizabeth asked, pondering whether she could somehow stop the rezoning and keep the farm. She'd figure out a way. She had to.

Mama set the coffee maker and came over to the table with her pad and pencil. "We've got time." She turned to a blank sheet of paper, figuring the numbers of seed for the acreage. She bit her lip. "I just don't know what to do."

Elizabeth grabbed the first bag and began dropping in two sugar cookies each. "We need to think outside of the box," she said, pinching another cookie as she racked her brain for ideas. Perhaps if she got a plan together for Mama, the universe would pitch in and help them keep all they'd worked for.

"What do you mean 'think outside the box'?" Mama asked. "What else can you do with the crops besides take them to the market?"

Elizabeth mentally combed through her experience with charity auctions, trying to come up with something. Suddenly, the idea hit her. "What if I made you a website and we did some sort of farm-to-table package?"

"How would I ever manage a website?" Mama asked. "I can't work the TV remote."

Elizabeth laughed. "I could help you."

The coffee maker beeped, signaling that it was ready. Mama got up and went over to it. "What would we even need it for?"

Elizabeth dropped a few more cookies into the bags, thinking through the idea, getting more excited by the minute as it solidified, goosebumps rising on her arms with the prospect that the stars were aligning just as she'd hoped. "People within driving distance could schedule times to pick up eggs, apples, and vegetables..."

Mama turned around and nodded slowly, her lips pursed as she thought it over, her interest encouraging Elizabeth to let her creative juices flow. This was the sort of thing Elizabeth had started out doing for her charities before Richard had taken over, yet in this context, she could see the ideas forming right before her eyes, and she could actually imagine herself and Mama working the farm. It had to happen. Like some cosmic Christmas gift to them both, it *had* to.

"What if we even opened the farm and had goat petting?" Elizabeth continued. "We could make cheeses from the goat's milk and serve wine and freshly squeezed apple juice for the kids."

Mama's eyes lit up and she hurried back to the table. "I love this idea," she said, jotting it down on the legal pad. "What if we don't plant hay, but rather a garden full of herbs and vegetables and expand on the idea of the farm-to-table? People can picnic on the grounds..." She drew a circle around the numbers she'd jotted down before and crossed through it.

"Exactly." Elizabeth nodded. "We could offer dried herbs for seasoning and even add them to candle wax—things like that—and make home-goods."

"And you and Naomi could bring the horses out and offer rides, teachin' the little ones the way you two learned to ride when you were kids," Mama said, her eyes sparkling while she listed her thoughts. "You two could split the profits."

Elizabeth was feeling more purpose with every word, everything now coming together. "I have ten thousand dollars," she said, her skin prickling with elation, still under the spell that somehow everything would be okay. "We could set up big awnings, picnic tables, large bench swings that overlook the valley. We could offer apple-picking tours..."

The coffee maker beeped again, and Mama did a little spin before she went back over and poured them a cup, her delight clear. "We'll have a full house," she said on an enthusiastic exhale.

"Yes!" Elizabeth knew without a doubt that she was *exactly* where she should be.

"Speakin' of a full house, do you need to get in touch with Paul to find out when he'd like to come over? I could make us a roast and some potatoes for dinner."

"I'll call him now." With a pep in her step, Elizabeth grabbed her phone and pulled up his number.

The phone rang three times before he picked it up.

"Hey, it's Elizabeth," she said when he answered, the sound of his voice like music to her ears.

"Oh, hi," he said, something lingering under his tone.

"You okay?" she asked.

Paul exhaled loudly into the phone. "Yeah, sorry. The investors are being difficult. Time is money," he said.

"But it's the holiday. Surely you get a day or two off."

"I do understand," he said. "They've put up a lot of capital for this deal, and I'm behind schedule."

"Well, they can wait one more day."

"I hope you're right," he said, but she could tell the weight on him hadn't been lifted.

"Want to take your mind off it and come over for some Christmas cheer?" she asked, hoping to lift his spirits. "My mom said she'd make her roast with turnips and potatoes, and it's always amazing."

"That sounds wonderful," he said, a lightness to his voice now.

"I'll text you the address. We're here all day."

"Perfect. I'll just finish up a few last things with work and I'll be there in a couple of hours."

"See you soon." Elizabeth ended the call, energized and enthusiastic. "He'll be here in a couple of hours," she repeated to Mama.

"While we wait, we should write some Christmas letters to go with the cookies like your nan used to do," Mama suggested. "And we can eat a slice of Lazy Daisy cake while we do it."

"Any excuse," Elizabeth teased as she fired off the address to Paul and put her phone on the table. "Should we read the next letter from Nan's stack?"

"Oh, go on," Mama said. "Open it and I'll grab us some paper and pens so once we're inspired by your nan's letter, we can get down to writin'."

Elizabeth grabbed the stack of envelopes and carried them to the kitchen table while Mama went off to her room, returning with a box of Christmas cards, a pad of paper, and two ballpoint pens. She set them down between them while Elizabeth opened the letter.

December 25, 1944

Dear Harriet,

I know this is not the time to share this with you, but the war does not care about our holidays or our loved ones. I have no practice in how to deliver this news, but all I know is that I would like to be the messenger so that you can hear it from someone who cares about both of you.

Jimmy was killed in battle.

I promised that I'd be here for anything you need. I intend to keep that promise. I'm so very sorry, Harriet. I'm here if you need me. It feels wrong to wish you Merry Christmas. I'm sure Jimmy is having a grand one up in Heaven, resting.

Thinking of you,
Roger

Elizabeth stared at the letter's date: December 25. "Look at the date of this letter." She turned it around for Mama to see. "She used to write Christmas letters every Christmas to tell people how much she loved them. And she tied them with a red bow as a symbol of that love…" She ran her fingers down Gramps's writing. "I'll bet it was to honor Jimmy."

Mama covered her mouth, speaking through her fingers. "We never knew the real significance of it…"

"She was such a strong woman." Elizabeth folded the letter, returning it gently to its envelope. "I want to know more now," she said.

"Open the next one," Mama urged.

As Elizabeth pulled another envelope from the stack, she could almost feel Nan urging them on, and she wondered if Nan was trying to teach them something.

April 8, 1946

Roger,

I hope these desserts will help a little to make up for my behavior the other day when you came to see me for the first time. I'm sorry I fell apart. My anger was at the war, and what it had taken from me—not you. I was delighted to put a face to the man who'd helped me through. I'm still devastated that this war has stolen Jimmy from us. And while it didn't seem like it, I'm glad it was you who gave me the news.

I have no idea what my future holds now. My fiancé died. I can't believe it. I'd imagined the two of us running the farm, living out our years here. I still feel like my life has been stolen from me and my future is so uncertain. I don't know what to do.

But I've given in to my grief in your letter, and I shouldn't have. I should be telling you how lovely you are. I know you've experienced unthinkable hardships overseas and you deserve to come home to warmth and happiness. I'd like you to come to dinner tonight. While neither of us is ready for merriment, it would be nice to be together, united in our comprehension of what we've lost.

If it's too much, I understand. But if you want to see me, I'll be here.

Love,
Harriet

"Wow, that's so sad," Elizabeth said, the swooping writing blurring in front of her.

"It makes sense that two grievin' souls would find each other," Mama said, emotion showing in her voice.

"Yeah." Elizabeth returned the letter to the stack. "I'll bet she felt so lost. But now I know why she was great at running the farm after Gramps died. She'd already learned how." Elizabeth fell silent as she considered the idea of it. "Did her parents run the farm before her?"

"You know, they passed away before I was born, and I have no idea."

"I would assume so," Elizabeth said.

"Your grandmother was the youngest of six kids, and she was the one to run the farm, so I'm not sure. They've all passed on now…"

"We should know more about our family," Elizabeth said, promising herself to do a better job from this moment on. "Once they're gone, they take all the history with them if we don't know it."

Mama nodded, then straightened her shoulders. "What I do know is that if she could do it alone, then I certainly can."

"Or you and I can do it together," Elizabeth said, praying for that miracle to keep the farm.

Mama's eyes lit up and Elizabeth knew she'd made the right choice in staying.

"I've been thinking a lot about it, and I've decided that this is the only place I want to be," she told her mother.

"Oh, Liz." Mama leaned over and wrapped her arms around her daughter. "Are you sure?" She pulled back. "What about seeing the world?"

"I can still do that," Elizabeth said. "But we can do that together too. I'd rather be around people whom I love." Elizabeth gave her mother a squeeze. "Maybe that's what Nan's trying to tell us." She waved the stack of letters in the air.

"Maybe," Mama said with an adoring look in her eye. "She'd be so proud of this moment if she were here."

"Well then, we need to make Nan even prouder and write some wonderful Christmas letters. Who should we start with? Beatrice?"

"Beatrice sounds like the perfect person," Mama said.

Elizabeth picked up the pen. "Mind if I write this one?" she asked.

"Not at all. What are you goin' to say?"

Elizabeth smiled, recalling the nostalgia in the old woman's eyes whenever she looked at her. She placed the pen onto the paper and started writing. "I'm going to tell her that she'd be pleased to know that I've learned something already from Nan's Christmas letters."

"Oh?" Mama asked. "What have you learned?"

Her mind raced through her time in Mason's Ridge—coming back home, Naomi… meeting Paul. Elizabeth wasn't sure what her future held, if anything could happen with Paul, or if she'd ever see those dreams of working on the farm come to fruition, but she knew that as long as she was absolutely true to herself and those she loved, her future would be a good one. "I've learned that we can't predict what life will give us, but we can trust it nonetheless."

Mama smiled. "I like that." She clapped her hands together excitedly, as if the moment had given her a burst of positivity. "Ray and Ella can come over tomorrow night. They said they'd bring Beatrice, as long as the snow doesn't get too deep overnight. Naomi can drive Percy and her dad in the truck, and Lenny, Sabastian, and Harvey might even stop by. Let's fill the house!"

"I love that idea," Elizabeth said, a twinge of fear snaking through her as she pondered where she and Mama might end up after the holiday. Because of the uncertainty, she wanted to spend every moment with the people she cared about.

When Elizabeth finished the letter, she slid it into one of the red envelopes her mother had set out for them.

"I have another one I want to write," she said, pulling a second sheet of paper in front of her.

"Who's this one to?" Mama asked, filling a few more gift bags.

It was time to be absolutely truthful to herself, even if she didn't have all the answers. "Paul Dawson."

Mama's eyebrows rose, forming three creases on her forehead.

The small message Elizabeth wanted to say to Paul was already coming through, so she began to write. Her mother leaned over her shoulder, reading while her pen moved on the paper.

Dear Paul,

I didn't expect to meet you this Christmas, but I'm so glad that I did. For the first time in a very long time, you made me feel heard and... special. That's the best Christmas gift I could've gotten. Thank you.

Merry Christmas,
Liz

She peered down at her signature with a smile. It had been a long time since she'd gone by Liz, but it was important that she did. And Paul would absolutely understand; she was nearly certain of it.

"It sounds like you might have met someone extraordinary," Mama said, fondness for her daughter showing in her smile.

"Maybe," Elizabeth replied, just a bit more hopeful than she'd been in a long time.

"Come on in," Ray said when Elizabeth arrived at Beatrice's with a plate of cookies and the Christmas letter.

Elizabeth followed Ray to the same chair where Beatrice had sat before, making her wonder if the woman ever had reason to get up. Beatrice's face glowed when Elizabeth sat down next to her. "I brought you some cookies," she said, handing the old woman the gift bag tied with a bright-red ribbon. "And I wrote you a Christmas letter."

Beatrice sucked in a little breath, her face brightening in pleasure as she took the envelope from Elizabeth. "You always did remind me of your nan."

"That's quite a compliment," Elizabeth said.

"Have you read all her letters?" Beatrice asked, setting both the bag of treats and the envelope on a side table.

"I've started, but I'm not finished," Elizabeth replied. "I've read the one that mentions Jimmy's death, though."

Beatrice nodded solemnly.

"Did you go to his funeral?" Elizabeth asked.

Beatrice nodded again.

"How was Nan?" she asked, already feeling her grandmother's heartbreak.

"She was a mess," Beatrice replied. "It was unusual… The casket was empty, with only his dog tags and her photo on his dress uniform, since the body had been completely destroyed in battle. A fellow soldier had found his tags among the rubble and taken them back to base. Roger had brought them home, along with her picture. Your nan held those tags, laid her head on the casket, and wept for hours."

"That's terrible," Elizabeth said, swallowing in an attempt to clear the lump in her throat, her own loss of relationship seeming completely insignificant in comparison. "She never told us about him."

"It was too much for her. She explained to me once that her life was split into two parts: the one with Jimmy and the one with your gramps. One was utterly tragic and the other was almost euphoric. She owed it to both men to keep the two separate or the guilt over both sides of her life would drive her crazy."

"Guilt?" Elizabeth asked, trying to make sense of it.

"She felt the need to honor her promise to spend her life with Jimmy, but she also fell utterly in love with your gramps and she wanted to give her whole self to him."

"That sounds like Nan," Elizabeth said with a small smile.

"She felt that telling anyone about Jimmy would muddle the two sides of her, and she knew Jimmy would have wanted her to go on with her life."

"I'm so glad she gave you the letters," Elizabeth said. "And I'm so glad you trusted me with them."

"Maybe all three of them are together now, smiling down on us."

"I hope so," Elizabeth said, feeling better for having come to see Beatrice. "Merry Christmas."

"Merry Christmas."

Elizabeth and Mama had delivered Christmas letters with bags of cookies to the farmhands. With a full heart, Elizabeth had come home to get ready for Christmas Eve while Mama filled the air with clove, nutmeg, and cinnamon as she stewed the mulled wine before rushing off to her bedroom to freshen up.

Elizabeth swiped her lip gloss over her lips and ran her fingers through her hair, fluffing it up. Paul would be there in about ten minutes. The candles were lit, a plate of cookies and his Christmas letter all ready to go, and Elizabeth had showered and put on a red sweater and jeans with a pair of dangly earrings, feeling as if somehow everything would end up the way it should. She couldn't wait for Paul to arrive.

Right on cue, the doorbell buzzed. Elizabeth took one more quick look in the mirror of her dressing table and then headed to the front door. "I've got it," she called down to her mother's bedroom.

"I've lit the fire in the firepit outside on the back porch, turned the outdoor heater on, and put the cushions out on the chairs for the party tomorrow. And I've set S'mores and skewers out there," Mama said from the bedroom. "Feel free to offer Paul some if you want to."

"Okay."

With every step down the hallway, excitement hummed inside Elizabeth and she couldn't help but feel that this was a turning point in her life. With a deep breath, she opened the door, her heart skipping a beat when she saw him.

But once she'd had a second for his demeanor to register, concern took over. He stood on the other side, looking as if he had the weight of the world on his shoulders.

"Is everything okay?" she asked.

"I just came by to say that I can't stay," he said. "I'm so sorry. Something's come up and I have to speak to someone at work. It's urgent."

"Can't you call them from here?"

He shook his head, clearly consumed with whatever was on his mind. "This isn't a short call."

"Please stay," she said. "My mom loves meeting new people and she's excited to have you. If she had her way, she'd have the whole town over."

"I can't. It's important." He stared at her, looking as if someone had just thrown a bucket of cold water on him.

She opened her mouth to try to convince him, but his phone went off and, without any further explanation, he gave her an apologetic glance, then turned back toward his running car.

"Wait," she called after him.

With his phone already to his ear, he got back in and took off, leaving her standing in the doorway.

Stunned, she closed the door as Mama came into the room.

"Where's Paul?" her mother asked.

"He left. He said he had something come up." The words left her lips on a whisper of disbelief.

"On Christmas Eve?"

Elizabeth shrugged, the disappointment swarming her, his actions chipping away at the hopefulness that she'd built up, making her wonder if that optimism had been nothing but wishful thinking. Regardless of whatever he was facing, he'd chosen work over spending time with her. She'd promised herself she wouldn't let another person put her in that position. She just never thought *Paul* would be the one. She walked over to the table and picked up the envelope with his Christmas letter, gazing down at it, tears unexpectedly pricking her eyes.

"Don't let him get you down," Mama said, but it was obvious by the sympathy on her face that she knew he had.

"I can't believe it." Elizabeth shook her head. "He'd mentioned that his investors didn't want to wait until the holiday was over, but he didn't even put his foot down."

Mama reached out and rubbed the tops of Elizabeth's arms as if she could rub the distress right off. "It's Christmas Eve. We've got lots of great food, hot cocoa, and a night of binge-watchin' movies ahead of us. And then tomorrow we have everyone coming over. There's lots to celebrate."

"I guess you're right," she said, ignoring the ache in her chest and tossing the letter she'd written Paul onto the table. It seemed that she should've listened to her gut when she'd first arrived in Mason's Ridge after all.

"I'm turning in for the night." Mama clicked off the TV and folded the blanket, draping it over the arm of the sofa. "Love you," she said to Elizabeth, kissing her on the cheek.

Elizabeth clicked off the lamp, the only light in the dim room coming from the sparkling Christmas tree. "Love you too," she said. "Merry Christmas."

Mama grinned at her with the excitement of a child. "Tomorrow is Christmas mornin' and I already feel like I've had the best holiday because you're here."

"I'm so glad," Elizabeth told her, giving her a hug. She'd had a lovely evening with her mom, even if she couldn't erase the pang of disappointment that Paul had left. "I think I might stay out here a while and enjoy the Christmas tree."

"Don't stay up too late."

"I won't. Just late enough to sneak a few cookies." Elizabeth winked at her mother, making Mama laugh.

When Mama had retreated down the hallway, Elizabeth plopped back down on the sofa, taking in the shimmer of the baubles in the lights and the silver streamers of the mistletoe. The only sounds were the flickering of the fire and the soft clamp of the latch on Mama's door as it shut. Today had been a whirlwind of emotions, but the one thing Elizabeth kept coming back to was the fact that this farm had brought her closer to her mother and to who she wanted to be, and she couldn't lose it.

Quietly, she padded over to Nan's writing desk that sat by the front window in the living room and looked down the hallway to be sure it was clear before pulling open the first drawer. She thumbed through the few files inside: the warranty and paperwork for the new tractor, listings of organic pesticides and feed processes, every landline phone bill Nan had received since the 1980s, Nan's healthcare cards and hospital forms, old tax paperwork…

Elizabeth pulled out the tax documents and flipped through them. The taxes were based on expenses, feed, fertilizers and other supplies, and repairs and maintenance—not a thing to give her any answers. She put them back, opening the only other drawer. But there was nothing in there either. Only thank-you notes, tissue paper, and gift bags.

Closing it, she padded over to the hall closet, holding her breath as the hinges squeaked lightly. She ran her hand through the hanging coats, Nan's scent wafting toward her, making Elizabeth feel as if she was somehow there with her, guiding her. She ran her fingers along the top shelf, feeling nothing but a few folded blankets.

Slipping her phone from her back pocket, she shined the light at the bottom, revealing the vacuum, a couple of long umbrellas standing on end, and a file box that she hadn't seen before. She slid the box out until she could get a hold of it and took it into the living room, clicking on the lamp and gazing down the hallway once more to be sure she hadn't woken Mama.

Elizabeth put her hands on the box and silently sent a message to Nan: *Please. Show me what's going on. Help me understand.* With a deep breath, she lifted the lid and her shoulders slumped when she found nothing but old hats, gloves, and Nan's shoes that she'd probably set aside to go to the second-hand shop. Unwilling to accept that Nan wasn't there to offer answers, Elizabeth dug around inside it anyway, and when she couldn't find anything, she dumped the contents out on the floor.

Nothing.

Disappointed, she folded it all and put it back in the box, returning it to the closet. Then she went into the kitchen and checked each drawer, searching for anything that would speak to the deed of the property being in someone else's name. With every drawer she went through, her hopes were dashed just a little more.

After rummaging around in every drawer and every cabinet, with nowhere else to check, Elizabeth turned off the lamp, and then unplugged the Christmas tree, sending the room into darkness. No closer to having answers, she headed to bed, hoping Christmas Day would bring something—anything—to help this all make sense.

Chapter Sixteen

Elizabeth's eyes burned, the morning coming too early after a restless sleep. Paul's conduct last night had her mind going until the wee hours of the morning. She couldn't help but wonder what in the world could've been so important that he couldn't even stay for dinner or text her back. The least he could've done was to provide her with a more suitable explanation so she didn't sit and worry about him.

As she lay there, her head heavy on her pillow, she considered the fact that she didn't know Paul as well as she thought she had. Suddenly, the same scenario of glittering first impressions giving way to work-over-people that she'd experienced with Richard was playing out in front of her once more. Perhaps it was a good thing this had happened now, although the knowledge of it didn't help to fill the crack that it had left on her already shattered heart.

The sound of the doorbell sent her jumping to her feet. Hoping somehow Paul had decided to come back and apologize, to restore her faith in him, Elizabeth threw on a pair of jeans and a sweater and ran her hands through her hair, rushing to see who it was.

When she arrived at the door, Mama had already answered it and, to Elizabeth's disappointment, their farmhand Sabastian was standing on the other side.

"Mornin' y'all," he said, his hands shoved into the pockets of his jeans. "You wanted to see me?"

"Merry Christmas," Mama told him. "I know y'all are headin' out to see your families, but I wanted to send you off with some coffee and cinnamon rolls. You're also welcome to come to our party tonight."

"You didn't have to do that, ma'am," he said with a big grin. "You already gave us cookies."

"I know, but I couldn't run the farm without you boys." She handed him three paper bags of cinnamon rolls and a thermos for each one of them. "There's also a little bonus in these cards. It's not much, but just somethin' to say thank you."

Elizabeth soaked in her mother's generosity, knowing Mama didn't have the money to hand out bonuses, but she'd done it anyway.

"You don't need to be spendin' your Christmas mornin' fussin' over us," he said with a grateful nod.

"Aw, it's nothin'," Mama said. "I was just plannin' on putterin' around the house. And Elizabeth just got up." She turned to Elizabeth, only then acknowledging her. "Mornin'."

Elizabeth, who'd been lingering at the back of the living room, greeted her mother and gave a little hello to Sabastian.

"And y'all deserve a little somethin' for agreein' to help us figure out what's goin' on with that barren land out back. That's not really in your job description," Mama continued.

"Well, if you've got a second, I did want to show you somethin'," Sabastian said. "Wanna grab your coats? There's quite a development with the corner of that field…"

Intrigued, Mama and Elizabeth bundled up and followed Sabastian, their boots crunching on the ice-covered snow, the frigid winter wind taking Elizabeth's breath away. When they reached the infertile area, Elizabeth's mouth hung open at the sight of the massive unearthing.

"I was gonna come over after Christmas to tell you. The boys and I were diggin' to find out what kind of rock this was, but it ain't no rock. It's a massive slab foundation. A layer of soil had covered it over the years. Looks like a building was gonna be built here."

Mama clapped a hand over her mouth.

"Nan never said anything about another house," Elizabeth said, completely perplexed after Sabastian had left. "Did she know it was there?" What had happened that Nan and Gramps had lived there all their lives but that foundation had sat untouched?

Mama set out two plates, placing a giant cinnamon roll on each, the white icing pooling onto the plate. "She'd have to have known… Could she and Dad have wanted to build something more?" She set a roll in front of Elizabeth, along with a mug of steaming coffee.

Elizabeth picked up the silver pitcher of cream. "Are you sure she knew? *We* live here and we didn't know." She added cream and then sugar, stirring.

Mama sat down and held her coffee in both hands, a far-off look in her eyes.

Elizabeth did not want to tell her, on Christmas Day, what she'd learned at the lawyer's, but she was starting to wonder how Nan had actually come to live there. Had she owned the farm at all? It didn't make any sense, as there were no records of payment to anyone. They hadn't been renting it. And, certainly, they wouldn't have been allowed to live there free of charge for more than half a century.

"Do we have any paperwork that states that Nan is the owner of the property? Maybe we can learn something from it."

"I've turned this house upside down and I couldn't find a thing," Mama said. She waved her hands in the air as if brushing it all away, the way she did when she got overwhelmed.

Elizabeth wondered if the same questions were going through Mama's head with or without the discussion with the lawyer.

"Let's enjoy Christmas Day and not worry about this until tomorrow."

"You're right," Elizabeth said, the weight still lingering on her shoulders, but she was determined to rally. "These look delicious." She cut into the creamy cinnamon roll, the spicy, vanilla scent of it floating up through the hearty aroma of the coffee.

When they'd finished, the two of them went over to the glimmering Christmas tree, and Elizabeth noticed a few new gifts. She gave Mama a questioning look.

"I can sneak and find you things too," she said with a mysterious twinkle in her eye.

"You know I didn't expect anything," Elizabeth said.

"I know, but I'm your mama. I want my little girl to have Christmas."

Elizabeth gave her mother a heartfelt squeeze, feeling in that moment that she was holding on for dear life, everything they knew hanging in the balance.

Mama took Elizabeth's hands and lowered the two of them onto the floor in front of the Christmas tree, the way they'd done when Elizabeth was a girl. "It's just us," she said.

"Yep. Just us."

"Until later! Everyone's comin' to the party. They all said they could."

Elizabeth grinned at her mother's absolute delight at having a full house at Christmas. "Think I should try to reach Paul to ask him to come?"

The happiness on Mama's face turned to concern. "He could stop workin' for one day."

Elizabeth fired off a quick text to him before she changed her mind. "I thought he was different," she admitted. "I want him to be different so badly."

"Maybe he'll come around." Mama leaned back and admired the tree before turning to face Elizabeth. "Just in case, I saved the Christmas letter you wrote him. I put it in the kitchen drawer."

Elizabeth thanked her mother, but her confidence in Paul had taken a turn. If he didn't come, at least everyone else would be there to share the holiday. Then she peered over at the chair where Nan used to sit while they all passed presents to each other. "Think Nan can see us now?" she wondered aloud.

Mama followed her line of sight, smiling at the empty seat. "I hope so." She clapped her hands together. "Nan used to always let us go first. Should we unwrap some presents?"

"Yes, and then maybe we could end our present-unwrapping with her next letter so it feels like she's here," Elizabeth suggested.

"That sounds perfect." Mama reached under the tree and pulled out the first gift, wrapped in shiny red paper with a silver ribbon. "Open this one," she said. "It reminded me of you."

Elizabeth took the present and gave her mother a kiss on the cheek.

Mama laughed. "You don't even know what it is yet."

"It doesn't matter," Elizabeth said. "I get to sit here at Nan's farmhouse with you, on Christmas. That's the best gift of all."

Mama gave her an adoring pout. "I hope you like the present."

Elizabeth tugged on the silver string, untying it. She slipped her finger under the fold of the paper until the tape came loose. When she pulled the wrapping away, she found a beautiful stationery set with a lace pattern cut out of the top of the paper and matching envelopes in a pale green.

"You've been so enamored with Nan's Christmas letters that I thought you might like to have paper when you write your own."

"Thank you, Mama," she said, giving her a hug, unable to hide her smile. "I love it." Elizabeth reached under the tree, pulling out another gift. She'd had it wrapped at the boutique where she'd bought it, the little box adorned in white glittery bauble print with a candy-cane-striped ribbon. She handed it to Mama. "I think you'll enjoy this..."

Mama unwrapped the present to reveal another box of stationery—this one with butterflies and flowers. She laughed and then held it to her chest fondly.

"I thought the same thing," Elizabeth said. Then, without warning, the question of whether they would be writing their Christmas letters at the farm next year ran through her mind.

When she surfaced from her thoughts, Mama was peering down at her gift, the same worry seemingly on her face.

"Maybe we should we read one of Nan's letters now instead of at the end, so it feels more like she's with us," Elizabeth said, trying to keep the atmosphere light.

Mama set her present aside. "It would be good to hear her, wouldn't it?"

Agreeing, Elizabeth grabbed the letters from the coffee table and pulled out the next in line.

July 1, 1946

My dearest Roger,

I'm writing to you today to tell you how alone I feel in this farmhouse all by myself. I look out at the corner field where Jimmy and I had begun building our dream home, the foundation sitting empty, exposed…

A thrill coursed through Elizabeth's veins. It was as if Nan had been waiting to offer them a little gift of her own. "This is at least a shred of proof that Nan owned this land. She and Jimmy had to own it to build on it, right?"

"It couldn't hurt," Mama said. "And now we know what that foundation is."

Nan's message came back to Elizabeth yet again: *Foundations aren't all we need. They're nothing if we don't give them shape and form, Liz. Build your foundation, but plan more than just the ground level, see it through, and nurture it.* She found herself giving shape and form to her life, just as Nan had told her, but now she needed the farm to be theirs to make it happen. Could this letter be what they needed? Could it possibly override a legal deed?

"What does the rest of the letter say?" Mama asked.

With a burst of hope, Elizabeth read on.

I'd been so devastated over the loss of Jimmy that I hadn't been able to see what God had put right in front of me: you. You've carried me through the unknown of the war, through losing Jimmy, and now through the loneliness of learning to live life on my own. I'd like to ask you to stay in Mason's Ridge. We both deserve to see what transpires—together.

What do you say?

All my love,
Harriet

Mama stared down at the letter. "I suppose his answer was yes."

"He was so good to her."

"Yes, he was."

Right then, Elizabeth knew that no matter what, she wouldn't go down without a fight. This farm belonged to Nan and Gramps. And she couldn't help but think that Jimmy would've wanted that too.

Chapter Seventeen

With the presents all unwrapped and stashed down the hallway in the bedrooms, Christmas music played on the radio while Mama and Elizabeth finished up preparations for the party, covering the kitchen and the living-room tables in festive plates of party food.

"I'm so excited to have everyone over," Mama said, while dropping crumbles of her homemade goat's cheese onto a ceramic platter with painted Christmas trees, arranging it with crackers and fruit.

"Me too," Elizabeth said.

Christmases in New York had been beautiful. Richard had surprised her with a different decorator every year who'd completely redesigned all the spaces in their penthouse with Christmas decorations.

"You don't have to do that. I love to decorate," she'd told him. But he'd always said that she had better things to do than to fumble around with garlands all day for weeks. What he'd failed to realize was that it had less to do with the décor and more to do with the time spent doing it. As Elizabeth looked around at the mistletoe and the little tree with lights, all the glamour in the world couldn't outshine the love that radiated from the farmhouse.

The buzzer sounded on the front door.

"I'll get it," Elizabeth said, leaving Mama to finish displaying the final few things on the kitchen table. She paced over to the door and opened it, stopping cold, her hand stilling on the doorknob when she saw Paul on the other side, holding two wrapped gifts under his arm. "You decided to come back?"

"Yes," he said, his chest filling with air under his coat. "I'm sorry I ran off. It was just… work…" He smiled, but his usual candor was absent.

A fizzle of excitement swam through her at the idea that he'd regretted leaving and decided to let it all go for the holidays, choosing friends and good cheer over his work commitments. "Well, make them all wait. It's Christmas," she said, beckoning him inside.

He nodded agreeably, and then shook his head as if dislodging the stress of whatever it was from his mind, though he didn't look convinced. Tentatively, he held out the two presents. "I brought you and your mother something."

"Thank you," she said, taking them from him and setting them under the tree, Paul following behind her.

"It was the least I could do for your hospitality. Especially after I ran off without an explanation." He seemed as though he wanted to look around, but was fighting the urge to keep his focus on Elizabeth.

"You must be Paul," Mama said, coming down the hallway, wearing her matching Christmas-tree earrings and pendant set. She stretched out her hand in greeting. "Loretta Holloway, Elizabeth's mama."

"It's nice to meet you, Loretta." He shook her hand. While it was clear that he was giving it his best effort, he wasn't as jovial as he'd been the other times Elizabeth had been with him.

Mama was as smitten as a kitten, clearly not noticing a thing. "Well, sit, sit," she said, buzzing into the kitchen. "I've got dinner in the oven and there's mulled wine brewin'. I'll get us each a cup."

"You have a lovely house," Paul called over to Mama as she dipped a ladle into the crockpot. His gaze finally wandered to the stockings hanging from the mantle.

"Thank you," Mama said. "It was my parents' house."

"Oh?" His attention moved back to her.

"Yes," Elizabeth added. "This farm's been in our family since my nan was young, and after she passed, my mother took over and she runs it."

"Well," Mama said, bringing Paul the first mug of mulled wine. "Elizabeth has been helpin' me. And I have the farmhands."

He walked over to the stone fireplace. "That's incredible…"

"My grandmother married my grandfather right on the porch outside," Elizabeth told him, thinking about how one day she, too, would like to have her wedding there, but the idea seemed so far away now. When she turned back to Paul, he was sipping his wine, peering over the desk through the window that faced the porch, pensive, the Christmas tree's gold lights shimmering outside. He sat down in one of the chairs and Elizabeth followed suit.

Mama came over and handed Elizabeth her mulled wine, sitting down in the chair opposite her and Paul. "How about you, Paul?" she asked. "Tell me about your family."

With a deep breath, he turned his focus back to Mama. "There's not a lot to tell, really. I grew up with my parents in Chicago."

"Are they still there?" Mama asked, her head turned to the side the way she did whenever Elizabeth told her a story.

"Not anymore. They've both passed away. My grandfather is my only relative left." He frowned, but then cleared it, producing a smile as if to lighten the mood. "I sound like a downer," he said, his features lifting again. "My life was anything but that. Growing up, my parents always took two weeks off work at the holidays and we had big family Christmases at our house."

"What did your parents do for a living?" Mama asked.

"My parents both worked with the family business," he replied, Mama's gentle demeanor slowly bringing him back out of himself.

Mama crossed her legs and folded her hands over her knee. "What's the family business?"

"It's a corporate development firm."

"How nice to be able to continue it for them," Mama said, clearly making conversation, her favorite thing to do.

"Yes. It's been in my family for three generations now. My grandfather started it back in the fifties as an agricultural firm. He told me once that throwing himself into his own company helped him learn who he really was," Paul said, taking a drink from his mug.

"I can certainly understand that," Elizabeth said. Running the farm with Mama was teaching her a lot about herself.

"That's exactly how I feel, too," Paul continued. "I'd never felt more in line with what I was doing than I did the minute I took over the business." He looked back at the porch for a tick as if he were wrestling with some thought and wanted to say something, but then returned to the conversation.

"Who's taking care of things at work while you're gone?" Mama asked.

"I'm working from here, handling our investors and timelines for each project, but I have a staff back in Chicago keeping everything else moving for me."

"Well, I hope you're not working too hard," Elizabeth said, suddenly distracted by the flutter of light snow illuminated by the Christmas lights outside. "Look." She pointed to the window.

Mama put her hand to her heart. "A white Christmas. How wonderful. The weatherman said we might get some more."

"I hope Ray won't have to tow me home," Paul said, the corners of his mouth turning upward, his first little joke since he'd arrived.

"Actually, I think Liz may have texted you, Paul, but I've invited Ray and a few others over for a little party and some drinks after dinner," Mama said. "I thought it might be nice to have a full house this holiday."

Paul's expression lifted just slightly. "Sounds great."

Elizabeth hoped that the festive atmosphere might get his mind off work and lighten his mood a bit more.

Mama reached over to the tray of cookies and pinched a sugar cookie. "I'm just gonna do one more check to be sure everything's ready."

"You don't need any help?" Elizabeth offered.

"No, no. You two relax." Mama fluttered over to the counter and lit one of the vanilla candles that Nan had kept for special occasions. Then she retrieved the Christmas letter from the drawer, bringing it in and setting it onto the table. "Here's Paul's Christmas letter."

"I have a Christmas letter?" Paul asked, that glimmer swimming through whatever had been worrying him.

Elizabeth slid it off the coffee table, suddenly feeling exposed, and wondering if she should give it to him or not after he'd run off yesterday, but he was here now, which was what really mattered. "You know my nan's letters? Well, she also wrote one to all her friends every Christmas and delivered each one with a plate of holiday goodies." Elizabeth handed him the letter and then moved the plate of cookies in front of him. "Have as many as you like."

"Thank you," he said, holding the letter, something showing in his eyes that Elizabeth couldn't decipher as he unfolded it.

"The tradition was that Nan would tell the person what they'd offered her that year that she was thankful for," Elizabeth told him, feeling a little nervous at the gesture.

He read the letter and then looked up at Elizabeth, locking eyes with her. "Liz?" he asked, noting her signature.

"You said I looked more like a Liz. And, here, I feel more like the girl I'd been so many years ago. Just wiser."

His lips parted as if he wanted to say something, but nothing came out. Instead, he seemed conflicted, puzzling her and making her want to kick herself for being vulnerable. But then she honed in on the original intent of her letter. Whatever the reason he was acting differently now, he'd made her feel great before, as if she could tell him anything.

He stared down at the letter.

She put a hand on Paul's arm to comfort whatever it was that was brewing inside that mind of his. "There's a lot going on in our lives that we can't always control. But one thing we *can* control is not letting the rest of the world get in the way of spending time with our friends and family. Despite how difficult everything else is, let's just try to enjoy Christmas."

He stared at her for a long time, making her wonder if her words meant more to him than she'd intended. "Okay," he said, that warm look surfacing, sending a tingle through her. "Thank you for this." He waved the letter in front of him. "It means a lot."

"You're welcome," she said. "One thing I'm learning is that, no matter what, in the end, everything *will* be okay. It might look different from what we'd thought, but it will be okay." When he didn't respond, she knew that if anyone could prove it to him, she could.

He looked as though he was about to ask her something, but just then, the buzzer rang. Mama ran over to the door, and greeted Ray, Ella, and Beatrice.

"The last time I was here at the holiday, I was having tea with Harriet," Beatrice said, unwrapping her scarf, her eyes misty as she looked around. "I feel like she's still here..." She waved to Elizabeth with her free arm, the other clutching her handbag full of knitting essentials.

Mama helped her into the living room, while Ray and Ella took off their coats and, after hellos and cookie browsing, settled into a comfortable conversation about how many logs it took to get a good flame going.

"Let me help you into a comfortable spot by the fire," Mama offered to Beatrice, guiding her gently by the arm, keeping the old woman steady as she lowered herself down in the chair.

"Hello, my dear," she called to Elizabeth.

Elizabeth got up and walked over, giving her a hug. "Merry Christmas," she said. "Beatrice, this is Paul. He helped me find your birthday gift."

Paul shifted seats and greeted the woman, sitting down next to her on the hearth as Ray and Ella gathered around the cookies with Mama.

The doorbell buzzed again. "I'll get it," Elizabeth said.

She found Percy, Naomi, and Travis on the other side, newly fallen snow in their hair.

"It's freezing," Naomi said with a little tap of her feet before kissing Elizabeth on the cheek and breezing past her. "Hey, y'all!" She dropped her coat onto the chair, gave a little wave to Beatrice, and headed straight over to the table, while Elizabeth ushered Percy and Travis inside.

Before she could shut the door, the farmhands were already making their way down the walk, along with the yellow lab. The dog bounded in and shook the snow from his fur before finding Beatrice by the fire.

"Oh, hello," Beatrice said to the dog. She set her handbag on the floor and reached out for the dog as it neared her. "You're a sweet boy..."

Lenny came in, followed by Harvey and Sabastian. Elizabeth shut the door, the house humming with chatter as everyone settled in, greeting one another while holiday music played like the Christmas underbelly of memories in the making.

"Who's that?" Percy asked Elizabeth, coming up beside her. He pointed to Paul, who was now slicing a piece of Mama's Christmas cake at the kitchen table while Mama told him all about the icing she'd used.

Elizabeth couldn't help but be amused by the skill in which Paul was able to look enthralled by Mama's baking chatter. She couldn't have imagined a better holiday gift than to see him relaxing. "Paul Dawson," she replied. "He's visiting."

Percy glared at him. "That's the guy who wanted to buy my land out from under me."

Elizabeth turned and stared at him, confused. "You sure?" she asked, nearly certain the old man was wrong.

"Absolutely."

"You must be mistaken. He said himself that he wasn't one of the people trying to buy up all the land," she countered.

"Naw, that's him, ain't it, Travis?"

Travis glared at Paul. "Mm hm. That's definitely him."

But then Elizabeth recalled Paul's exact words: "I have to admit, I tried to delve into it a little…" The room faded to an undecipherable buzz as Elizabeth processed what Percy and Travis had just told her.

Chapter Eighteen

Had Paul lied to her? What was he really doing there? All of a sudden, his phone conversations began to filter back through her mind: *I need three weeks at least… It's Christmas. There's nothing I can do. See if you can stall them.* And then his face when he'd shown up at her door… What had that been all about?

She made a beeline to Paul.

He turned to her, his expression unsuspecting and warm like it had been the night she'd met him, the sight of it causing her hands to tremble as the sense of her Christmas crashing down around her began to surface.

"I need to speak with you," she said, ignoring the others. The way his face dropped as if she'd just caught him red-handed made her stomach feel like a boulder had settled in it.

"Excuse me," he said politely to the others.

Mama followed them with her eyes while Elizabeth pulled Paul down the hallway. On a gut feeling, she asked him, "Who is William Worsham?"

His jaw clenched and he said nothing, looking as though he were deciding something. He probably knew good and well why she'd asked.

"Tell me," she demanded.

Paul took in a long, slow breath and let it out, thoughts clear in the lines forming on his forehead. He broke eye contact, his shoulders tense. "He's my grandfather."

Her heart fell into her stomach.

"What's going on?" he asked, but the fear in his eyes told her he already knew.

Elizabeth grabbed Paul's arm and walked over to the coat hooks, grabbing his coat and tossing it over to him.

Her mother gave her a suspicious stare from across the room, but Elizabeth dismissed it.

"Don't freeze out there," Mama said, as Paul followed Elizabeth through the group of people in the kitchen and out to the back of the farmhouse.

She stood under the tin roof of the porch, by the roaring fire in the large stone firepit, as the snow fell in giant flakes all around them. The strings of bulb lights were lit above them, the fire casting warmth and flickering shadows on the wooden boards. Mama had set out her little table full of marshmallows, chocolates, and graham crackers, the mere idea of it causing a twinge of acid to hit Elizabeth's already unsettled stomach.

"Your grandfather is William Worsham," she stated just to make sure she could trust her brain.

"Yes," Paul said.

She needed to sit down. Lowering herself into one of the Adirondack chairs, she scooted it next to the fire for warmth. Paul sat down beside her.

"And you're not on vacation," she guessed.

He shook his head, looking down at his feet.

"Why *are* you here?" she asked.

He lifted his head back up, the flames from the fire dancing in his worried blue eyes. "I was supposed to be here to view Crestwood Farm for development, although I hadn't been able to, given the fact that there were residents."

Every nerve in Elizabeth's body was on high alert, a slight pounding beginning in her temples. But then, suddenly, the fear gave way. Paul had seemed to have a connection with her. Maybe she could make him understand that she needed to keep the farm. "Is that why you didn't stay yesterday? You didn't expect to find me here?"

"Yes," he said, his breath dissipating into the cold air. "I'm so sorry. I had no idea that you were the one living here."

"I do live here," she said. "And my mother lives here. Before her, my nan lived here nearly her whole married life. Can you help me understand how this property is in your grandfather's name?"

Paul shrugged helplessly. "He owns all kinds of property. He bought and sold farms for a living."

"He can't own this land. It has to be a mistake. We can correct it, right?"

Paul shook his head again as if putting a halt to her plea. "I found the purchase records and tax documents in our online database. My grandfather bought Crestwood Farm for his agricultural business, using a loan from his father that he paid back over ten years. But none of the documents mention an occupant."

"When did he buy it?" she asked.

"It's hard to say. I'm guessing it was before we had the computerized system, because some of the cells were blank."

"Okay, well, can we buy it from him?" Elizabeth asked, having absolutely no idea how she or Mama would afford it.

"We're building a resort on this land. I've got investors, architects, and the county zoning ordinance board involved, just to name a few," he replied. "The plans are drawn. We were supposed to be breaking ground in three weeks."

She wondered if the agony she saw on his face was because it was happening or was it because she was in the way?

"I can't back out."

She stared into his eyes, tears forming in hers. "You're putting Mama and me on the street."

Indecision consumed his face. "I'll help you both find somewhere else to live," he said.

Despair pulsed through her. "We can't live anywhere else, nor do we want to. All Mama knows is farm life. She has no other way to make a living."

Paul's gaze roamed the floor. "My hands are tied," he said in almost a whisper, his voice strangled.

Everything seemed to be slipping away. "Maybe we could talk to your grandfather and find out more."

"I've tried," he said. "We aren't speaking, remember?"

"Why aren't you two speaking exactly?"

"He didn't want me to move into commercial development. He'd rather the land remain agricultural." Paul picked a tiny twig from the arm of his chair and tossed it into the fire. "But the board felt that it was the most lucrative way to invest, and even though I wasn't certain about the board's idea, things couldn't continue the way they were going. He left me to run the company entirely, wanting nothing to do with it."

"Why didn't you listen to him?" Elizabeth asked, the whole idea of choosing business over family pricking a nerve.

"We were hemorrhaging money, Elizabeth, including all his retirement savings. The company was going under, but it's profitable again, so it was worth it."

"It was worth losing your relationship with your grandfather?" she asked incredulously.

He sat there, silent. "You don't understand. He stood to lose everything."

Despite it all, there was something in Paul that Elizabeth felt, or at least hoped, was good—she'd seen it with her own eyes. She knew that the last opportunity she had to save the farm was to connect with his grandfather and plead her case—maybe it could help. Perhaps having all of them together, all sides represented, could change things. "I want answers. I want to know how he acquired the farm and whether he knew my nan and gramps were there. I figure he must have if he paid the taxes on it. Were Nan and Gramps allowed to live here for some reason?"

The back door opened, interrupting them. Mama poked out her head. "Is everything okay?"

While Elizabeth attempted to formulate a suitable answer to that question, she overheard Percy talking to someone inside. "She's checking on Elizabeth… I don't know what he's even doing here. He doesn't belong with us…"

"We're fine, Mama, thank you," Elizabeth said, attempting to drown out Percy before he could do too much damage.

"Okay, y'all come in if you get cold." She shut the door, leaving them in silence.

Paul stared at her, and it was clear that he'd heard. He stood up abruptly. "I'm in the worst position, with no answers, ruining your holiday… I need to go and let you all enjoy the party," he said gently.

She could've sworn his gaze had been conflicted before he'd turned to let himself back into the house. Elizabeth jumped up and scrambled after him. Everything she'd seen of him had told her that the last few days couldn't all be fake. "Why won't you stay and try to figure this out with me?" she asked to his back as he made his way past the people gathered at the table and through the living room, without a word to Beatrice, Naomi, or Percy, who'd stopped to watch what was going on.

With Elizabeth on his heels, Paul turned the knob to the front door and walked out onto the porch. He looked her way but wouldn't meet her eyes. "I don't deserve to be here." When he finally did make eye contact, the pain in them was clear. "I didn't come to ruin everyone's Christmas." Then he left her and walked toward his car, got in, and pulled out.

As she gazed at the fresh tire tracks in the snow, the weight of it all hit her hard. She'd wanted to make this the best Christmas ever, but now it was one she wanted to put behind her.

Chapter Nineteen

Elizabeth sat on the sofa beside Mama after their chores the next morning, her head pounding from finally filling her in on everything the lawyer had told her, what they'd overheard Percy say, and what had transpired between her and Paul last night. She hadn't been able to keep it from her any longer; not now that it seemed the farm's future hung in the balance.

"Oh, my God," Mama said. "What are we gonna do?"

Elizabeth rubbed the pinch in her neck. "The only person with answers is William Worsham. We need to talk to him."

"How do we do that?" Mama asked, her features downturned in her anxiety, making her look older.

"I don't know." Elizabeth had stayed up until the wee hours, scouring the internet in the hopes of making some sort of breakthrough, but when nothing had come, she'd called Paul this morning and left a message. "I've tried to search his name online, but I don't even know if he lives in Chicago. I can't find any contact information. And I can't get a hold of Paul."

Mama's shoulders fell. "I'm sorry things didn't work out with you and Paul. You had such a glow whenever you mentioned him. I was hopin' he'd come in and sweep you off your feet."

"It was bad timing," Elizabeth said.

Mama shifted on the sofa, tugging her bathrobe tighter around her thin body. "Timin' is never right," she said. "If you wait for the timin' to be perfect for things, you'll spend your life waitin'."

Elizabeth let out a long breath, but it did nothing to relieve the concern she had over not talking to Paul. "It wasn't meant to be. Probably better that I didn't waste another seven years before figuring it out." Even though she was trying to let it go, there was a part of her that still held on to the dream that Paul was a good guy and, somehow, they could find a way through. She needed to concentrate on what really mattered now. "What would Nan say about all this? She always had an answer for everything, but I bet she'd be stumped with this one."

"We've got a few more letters to read," Mama said. "Maybe she'll tell us."

Doubting they'd get any answer at all to this conundrum, but wanting to hear Nan's voice more than ever, Elizabeth got up and took the letters back to the sofa, pulling the final two from the stack. She opened the first one and her eyes widened as she scanned it. "It's from Gramps. And he mentions the farm."

March 7, 1947

Harriet, my love,

Every year, we have four seasons: the summer, where everything is glorious and golden; the fall, when the bold and stunning colors of the trees overpower the fact that we're watching the leaves wither and die; the winter, where we draw inward, into ourselves; and spring, a time of blossoming and rebirth.

I've watched you, too, go through the seasons of life. Your vibrant love for Jimmy faded into fear that was followed by the anguish of death. But then, when we are together, I've seen the light return to your eyes and the life blossom in them, just like the springtime. Now you are shining once more.

You are a rare flower in my eyes. I'm filled with wonder and elation whenever you laugh, and I crave the moments when I can see it again. I've taken care of everything with the farm. You don't have to worry about a thing. And I promise you that I will stand by your side as long as you'll have me.

All my love,
Roger

"What does he mean he's 'taken care of everything' with the farm?" Elizabeth asked.

"I don't know," Mama replied. "I'm sure takin' care of everything by herself was quite a task for your nan. Until you got here, I've been workin' around the clock, even with the help of the farmhands. It's not for the faint of heart. And there's so much more to do durin' the growin season."

"Could he have sold the farm to William Worsham and rented it back or something?"

Mama shrugged, baffled.

"It would be just like Gramps to take matters into his own hands. If Nan ran the entire farm after Jimmy died, it would certainly be a lot to pay for. Gramps might have done some sort of business deal to allow them to live on it."

"But how did Dad know William Worsham when no one here has ever heard of the man?" Mama asked.

"There's only one person who can answer that and that's William himself," Elizabeth said. "May I take the car if I can get it out?" she asked Mama, setting the letter on the coffee table. "I'm driving over to see Paul." She was determined, unable to believe that everything would end like this.

"Of course," Mama said, taking her purse from the hook near the front door and digging around for her keys while Elizabeth pulled on her coat. "The snow was light last night; you should be able to get out if you drive down the snow tracks Ray left with the tractor." Mama handed the keys to her. "Want me to come with you?"

Elizabeth shook her head. "I'd like to talk to Paul alone, if that's okay." Her heartrate quickened at the mere thought of seeing him again and the unknown of how he would react.

"Yes. Go. Let me know if you need me."

Elizabeth lumbered through the snow, climbing into Mama's old Buick, and starting the ignition. Shivering, she didn't wait for the engine to warm before she put the car in drive and slowly rolled down the tractor's tread to the main road.

On the way, Gramps came to mind. He'd always been there for Nan, from the very beginning. Elizabeth had yet to find someone like that, someone who would risk everything for her and not sleep until he'd made it all okay. Gramps had said himself that he promised to be by Nan's side as long as she'd have him. Were there still people in the world like him?

Elizabeth pulled up outside the rental, immediately noticing the absence of Paul's Mercedes. She cut the engine and got out anyway, stepping up to the door and pressing the doorbell. With her hands in her pockets, she held her breath, unsure of what she would even say first. When no one came, she cupped her hands, peering into the dark house, and her hopes fell. All signs of a tenant were gone. Paul had returned to Chicago without even a goodbye.

Fighting off the disappointment, she walked over to High Peak Coffee on the off chance he was there. She went inside and scanned the crowd, looking for that crop of sandy-blond hair, but there was no one matching the description. Her gaze fell on the little map by the fireplace and she had to force the swell of emotion back down as she considered how much that map would change by Paul's hands.

"Excuse me," she said to the barista. "Do you know if anyone named Paul Dawson is here?"

The woman with the spiky hair pouted, shaking her head. "Never heard of him."

"All right. Thanks." Elizabeth turned to walk away, but the barista stopped her.

"Wait," she called. "Is he the guy who's been here every day? The one with the blue eyes and the laptop?"

"Yes." Elizabeth's skin tingled with the anticipation that he hadn't actually left and that maybe she'd get to talk to him.

"He drove to the airport early this morning. Got a coffee on his way out."

"Okay," she said, hanging her head. "Thanks again."

With a heavy heart, Elizabeth got back in Mama's car and sent Paul a text, asking him to call her. Then she headed home, feeling like she'd lost something big today—not only the farm, but the thrill she'd felt whenever Paul was with her. And that was almost as difficult to bear.

"Maybe the lawyer can connect us with Mr. Worsham," Mama suggested when Elizabeth had arrived home.

Elizabeth flopped onto the sofa and threw her head back in frustration. When she sat back up, her gaze fell on the two presents that Paul had brought them under the tree. She didn't feel much like opening them now.

Mama followed her line of sight. "It would've been nice if he'd stayed long enough for us to unwrap them so we could thank him for them."

"Let's just leave them there for now," Elizabeth said, secretly hoping that the two untouched gifts would send Paul some sort of cosmic message that they were waiting for him and bring him back to the farm. As she stared at them, she thought out loud, "What do we do?"

Mama frowned, clearly thinking. "We've got one last letter. The others have given us some sort of understandin' of what's goin' on. We could see if there's any more information that could help us."

Elizabeth got up and grabbed the stack of letters, pulling the last one from under the crimson ribbon that bound them all. For a moment, she held the envelope in her hand, not wanting to open it. This was the final message from Nan and after that, the silence might drive a knife right through her heart. After everything she'd lost, she couldn't bear to lose her grandmother too, not when she'd felt like she'd gotten her back these last few days.

"It's okay," Mama soothed her.

With unsteady hands, Elizabeth opened the envelope and slid the letter out.

December 25, 1947

My sweet, sweet Roger,

How absolutely incredible the journey was to get the two of us here—in love. You are the kindest, most genuine person, and I am thankful every day that you answered my letter to Jimmy. Sometimes I feel as if his angels somehow orchestrated it, and you were handpicked to make me whole when the evil of this world wanted to tear me apart. And I'd like to think that Jimmy was there to give his blessing on our wedding day.

When you finally told me you'd sold the farm, I couldn't believe it. I was so upset with you… But I have to trust that the person chosen just for me would know exactly what to do. You know I'm never good with the finances, so I'll let you handle all that. But I'll hold you to your promise that we'll always live here for generations to come. I don't know how you know that, but I trust that you do.

What Jimmy and I started here was only the seed, but you and I will grow our family and I will spend every day here, honoring Jimmy by caring for my loved ones.

Elizabeth looked up from the letter, fear draining the blood from her face, leaving her skin cold. "So Gramps must have rented the farm from William Worsham."

Mama's lips fell slack, the understanding of the situation hitting her. "So we really do have to leave." She swallowed, her eyes glistening with tears as she pressed her lips together into a frown. "What does the rest of the letter say?" she asked, her voice breaking.

Unable to form a sentence, Elizabeth shook her head, turning the letter around to show the final lines and Nan's signature—none of it giving them any further information. All she could piece together was that with Gramps and Nan now passed and the fact that the land was someone else's, Elizabeth and Mama would need to start packing their bags. They'd spent their last ever Christmas at Crestwood Farm.

Chapter Twenty

The next day, Elizabeth and Mama tended to the animals first thing, before breakfast, as always. The sky had cleared, leaving golden beams of sunshine to cast a shimmer across the fields, showing off the farm in all its splendor and illuminating everything that she and Mama would miss.

A lone stream of light filtered through the barn door. Elizabeth brushed Buttons' mane, wondering when they should drop the news to the farmhands that they were going to have to let them all go. She and Mama would also have to find the animals new homes. Buttons snorted, shifting his hooves, and she knew without a doubt that she'd miss him terribly. Certainly, Naomi could take the horses, and they'd relocate the other animals to good homes in the area. The farmhands would go on to find other jobs, but where did that leave Elizabeth and Mama? What were they supposed to do? Elizabeth bit back tears as she dragged the thick bristles through the horse's mane.

Nan, where are you? she wondered. *You always had the answers. We need you now.*

Buttons shifted again, startling Elizabeth and causing the tears to fall down her cheeks. She wiped them away with her icy fingers, numb not from cold, but from the anguish she felt at leaving. Nothing would ever be the same.

Elizabeth racked her brain for any way to fix this. Could they attempt to buy the land back? She could ask Richard for the money to bail her out… But he probably wouldn't, and she didn't want to be in debt to him like that, nor did she want to admit to him that she needed his money. Her savings were nonexistent, and all she had was what was left of the ten thousand Richard had given her. Mama had very few savings to speak of—she'd said herself that she'd sunk most of her money into the farm.

"I'm freezin'," Mama said, walking over to her. "You almost done with Buttons here?" She patted the horse's side affectionately. A heaviness lay between them this morning, even though both were trying to carry on as normal.

"Yeah," Elizabeth said, putting the brush in the bucket nearby and running her fingers down Buttons's mane. "I'll see you later," she told the horse sweetly, but her heart ached knowing that she most likely wouldn't be seeing Buttons much in a few weeks' time.

Elizabeth and Mama walked back across the field to the house, letting themselves in and settling next to the fireplace. As Elizabeth warmed her quivering body, tears slipped down her cheeks.

"Honey…" Mama took her ice-cold hand.

Elizabeth shook her head. "Everything's gone wrong," she replied, unable to keep herself together for Mama's benefit anymore. "We can't lose this farm, and I can't reach the one person who could help me save it."

"I'm surprised he up and left without a word, no matter what Percy might have let slip," Mama said with a frown. "Did you text him?"

"Yes. He never responded." Elizabeth's voice broke on her words, the pain overwhelming her. "I couldn't admit this until now, but I miss him, even though I shouldn't. I just can't admit to myself that I was wrong about him."

Mama pulled Elizabeth into her and she put her head on her mother's shoulder.

"I shouldn't miss him. I should be angry with him for taking away the one thing that makes us both feel whole."

"We can't always help how we feel, Liz. Sometimes our hearts speak for us."

Elizabeth wiped a tear from her cheek. "I'm starting to notice that I have a knack for picking the wrong guys."

Mama leaned in and squeezed Elizabeth tighter. "Don't beat yourself up and start generalizin' after two people. You'll find your person."

"What if I'm not meant to have a person?" she asked.

"You're open to love, so you're definitely meant to have a person. You just have to be patient for the right one to come along." Her eyes crinkled at the corners as she grinned at Elizabeth. "If anyone can be patient enough, it's you."

Elizabeth gave her mother another hug. "Thank you for making me feel better." She was so glad to have Mama to go through it with her. Her mother *did* help Elizabeth to feel more confident, but there was still that lingering thought that things could've been different between Elizabeth and Paul if he'd just given the farm a chance.

"Whatcha doin'?" Mama asked that afternoon, leaning over Elizabeth as she sat at the desk, clicking the keys on her laptop.

After feeling sorry for herself earlier, Elizabeth knew she couldn't just sit back and stew in her own turmoil. "I'm trying to figure out what I want to do with my life," she replied, turning around. "I keep thinking about what Nan told me: 'Build your foundation but plan more than just the ground level, see it through, and nurture it.'"

"That reminds me of the foundation out back," Mama said. "Do you think Nan was referrin' to that when she said those words?"

"I don't know, but I have to wonder," Elizabeth answered. "She didn't get to build a home with Jimmy, but she certainly did with Gramps, so she knew both sides of that advice."

"That she did." Mama sat down in the chair next to the desk. "So, what are you working on?"

"I've been trying to find a career that fits who I am," Elizabeth replied. "I've been thinking about charities, maybe even trying to coordinate one like I used to, but, to be honest, when you and I were talking about the changes to the way we use the farm, it was the most excited I'd been about work in a while. I could really see myself heading that up, working with branding ourselves and really giving shape to Crestwood Farms. In time, we could build enough revenue to include charities in our work… It seems like a dream job."

"It did seem like a really great idea," Mama said wistfully.

"It would be *the perfect* idea, but none of it can happen without the farm." A shot of fear pelted her. "Will we really lose it?"

Mama's face downturned, her sadness clear.

"Maybe Naomi, Travis, and Percy would let us work their farm," Elizabeth said, shutting out the loss that came with admitting that they might lose Nan's home—their home.

Just then, Elizabeth's phone rang across the room. Hoping it was Paul, she jumped up and ran over to get it, abandoning their conversation. "Hello?" she answered.

"Hi, Elizabeth, this is Shirley Clark from Pierce and Hughes. I was calling to see if you'd found any documentation contesting the deed."

Elizabeth's shoulders fell. Nan's letter had pretty much given her the answer. "No, ma'am," she said. "We don't have anything stating we own the land."

"All right," the woman said gently. "I suppose we should discuss a plan for vacating the property. Although, I did mention to my client that you may be interested in pursuing Adverse Possession laws…"

"Adverse Possession?" Elizabeth asked, holding up a finger when Mama sent her a questioning glance.

"There's some debate with it being legal in Tennessee, but if you've resided on the property for twenty years or more, and you've made substantial improvements to the property, you might actually have some rights. At the worst, you'd be considered a 'squatter' and, if you have any records of paying rent on the property, you could be a 'holdover tenant.'"

Even though it wasn't a guarantee that anything good would come of it, and she wasn't sure she could fight a major corporation in court, the small olive branch that Shirley had extended made Elizabeth want to reach through the phone and hug her. That lawyer was also a small-town woman, and she knew exactly what Elizabeth and Mama were facing.

"How long do I have to look into it?" she asked.

"If you haven't gotten legal counsel, I'd say do it today, and then you have as long as it takes to plead your case to the courts."

"Thank you, Shirley," Elizabeth said, relief flooding her.

"What was that all about?" Mama asked as Elizabeth ended the call.

"We need to look up Adverse Possession," she said, going back to the desk and grabbing her laptop. She sat down on the sofa, explaining to Mama what Shirley had told her while she typed in the search term. "It says here we'll need a real-estate attorney because the laws can get tricky," Elizabeth said before looking over at her mother. "Think we could challenge it? Maybe explain that Nan and Jimmy owned the land and Gramps sold it, but he has some sort of permission to stay…?"

"How do we find out who granted him permission?" Mama asked.

"I think we need to call Worsham Enterprises and see if we can talk to Paul, and if he won't talk, we need to speak to someone else, or they can talk to our lawyer. The least they can do is give us the rental history." Elizabeth squared her shoulders, a new wave of determination spurring her on.

Chapter Twenty-one

"I left a message at Worsham Enterprises, but no one's called me back."

"Don't worry," Naomi said later that afternoon while they sat at a table for two at High Peak Coffee. Elizabeth had told her everything. "We'll find an answer."

"I also got a lawyer," Elizabeth said. "I'm just hoping that she can do something for us." She fixed her eyes on the map by the fireplace. "I let myself fall for Paul. I really thought he was someone special, but I haven't heard from him at all."

"You know how once we've used up all the nutrients by plantin' crops, the dirt in a field isn't always great for replantin' and we've gotta let it rest, then add fertilizer, and till it to make it good again?"

"Yeah," Elizabeth said, wondering where Naomi was headed.

Naomi leaned in locking eyes with her. "There's nothin' wrong with the soil. It's just not doin' what we want it to at that moment, but if we care for it, we can get it to do what makes sense for us."

"So if I care for Paul, he'll let us keep the farm?"

The corner of Naomi's mouth twitched upward. "If you care for Paul, and you open yourself up to him, you might change his mind."

Elizabeth shook her head. "I tried to change his mind," she said. "I explained it to him and he left. It seems that our soil is a little too rocky to grow anything on."

Naomi blew air through her lips. "It didn't seem like it when he was with you. He lit up whenever you came near him. When everyone was talkin' about it back at home, I stuck up for you and told Dad and Grandaddy that he seemed like a good guy."

"Maybe he had us all fooled." Elizabeth took a drink of her coffee, unable to deny the sinking feeling that she wouldn't be able to fix this. "I just wish he'd respond to me," she said.

Ever the optimist, Naomi leaned onto the table to get Elizabeth's attention. "Perhaps he will. Give him some time. And focus on you right now."

Elizabeth smiled despite her emotional state because even though she stood to lose so much, she had gained one very important thing: her best friend. She picked up her mug of coffee, taking another sip of the warm liquid. "What am I supposed to do in the meantime? I need to find a job."

"Your mama told Dad that you like organizin' events."

"Yes," Elizabeth replied from behind her mug.

"And I'll bet, after what your mama has said about the charity work you've done, that you're great at the PR... You can make logos and websites?"

Elizabeth could practically see her friend's mind whirring. "What are you thinking?"

"*You* could be the face and the brand of Thistle Farms. You and your mama could take care of the business side of the farm—none of us are good at that. We've been lookin' for someone, and you two would be perfect. We could pay you both."

Although it wasn't quite as good as staying at Crestwood Farm, the idea excited Elizabeth and seemed right up her alley, given that she'd even suggested something similar to Mama. "Where will we live? If a lawyer can't grant us rights to stay on the farm, we'd need to find something else," she said, thinking aloud.

"We'll get Ella to find you a house. She's a real estate agent."

"I'd totally forgotten," Elizabeth said, recalling Ray's story about how he'd met his wife.

"Definitely think about it. My dad would be thrilled to have you and your mama workin' for us."

"Think that could get weird with Mama and Travis working together?" Elizabeth asked. "Mama might not want to work for the man she's got a thing for."

Naomi cracked a smile. "She's an independent woman, for sure. But maybe it's somethin' to think about, anyway."

"Thank you, Naomi. It's a wonderful offer. I'll talk it over with Mama tonight." Elizabeth looked down into her near-empty coffee mug, the end coming too quickly. After eleven years in New York, she should've been used to making decisions hastily and adapting to ever-changing environments, but her emotions were holding her back. If she got too eager to take up Naomi on her offer, it would feel as though she wasn't fighting hard enough for Nan's farm. Gramps had promised Nan she'd have the farm for generations, and Elizabeth felt that it was up to her to help him keep his promise. She just wasn't entirely sure if she could.

"Hey," Naomi said, "we're havin' game night as soon as I get home. It's at Beatrice's if you and your mama wanna come. It might take your mind off things for a while."

Elizabeth produced a smile, her mind still on the farm. "Thanks. We might just do that."

Elizabeth arrived home to find Mama sitting in the hallway with piles of Nan's things surrounding her, tears streaming down her face. Elizabeth rushed over to her.

Mama balled one of Nan's sweaters in her fist and put it up to her nose, inhaling it through her sobs. "I thought I could be productive and begin to sort through some things, but it's too much. My life is this farmhouse. I don't know what I'll do without it. And what about Travis? I've only just realized how wonderful a man he is. Will I have to leave him?"

Elizabeth bent over and gently pulled her mother up by her hands, wrapping her in an embrace. "I know," was all she could say, tears springing to her own eyes.

Mama pulled back. "What are we gonna do?"

"We'll figure it out," Elizabeth said automatically.

"No," Mama said, her voice manic. "I don't think we will this time. I think we've officially lost the farm and there's nothin' either of us can do about it."

Elizabeth had never seen Mama like this before. While Elizabeth had been at the coffee shop with Naomi, Mama must have tried to busy herself, the way she did when things bothered her, but in the end, she'd fallen apart. The mere fact that Mama hadn't been able to follow her usual coping strategy spoke to the weight on her.

"We still have to talk to the lawyer."

Mama's shoulders fell in defeat. "You think she can really do anything for us? We don't own this land."

"We have to fight for it."

Mama dropped onto the sofa. When Elizabeth followed her lead, the gifts Paul had brought them caught her eye from under the tree.

Noticing too, Mama took in a jagged breath. "What in the world could Paul have brought for us?"

"Probably just a Christmas potholder set or something."

Mama sniffled, a smile surfacing on her lips. "Maybe they're matching ugly Christmas sweaters."

"You're joking through all this—I like it." Elizabeth embraced her mother. She needed Mama to keep it together for the both of them or she wouldn't be able to manage.

"Should we open them?" Mama asked, finding her way back to her typical approach of handling stressful situations. "It might take my mind off of everything for a second."

Elizabeth hadn't wanted to think about the fact that she hadn't opened them, holding onto the thought that she could open them with Paul at some point, but that wasn't looking like a possibility anymore. "I guess so," she replied, giving in to her mother's attempt to lighten the mood. She needed something to ease the pain as well, so agreeing wasn't so difficult to do.

Mama got up and grabbed the two gifts, handing Elizabeth the one marked for her. "You first," she said, clearing her throat as she still obviously battled her emotions.

Elizabeth held the gift, an uneasiness spreading over her. "I know you're trying to distract me, but it's… odd and joyless to open Paul's gift like this. It just doesn't feel right."

"So are we just goin' to leave them wrapped forever?" Mama asked, getting comfortable on the sofa.

Elizabeth considered the fact Paul hadn't contacted her since he'd walked out two days ago, and she probably would only hear from lawyers from there on out. She fiddled with the ribbon, deciding. "You're right," she said, giving in. "Let's open them at the same time."

Mama took hers into her lap and ripped the paper off, balling it up and tossing it aside while Elizabeth pulled the gift paper of hers until it fell loose in her hands. Elizabeth lifted the lid of the box, revealing the back of a small store-bought picture frame. Mama's was the same.

Interest swirling around inside her, she flipped it over and sucked in a breath of surprise.

"It's the map of Mason's Ridge that I always used to stop and look at in the general store. They've got a copy of it on the wall in the coffee shop." Elizabeth touched the glass, her lips wobbling as her finger came to a stop on the small spot of land where Crestwood Farm was located.

"I got one too," Mama said before falling silent beside Elizabeth.

"I'd told him about it…" She swallowed, trying to keep her disappointment over his silence from overpowering the moment. "I didn't expect something so meaningful," she said, the gesture bittersweet, given his plans for the area. Mason's Ridge would never be the same again. "He really thought about the gift, didn't he?"

Mama nodded, cradling her own. "Yes, he certainly did."

Full of tension, Elizabeth stood up and paced across the room, setting the frame on the kitchen table next to the list she and Mama had made with their ideas for the farm. The sight of them together caused tears to surface.

Mama got up and wrapped Elizabeth in a hug, emotion in her own eyes. "Let's not spend our last days at the farm sad. Let's try to enjoy them." She took in a deep breath and let it out, turning toward the hallway. "Want to help me pick up Nan's things and put them away? Then we should try to find somethin' to do to clear our heads."

"All right," Elizabeth relented, not feeling any better but putting on a brave face for Mama. The two of them set in, cleaning up the piles until they'd been neatly returned to their places. "Naomi's at Beatrice's, and they're going to have a game night. She's invited us to come," Elizabeth said to Mama after they'd gotten everything put away. "Why don't we go over and see them?"

"That sounds nice," Mama replied, closing the closet door and heading into the living room with Elizabeth. "I'll bet Travis will be there." Mama allowed a small smile. "Would you like to style my hair?"

"I'd love to," Elizabeth said.

"House!" Ella yelled from the sofa, while Ray scribbled on the large pad of paper. "Apartment! Box! Rooftop!"

"Time," Travis called.

Ray's arms fell by his side, the uncapped marker still in his hand. "The word was 'lawnmower.'"

Ella squinted, turning her head to the side, clearly trying to make out the image Ray had drawn.

"That's the handle," he said, pointing to the roof of the house.

"I see it now," Ella said before turning to the rest of them and bursting out laughing.

"Liz, your turn," Travis said with a chuckle.

Elizabeth took the pen from Ray and pulled the slip of paper from the dish, opening it up. *Labrador*. She began to draw the floppy ears and snout of a dog, swiping her pen quickly over the paper.

"Horse!" her partner Naomi called, making Elizabeth laugh at the sight of her drawing.

Elizabeth shook her head and continued to draw.

Naomi slid off the sofa onto her knees in excitement, inching closer to Elizabeth as she drew. "Dog!"

Elizabeth turned around and widened her eyes to get Naomi to say more.

"Canine! Puppy! Um..."

Elizabeth turned back to the page and drew two more dogs in different sizes, pointing to the larger one and coloring it in with her black marker.

"Five seconds!" Travis said, holding the stopwatch.

"Oh, oh!" Naomi wiggled. "Labrador?"

"Yes!" Elizabeth spun around, jumping up and down.

"They beat us!" Mama turned to Beatrice in counterfeit shock.

"By one point," Beatrice said with a smirk. "If I'd have been able to get up and draw," she said to Mama, "with your quick mind, we'd have pulled it out for the win."

Mama grinned at Beatrice.

"That was fun," Naomi said, taking her spot back on the sofa.

"Thank you for inviting us over tonight," Elizabeth said to her friend, so glad for the reprieve. As she looked around at everyone, she couldn't remember when she'd had such a great time.

"We should make it a weekly thing," Beatrice offered, looking younger than she had when Elizabeth had first arrived in town.

"Maybe we can," Elizabeth agreed, although she knew that it probably wouldn't be a reality unless she and Mama could manage to scrape up enough money to buy a house in the area, which, given the rising demand for land, wasn't going to be easy.

As if he were reading her mind, once everyone had begun to chat with one another, Travis came over to her. "Your mama told me about the farm."

She nodded, not wanting to say anything for fear she'd burst into tears.

"I'm sorry I was hard on you when you came back," he said. "And Naomi told me about the job idea you two discussed. You know I'll do anything I can… We all will."

“This was as close to family as she'd get, and she couldn't imagine a better group of people to spend her time with. If only she knew how much time they actually had together like this…

Chapter Twenty-two

The next morning, Elizabeth's mind was too full of worry over the farmhouse to do anything else. Not helping matters, she'd missed a call from Shirley Clark at the law office, telling her that she'd need to call her. Without any documentation stating they owned the farm, or any headway with Worsham Enterprises, Elizabeth was nearly certain that her next phone call with Ms. Clark would be to determine a date for eviction, so she had left a message for her own lawyer, asking what they should do.

Unable to focus on anything else, Elizabeth bundled up to join Mama outside, worried she was freezing by now. Her mother had been out there all morning, deciding to spend some time in the barn after they'd finished their chores.

Finding Mama near the chicken coop, Elizabeth huddled next to her. "Whatcha doing?" she asked.

"Enjoyin' the animals," Mama replied.

Knowing just what she meant, Elizabeth reached in and took the baby chick they'd named Holly out of the coop, cradling it in her arms. "Isn't she just the cutest thing?" she asked, stroking the chick's downy fur. The chick cheeped, making her smile, but it faded when she thought about how that little being had no idea that its life was about to be upended.

Out of nowhere, the sound of tires on gravel pulled her attention to a car coming down the drive. She shielded her eyes from the bright light reflecting off the remaining snow and squinted to see who it could be. It wasn't a car that she recognized. Mama clearly wondered as well, giving Elizabeth a questioning glance, since no one ever came to the farm except their closest friends.

When she was finally able to make out who it was, Elizabeth held her breath and steeled herself at the sight of Paul and another man through the car's tinted windshield, her heart pounding like a snare drum. She put the chick back into the coop and took Mama's hand. This was it: that moment that would be burned into her mind for a lifetime. He was driving up to tell her that they had to leave. Mama squeezed her hand before letting go, as if she were thinking the same thing.

The car came to a stop and Paul got out, locking eyes with Elizabeth immediately. Without a word, he went around to the passenger side of the car, helping out an elderly man, the two of them walking carefully on the snowy surface toward Elizabeth and Mama.

Guardedly, Paul came to a halt in front of them, his eyes on Elizabeth.

She shoved her trembling hands into her pockets and forced herself to look directly at him, hoping she'd done a good job of pushing her fear away.

"This is my grandfather, William Worsham," he said.

She gave him a cautious look, remembering that the two men weren't speaking—Paul had told her that. The old man seemed tired, his face turned downward with fatigue, but his eyes were highly alert as he looked at her with interest.

"Could we speak to you two in the house?" Paul asked.

"Yes, let's go inside," Mama suggested, her voice strained, making Elizabeth's hands shake even more.

The two men followed as Mama led the way past the Christmas tree on the porch, the festive spirit of it now seeming out of place. Paul had his arm around Mr. Worsham, guiding him. Mama opened the door, the four of them heading into the farmhouse. When they were all inside, she offered them a seat at the table, the mistletoe streamers dangling over them, but there was no sense of festive cheer.

Mr. Worsham's gaze roamed around the farmhouse, and Elizabeth wondered if he were assessing the surroundings before his old company ripped it down. She bit her lip to keep her emotions in check.

"I heard the message you left at Worsham Enterprises," Paul said, "but I couldn't respond properly. I was in airports, flying home to see my grandfather and then traveling back here."

He didn't have to spell it out for her; it was pretty easy to understand. But William distracted her from responding, placing his weathered hands on the table, a softness in his eyes when he looked at her that she didn't want to trust, given the situation.

"You're Harriet's granddaughter?" he asked.

"Mm hm," she answered warily.

The man's attention moved over to Mama. "And you're her daughter?"

"Yes," Mama said, seemingly as confused as Elizabeth by the mistiness forming in his eyes as they moved back and forth between the two of them.

"I knew your grandparents."

"I know," Elizabeth said. "My gramps sold his land to you."

The lines between the old man's eyes creased, but then released as if something had dawned on him, a very small smile showing at the corners of his lips, giving him a resemblance to Paul. "Your grandfather was a great man."

Elizabeth looked over at Mama and then away when she saw the tears in her mother's eyes just as Mr. Worsham started to speak again.

"My full name is William *James* Worsham. As a kid, I went by Jimmy."

Elizabeth's blood ran cold at the mention of that name. It couldn't be…

"My grandson tells me that you've read some of my letters." His eyes became wet with tears and he pursed his lips, the edges of them wobbling before he cleared his throat and straightened them out.

"What's goin' on?" Mama asked, obviously in as much shock and confusion as Elizabeth.

"Jimmy died in the war," Elizabeth said. "Nan and Gramps went to his funeral."

The old man shook his head. "I was taken prisoner and stripped of my uniform, and it took me almost two years to get home. By the time I had returned, your grandmother had already begun to build a life with Roger."

Mama gasped and clapped a hand over her mouth.

Elizabeth turned to Paul, wondering what in the world was happening.

"I came to see her," the old man continued, "but she never knew. She seemed so happy…" He folded his hands, covering his lips as if the sight were right in front of him. "All I wanted was her happiness. There were nights when I wondered if time would work its magic and do what it was meant to do, and I feared that I'd never get over her. But the last thing I wanted was to make her choose between Roger and me." He took in a jagged breath, clearly needing a minute.

"Let me get everyone a nice cup of cider. I'll warm some on the stove," Mama said impulsively, the way she did when she was overwhelmed. She pulled a pot from the pothanger above the stove and set it on the burner before returning to the table.

"When it was thought that I'd died, she received the farm because I'd left it to her in my will. When I came home, I realized that this would be an issue, and I didn't want her to find out I'd come back. She'd already grieved over me and she'd made it to the other side of that grief. So, I reached out to Roger."

"What in the world did he say?" Elizabeth asked, all of this too much for her to comprehend.

"He was surprised, as I'm sure you can imagine." William took in a deep breath and blew it through his lips. "Roger and Harriet were already married... We met secretly and I made him promise to never tell Harriet."

Mama got up again and brought William a mug of cider, setting it down in front him, then she rushed back over to the counter, her attention remaining on him.

"I still owned the land outright, but Roger took over all the finances of running the farm, and I paid the taxes, from my new home in Chicago, the two of us working together while I claimed to be his financial consultant. He never told her the truth. She didn't know a thing."

Paul finally spoke up. "When I found out my grandfather owned this land, on the board's suggestion, I immediately began working up a plan for development. He was totally against it, and I never understood why, until now. After spending time in Mason's Ridge and then learning that you two lived here on the property, everything I'd thought I'd wanted went out the window." He looked at Elizabeth, sorrow and adoration for her in his eyes. "I needed to talk to the board before I came back, and I had to go home and find out the truth. It took some convincing to get him to tell me his secret."

"I promised Roger that I'd take it to the grave," William said. "But when Paul told me about you all, I had to say something."

After bringing the other mugs to the table, Mama folded her hands anxiously in front of her. "We found a foundation at the edge of the field," she said. "What is that?"

William's gaze moved above her head as if he were chasing the memory. "That was supposed to be mine and Harriet's house. But once it was thought that I was dead, Roger never built on it out of respect for me, even though I told him he could when I'd returned."

Paul gave William a warm smile. "I understood him so much more once I knew his story, and I totally understood why the farm mattered to him and that I couldn't destroy it."

They all fell into a thoughtful silence, the four of them peering at each other, their common bond of Nan and Gramps uniting them.

"I haven't had a chance to say my piece to you, though," Paul said to Elizabeth, his gaze moving over to the unwrapped map that he'd gifted her leaning against the wall. "I know how important the farm is to you. And I'm prepared to refund the investors and take a loss if that's what you two would like me to do. Even if it means Worsham Enterprises goes under."

Elizabeth stared at him, hanging on his every word. The last thing she wanted was for his company to go bankrupt after all the work he'd put in. Would William have enough to retire on if that happened? How would Paul manage? She could hardly bear it. But it was a terrible situation to be in, where one of them would lose. "This is an impossible choice either way."

"Yes," he agreed. "But if you're willing to hear me out, I might have an idea."

"What is it?" she asked.

"It's just a thought…"

"Tell me," she urged him, leaning across the table.

"You'd mentioned how your mother loves to entertain," he said, turning his attention to Mama. "Isn't that right, Loretta?"

"Yes," Mama answered, a question in the word.

"When I first met you, I'd worked so hard that I was burned out in my career," Paul told Elizabeth. "And my wife leaving me made me feel like I wasn't worth much, so I dove into more work, despite being so tired. But when I met you, I was inspired by you leaving New York for a slower pace of life, and now I realize that it could be something I want as well."

Elizabeth leaned on the table anxiously listening. "So what are you proposing?"

"After having a long talk with my grandfather, we wondered if we could repair the foundation on the other side of the farm and, instead of a resort, build a bed and breakfast."

"How would that benefit us?" Mama asked.

"Well, I'd like someone knowledgeable about the area to run it with us."

The ideas that Elizabeth and Mama had written down flooded her mind. Trying not to get too excited at his proposition just yet, she got up and grabbed the legal pad, scooting her chair next to Paul's. "Mama and I were thinking we could use the farm for things like this," she said, running her finger down the list of goat petting, apple juice, picnic tables, horse rides…

William's weathered lips turned up into a smile. "That sounds like something Harriet would've thought to do."

Emotion sprang up at the mention of Nan, and Elizabeth could feel it in the air—something good was happening.

Mama gave her a cheerful look. It was as if Nan and Gramps were right there with them, cheering their whole family on, as if they'd orchestrated the whole thing from above somehow.

Interrupting them, Elizabeth's phone went off. "Sorry," she said, after retrieving the phone from her pocket and finding a familiar number. She answered.

"Hey," Naomi said on the other end of the line. "I saw the car in the drive and didn't want to interrupt, so I left the stack of letters on your porch. Beatrice said she felt like you'd want to be the one to keep them."

Nan was right there on the front porch, it seemed. "Okay, thanks," Elizabeth said, the wonderful feeling of anticipation filling her up.

"Everything all right?" Naomi asked.

"Very possibly."

Ending the call, she walked over and opened the front door. There, on the boards of the porch, tied with that familiar red ribbon, the Christmas lights still glittering against the green clapboard, Elizabeth reached down and picked up the letters, taking them back inside. She considered her theory of why Nan had begun writing Christmas letters and how she was honoring Jimmy. They were between her grandmother and the two men she loved. Then, it occurred to her what Nan would probably want her to do with them.

"I think you might like to have these," she said, holding them out to William.

The old man took them into his trembling hands, peering down at them lovingly.

"There are a few from Gramps in there too," Elizabeth said.

William held them to his chest. "Thank you."

Mama lifted her cider in a toast. "Merry Christmas."

"Merry Christmas," Paul returned, and they all clinked their mugs. His eyes met Elizabeth's and right there, she could see the man she'd first met.

With everyone gathered around the table, asking each other questions and getting to know one another, Paul stood up and took Elizabeth's hand. "Talk to me for a minute?"

She got their coats and followed him outside to the back porch where she struck a match and lit the fire in the firepit. The logs popped and sizzled under the heat of the flame, catching slowly until the fire devoured the limbs in its blaze.

"I'm sorry I ran off," he said, facing her. "Once I'd realized what I'd done, and overhearing Percy's thoughts, I knew that turning this farm into a resort was absolutely wrong and not representative of what I stand for. I needed to convince the board to drop this immediately and let them know that I couldn't move forward. While I wanted to set your mind at ease before I left, I also needed to speak to my grandfather to figure out why you didn't seem to know him at all. I had to hear the whole story to be sure I made the right decision for you." He took a step toward her. "I didn't mean to worry you. I just… needed time to make a plan."

"Please promise me you'll never do that again," she said. "There's nothing we can't face together."

"You're right." He looked down at her fondly. Then he peered up at the silver streamers dangling from the porch roof above them, the corners of his mouth turning up into a grin. "What about that?" he asked, pointing to the ball of mistletoe that Mama had hung for the party. "Can we face that together?"

His suggestion made her so happy that she laughed. "Absolutely," she answered him.

He reached out and gently placed his hands on her waist, drawing her in. His fingers moved up to her face and he gently pressed his lips to hers, their every move together like notes in a symphony. This kiss was different from any Elizabeth had ever had before. The warmth of his lips on hers, the way their breathing was in perfect time with one another, the soft caress of his hands—it was as if he'd been made for only her, and everything she'd done before had been in preparation for this person.

When they finally slowed to a respectable pace, she pulled back. "Where will you live?" she asked.

"What?" He swallowed her with his gaze.

"When we build the bed and breakfast, where will you live?"

"Anywhere. As long as I can see you."

"Well, if you ever need a place, I know an old farmhouse that might offer up a room," she said, waving her hand through the air.

With a chuckle, he leaned down and gave her another kiss. As she looked into his eyes, she knew that this moment was the beginning of the rest of her life.

Epilogue

One Year Later

"Hey, Mama," Elizabeth said playfully, the phone pressed to her diamond-studded ear, as snow fell against the glittering decorations outside Crestwood Bed and Breakfast. She put one stiletto heel outside the car and took Paul's hand, the two of them walking past the sign that read *Grand Opening*. A Christmas party like no other was beginning inside, in about five minutes. Elizabeth smoothed her red ball gown and walked up the steps of the bed and breakfast, blowing a kiss to Paul as he held the door open for her, looking handsome in his tuxedo. "I'll call you back in just a second, Mama, I promise."

"Liz," her mother breathed down the line in that southern accent of hers.

"Just come over. The party's starting already."

"I know, but I'm struggling to find the perfume you told me to wear, and Travis is already on his way."

Elizabeth held the phone out so Paul could hear, grinning at the thought of her mother's frantic search for the perfect scent to impress her new beau. Travis had helped Mama with all the heavy lifting as they'd organized the farmhouse, collected items to keep and others to put in storage to get Mama and Elizabeth settled. And in their off time, he'd taken Mama out to eat and to the movies—things her mother hadn't done for many years. He'd become quite a big part of Mama's life, and the sparkle that was in her eye these days gave away how she felt about having him near.

"Do I need to run back home and help you look for it?" Elizabeth asked.

"Oh! Never mind! I found it."

"Are you wearing the pearl earrings I laid out for you?" She giggled, as Paul reached out and tickled her sides once they were in the building.

"Yes," Mama said.

"And the dress? Everything fits okay?" Paul nibbled her neck and she turned around to face him, the phone pressed to her ear while she playfully fought him off.

"Yes. All good. I'll be over as soon as Travis gets here. Sorry to bother you."

"You never bother me." She gave a loud kiss into the phone and then ended the call as Naomi swished up to her.

Elizabeth's eyes bulged with the beauty that stood in front of her. Naomi was wearing a hunter-green sequined gown with heels.

"Do you have on eye shadow?" Elizabeth asked over the band that was playing holiday music.

"Don't expect it every day," Naomi said with a wink.

"You look gorgeous."

Naomi blushed. "You're dazzling, as always. And, Paul, you look very dashing."

"Thank you," Paul said. "It's easy to seem dashing with this stunner on my arm." He gave Elizabeth a twirl.

Elizabeth swooned, peering up at him in utter adoration, having never been happier. She and Mama had spent the last year working hand-in-hand with Worsham Enterprises to design the bed and breakfast and plan all the amenities. They'd managed to incorporate everything from the original list that they'd made, and they'd even added in ways to involve the local school children, with field trips to the farm where they would learn about agriculture and conservation. All the proceeds from those tours, along with a percentage of the sales from the gift shop on the premises, would go toward the upkeep of local farms, the money available through yearly grants for the farmers.

Her time in New York now a distant memory, Elizabeth had settled in in Mason's Ridge. As a young woman, she'd run off in search of the life that was meant for her, but her dream life had been waiting for her right there all this time. With the legacy of her grandmother and the help of her mother, she'd found her place.

She'd realized that her friendship with Naomi had been the truest and most meaningful friendship she'd ever had, the two of them putting all their past experiences behind them, both of them looking forward to quite a bit of time together.

It had been Naomi who'd pulled off the biggest surprise of Elizabeth's life so far, luring her to the empty coffee shop where, inside, all the tables had been cleared for a make-shift dance floor, the entire place covered in flickering candles, and a band in the corner for just Elizabeth and Paul. He'd taken her into his arms and danced with her—the waltz. Then, with Naomi looking on, tears in her friend's eyes, he'd gotten down on one knee and proposed.

Elizabeth and Paul had been inseparable since. While he could romance her like no one else, Elizabeth's work with him on the bed and breakfast was also incredibly fulfilling. She'd found her place, incorporating her love of the farm and family with her charity work. Planning it all had given her the purpose and inspiration that she'd always wanted. Paul had been by her side in all of the planning, guiding her but also letting her lead when she wanted to and seeing her strengths along the way.

Paul had sold his property in Chicago, purchasing a large plot of land across town where he and Elizabeth planned to build their forever home. It was a sweeping farmhouse on the edge of town, with a small suite out back for William.

"I want to introduce you to someone," Paul said. "He's a new board member at Worsham Enterprises." He led Elizabeth and Naomi past a group of people all dressed in their holiday finest, through the silver trays of hors-d'oeuvres, to a man who looked to be about their age, with dark hair and bright-green eyes that matched his Christmas-themed tie.

The man turned toward them when they walked up, his attention immediately on Naomi as if she were the only person in the room. "Hello," he said, clearly taken by her natural beauty.

Paul cleared his throat. "Brian Simpson, this is Naomi White and Elizabeth Holloway."

"Call me Liz," Elizabeth said, the name of her youth fitting her perfectly.

"It's nice to meet you both." Brian turned to Naomi. "Would you like a drink?"

"I'd love one," she said with a smitten grin that Elizabeth had never seen before plastered across her face. When Brian headed toward the bar, Naomi grabbed Paul by the lapels and mouthed, "Thank. *You.*" Then she ran off to join him.

Elizabeth laughed, so happy to see Naomi enjoying herself.

Just then, Percy and Beatrice came up from behind them, holding glasses of champagne, both of them livelier than she'd seen them in ages. They were followed by William, Ray, and Ella. Percy was the first one to clap Paul on the back.

"It's absolutely beautiful in here," Beatrice said.

It was only then that Elizabeth took the time to look around. The two-story railings in the massive entry were draped with cedar garland, long silver ribbons cinching it up at every post with an explosion of matching balloons above each one. They'd put up five of Percy's Douglas Fir trees, all with white lights and blue and silver baubles.

"I'm glad you like it," Elizabeth said with pride. "We've been working so hard to get it all done for the holidays. Every single room is full." She smiled over at William and he gave her a knowing look. Renting a house nearby with Paul, he'd been there every step of the way during the construction of the bed and breakfast on the original foundation that he and Nan had started. Elizabeth had adored hearing all his stories about Nan, feeling more connected to her than she had in long time.

"That's wonderful." Beatrice took Percy's arm. "I can't wait to see what's in the great room. The band sounds positively delightful."

"I agree," Paul said, taking Elizabeth's hand and leading her into the room toward the band. "I feel a waltz coming on." He gave her wink.

There, under the holiday lights, Nan's words came to mind: *Foundations aren't all we need. They're nothing if we don't give them shape and form, Liz. Build your foundation, but plan more than just the ground level, see it through, and nurture it.*

As Paul took her onto the dance floor, giving her a spin, her red satin dress that she never thought she'd get to wear again puffing out around her, she knew that she'd made Nan proud tonight, and that somewhere in the heavens, Nan and Gramps were with them, cheering their family on—a family that was now whole.

A Letter from Jenny

Hi there!

Thank you so much for reading *The Christmas Letters*. It was a delight to write. I hope it pulled you right into the merriment of the Christmas season and left your heart a little fuller.

If you'd like to know when my next book is out, you can **sign up for my monthly newsletter and new release alerts here:**

https://www.itsjennyhale.com/email-signup

I won't share your information with anyone else, and I'll only email you a quick message once a month with my newsletter and then whenever new books come out. It's the best way to keep tabs on what's going on with my books, and you'll get tons of surprises along the way, like giveaways, signed copies, recipes, and more.

If you did enjoy *The Christmas Letters*, I'd be very grateful if you'd write a review online. Getting feedback from readers helps to persuade others to pick up one of my books for the first time. It's one of the biggest gifts you could give me.

If you enjoyed this story, and would like more happy endings, check out my other novels at http://www.itsjennyhale.com/books.

Until next time,
Jenny xo

7201437.Jenny_Hale

jennyhaleauthor

@jhaleauthor

jhaleauthor

www.itsjennyhale.com

Acknowledgments

As always, I am forever indebted to Oliver Rhodes for shaping me into the author I am today and setting the bar for my own publishing journey. His example continues to inspire me and gives me the blueprint for every single decision I make.

I owe an enormous thank you to my amazing editors: Megan McKeever, who lent her incredible experience to the book, Jade Craddock, line and copyeditor extraordinaire—I'm over the moon to work with her again—and my dynamite proofreader, Lauren Finger, the best of the best. I couldn't have had a better team to help me get this story ready than these women.

I'm so very thankful to have cover designer Kristen Ingebretson at the creative helm. Her ability to take a rough idea and make it into a masterpiece is incredible.

And to my husband, Justin, who has to listen to my endless chatter about building a publishing imprint, acquiring new authors, and fluttering around with the mantra "I have to get my thousand words!" I am blessed to have his support (and his dishwasher and laundry skills).

Made in United States
North Haven, CT
08 November 2022

26400107R00161